To Seduce a Texan

Books by Georgina Gentry

CHEYENNE CAPTIVE
CHEYENNE PRINCESS
COMANCHE COWBOY
BANDIT'S EMBRACE
NEVADA NIGHTS
QUICKSILVER PASSION
CHEYENNE CARESS
APACHE CARESS
CHRISTMAS RENDEZVOUS (novelette)
SIOUX SLAVE
HALF-BREED'S BRIDE
NEVADA DAWN
CHEYENNE SPLENDOR
SONG OF THE WARRIOR
TIMELESS WARRIOR
WARRIOR'S PRIZE
CHEYENNE SONG
ETERNAL OUTLAW
APACHE TEARS
WARRIOR'S HONOR
WARRIOR'S HEART
TO TAME A SAVAGE
TO TAME A TEXAN
TO TAME A REBEL
TO TEMPT A TEXAN
TO TEASE A TEXAN
MY HEROES HAVE ALWAYS BEEN COWBOYS
(novelette)
TO LOVE A TEXAN
TO WED A TEXAN

Published by Kensington Publishing Corporation

To Seduce a Texan

GEORGINA GENTRY

ZEBRA BOOKS
Kensington Publishing Corp.
http://www.kensingtonbooks.com

ZEBRA BOOKS are published by

Kensington Publishing Corp.
850 Third Avenue
New York, NY 10022

All Kensington titles, imprints, and distributed lines are
available at special quantity discounts for bulk purchases
for sales promotion, premiums, fund-raising, educational,
or institutional use.

Special book excerpts or customized printings can also be
created to fit specific needs. For details, write or phone the
office of the Kensington Special Sales Manager: Kensington
Publishing Corp., 850 Third Avenue, New York, NY 10022. Attn.
Special Sales Department. Phone: 1-800-221-2647.

Zebra and the Z logo Reg. U.S. Pat. & TM Off.

ISBN-13: 978-0-8217-7992-7
ISBN-10: 0-8217-7992-3

First Printing: January 2009
10 9 8 7 6 5 4 3 2 1

Printed in the United States of America

This story is dedicated to
every reader who secretly daydreams of
a handsome hero,
but thinks herself not worthy or pretty enough
to get the guy.
Honey, I wrote this story just for you.

and

To the memory of Western stars
John Wayne and Randolph Scott,
the two men I used to pattern my hero,
Waco McClain.
They're gone,
but the movies and the memories linger on.

Prologue

Late September 1864
The Texas side of the Red River

"So we're gonna rob a bank." Waco McClain leaned his tall frame on his saddle horn and tilted his Stetson against the bright September sun.

"What?" All three of his *compadres* started in their saddles and stared at him.

"You heard me," Waco snapped. "We're ridin' up to south Kansas. I've been told there's a fat bank in the town of Prairie View on the Arkansas River."

Zeb, the younger but taller of the grizzled old Webb brothers, spat tobacco juice in the river and looked north. "That's a mighty long way from Texas. We got to cross Indian Territory with them Yankee and Reb troops everywhere."

"It ain't as though we got a lot of choice, considerin' what happened." Waco sighed, not wanting to remember, then he shifted his lanky body on his restless bay stallion, Amigo, and began rolling a smoke. In his almost thirty years, he'd never been in this much trouble before. Zeke Webb ran his hand through his ragged beard and looked down at his denim shirt and pants. "I was wonderin' what we was doin' in these duds."

"Wonder no more," Waco drawled in his deep voice. "Besides, these clothes feel good after all this time."

Young Tom shook his red head doubtfully. "We get caught dressed like this, we might get shot."

Waco finished rolling his cigarette. "Tell me somethin' I don't know."

Zeb looked at the rolling red water. "There's a ferry downriver."

"Yeah," Tom said, "I don't fancy gettin' wet."

"Do you fancy gettin' caught?" Waco stuck the smoke in his mouth and scratched a match on his pant leg. "Don't want anyone to see us; gossip travels faster than a skunk at a ladies' garden party. We'll swim it."

"Oh, hell," grumbled Zeke, the older brother. "To think I could be settin' in a rockin' chair back at the ranch, playing my fiddle."

"Oh, shut up," Zeb said. "It's this or get hung. You can play your mouth organ."

"Sorry, boys." Waco took a deep puff. "This mess is my fault."

"No, it ain't. We wouldn't have done it any different," Zeb assured him, and the other two nodded in agreement.

"You know, this might be fun." Tom grinned.

The other three frowned at him.

"Fun as rasslin' a bobcat," Zeb said with sarcasm.

"Just tryin' to look on the bright side." Tom's freckled face turned red as a whore's drawers.

"Young'uns!" Zeke snorted.

"Enough jawin,'" Waco ordered, tossing his smoke away. "We got a long way to go and a short time to get there. I'll lead out. If your horse balks, get off and hang on to the saddle."

"I can't swim," young Tom admitted.

"Oh, hell," Zeb said. "Fine time to tell us that."

"Gawd Almighty! Shut up, all of you," Waco snapped. "Remember, if we run across any patrols, Yank or Reb, our story is we're just four cowboys from Texas tryin' to sell some beef. Now let's go." He took his gold watch out of his pocket, rubbed it for good luck, and took off his hat. He put the watch under his hat and pulled the Stetson firmly down on his sun-streaked hair. "Don't want it to get wet," he said. "My grandpappy give me that watch. I set a heap of store by it."

"Them fancy silver spurs of your'n," Zeke nodded, "the reflection is liable to catch a patrol's attention."

"I'll give you that." Waco reached to take off his ornate silver spurs, then put them safely in his saddlebags. "We can't be too careful." Then he turned his fine bay into the swirling water and it waded out hesitantly, then began swimming toward the far shore.

He glanced back. Behind him, his three friends strung out in a line, plunging their horses into the Red River and swimming toward Indian Territory. He'd gotten them into this mess and now he'd try to get them out. It all depended on robbing that fat bank in south Kansas.

Chapter One

Early October 1864
The president's office of Prairie View Bank

He was either going to have to murder Rosemary or marry her. Right now, he couldn't decide which would be the most distasteful. Banker Godfrey St. John leaned back in his fine leather office chair and cleaned his nails with his pocket knife. He gazed out into the busy lobby where customers gathered, excited about the coming celebration. From every post and beam hung large banners adorned with bright ribbons shouting, "Welcome Home, Rosemary!" "Rosemary, We Missed You!"

Like I'd miss an impacted tooth. Godfrey grimaced and brushed a speck of lint off his expensive striped suit. As far as the town folk, they hardly knew her, but any kind of a celebration was welcome with the war dragging on.

It was a hot day for early October, he thought as he snapped his pocket knife shut and dropped it in his coat pocket. With a resigned sigh, he pasted a smile on his handsome face, ran his finger over his tiny mustache, and walked out into the lobby to mingle with the customers. He hated being so close to such hicks. "Ah, good day, Mrs. Hornswaggle, you're looking well."

The fat widow gave him her brightest smile. "Thank you, Mr. St. John. But I'm feeling poorly. My lumbago, you know."

"So sorry." He walked past her before she could engage him in more conversation. As a rich widower, he knew he was a target for every woman in town.

"We're all excited about Rosemary's return," she shouted after him.

"Aren't we all?" He turned and nodded, thinking about his stepdaughter, and frowned. Plump and plain Rosemary was due in on the noon stage and he could only hope it got attacked by Indians or fell off a cliff, which wasn't too likely on the flat plains of southern Kansas. Damn her mother, anyhow. Agatha must not have trusted Godfrey after all since he'd discovered after her death that her only child, Rosemary, was to inherit the bank on her twenty-first birthday, less than three weeks from now. Godfrey only inherited if Rosemary should die, and she was healthy as a draft horse and about as appealing. Ye Gods! He was out of luck unless he took matters into his own, well-manicured hands. And after all the trouble he'd gone to get his fingers on this fortune.

So to maintain control of the bank and the estate, Godfrey would either have to marry Rosemary or murder her. There would be gossip, of course, if he married his own stepdaughter with her mother dead a little over a year, but he had gone too far to give up all this money now. Besides, he was such a pillar of the community that folks would soon forgive him. He thought about wedding Rosemary and frowned. Ye Gods! Maybe he ought to reconsider murdering her.

Godfrey continued walking through the lobby, greeting people, shaking hands.

The local minister hailed him. "Great day, isn't it, Mr. St. John, Rosemary due home and all?"

Godfrey shook hands with the frail man. "Yes, indeed, Reverend Post, I've missed her so much. However, you know, I thought a Grand World Tour would be good for her after the death of her mother. Agatha's loss was so tragic for all of us."

Reverend Post murmured agreement.

Actually Godfrey had hoped Rosemary wouldn't survive the Grand Tour. He'd hoped she might fall off the Great Wall of China, clumsy as she was, drown in a Venice Canal, or get carried off to some sheikh's harem or maybe trampled by an elephant. No such luck.

"So tragic, Agatha's death," the old minister said.

"Certainly was," Godfrey nodded, "but life goes on."

Or would, if I could figure out what to do about my stubborn, plain stepdaughter. He returned to his office, sat down in his expensive chair, and reached for his pocket knife. He cut off the tip of a fine Havana cigar and lit it, considering his options. The new Union fort that was being built just outside town was drawing more settlers and more money. With that in mind, Godfrey didn't intend to give up control of the only bank in Prairie View.

In the early autumn heat, his office window was

open and he watched four weather-beaten men ride down the dusty street and rein in near the bank's entry. Looked like country yokels, maybe cowboys, Godfrey thought as he watched them dismount.

The tallest of the four tipped his Stetson and nodded to a passerby. "Howdy, stranger, where can we find a stable for our horses and a good saloon?"

Texans, Godfrey thought, sneering at the drawl. *Now what are they doing so far from home, especially with a war going on?* The quartet looked tan and dusty like they'd been on the road a long time. The tall one listened to the local and nodded. "Much obliged. We're mighty thirsty." Then he led off with long strides, followed by a younger man with red hair and big ears and two old codgers sporting ragged gray beards.

Godfrey glanced at the big clock in his office and sighed as he smoked. If Indians and nonexistent cliffs didn't stop her stagecoach, his stepdaughter should be arriving within the hour.

Rosemary's stage rolled down the dusty road at a fast clip, moving toward Prairie View. She was the only passenger as she leaned back against the coarse horsehair cushions and sighed, wishing she was headed some place, any place but there. It was hot, so the isinglass curtains had been rolled up. While she sweated, fine dust blew in to coat her face, clothes and big plumed hat.

Ladies don't say "sweat." She could almost hear her dead mother's scolding voice. *Men and horses sweat, ladies glow.*

"Well, I sweat, Mother," she said aloud and then felt foolish to be talking to herself. She and her mother had never had a good relationship, and it had worsened when Agatha Burke had married that sleazy Godfrey St. John. But then Rosemary had always disappointed her mother for looking too much like her plain and rotund father. She had disappointed her father, too, who wanted a daughter as beautiful as his upper-class wife. Rosemary could never please either of them, no matter how much she tried. When Rosemary finally realized that, she had retaliated by becoming stubborn and difficult. Even being sent off to the fancy finishing school that Mother had attended back East hadn't done much to turn Rosemary into the fine and elegant lady Mother had longed for. Neither had that Grand Tour her stepfather had insisted she take after Mother's death.

Rosemary took out a handkerchief and mopped her steaming red face. Her corset was so tight she could hardly breathe, but her silhouette was still rotund.

Well, she didn't like herself much either. With the disapproval and disappointment of her parents, Rosemary never felt loved, and so she comforted herself with food and romantic novels, which only led to more disapproval.

Speaking of food, she wished she had a sandwich or some cookies right now. That would keep her mind off her unhappiness. Godfrey would think she should have worn the light gray of mourning, but she'd gotten grease from a fried chicken leg on her light gray silk dress and she wasn't certain it could be cleaned.

Maybe Agatha was right, Rosemary would always be a disappointment and no one would ever love her except for her money. So now, as the stagecoach bumped along toward Prairie View, Rosemary daydreamed as usual that she was someone else.

Today she was Lady DuBarry, the beautiful mistress of kings and the most slender, elegant woman in all France. Of course her powdered wig was coiffed in curls beset with diamonds, and a beauty mark accented her lovely face.

She leaned back and smiled in her fantasy. She wore a gold and silver ball gown, rolling along in her private carriage toward the chateau where a giant ball in her honor was waiting. There handsome dukes and earls, no, it would be marquises, would vie for Lady DuBarry's attention while she laughed behind her dainty fan and men begged to drink champagne out of her tiny slipper and threatened duels in her honor.

"Oh, please, gentlemen, no sword fights over my affections." She laughed behind her lace fan. "There really are other mademoiselles here."

"Ah, my cherie," the most handsome one bent over her fingertips for a kiss, "but none so beautiful as you."

She blushed prettily and drew her hand back. Which dandy would receive her favors tonight while other women looked on and frowned with jealousy?

The billowing dust brought on a fit of coughing, and that jerked Rosemary back to harsh reality. France with its chateaus and vineyards faded into the dusty Kansas plains as the stagecoach bumped along. She coughed again, straining the tight laces of her corset, and wiped her round face with a lace hankie, which only made muddy streaks, she knew. No doubt her plain brown hair was full of dust, too. Rosemary tried to straighten her hat with its big plumes, then she raised one arm and looked at the dark circle under the armpit. She should have worn a lighter color. Plum probably wasn't a good color with her complexion anyway.

Oh, Daddy, I never really got to know you. Mother always had me back East in fancy schools. How was I to know you would drop dead suddenly of a heart attack in the bank lobby while I was away?

That had been more than three years ago. Then Mother had married that slick and too handsome teller, Godfrey St. John, and made him president of the bank.

Rosemary scowled. All that was about to change. She had never liked Godfrey, and now she vowed that on her twenty-first birthday, she would send the rascal packing. With the help of that old reliable teller Bill Wilkerson, Rosemary would take over control of the bank herself. Was she smart enough to do that? Mother had told her over and over that she was not clever at all.

All right, so if she wasn't clever or pretty, she'd have to rely on her stubbornness and common sense. After she fired St. John on October thirty-first, Rosemary would make some other changes. First, she would get herself a dog. Her parents had never allowed Rosemary to own a dog; they complained that pets were dirty and shed hair.

Yes, a dog, and not the prissy little pup that ladies favored, but a real dog—a big, hairy dog to romp and play with, and yes, it could sleep in the house and it would love her no matter how plain and stubborn she was. She smiled to herself. Her parents would probably roll over in their graves.

She stuck her head through the open window of the rolling stage and looked down the road ahead. In the distance, she could see the barest silhouette of the town. Her brown hair blew loose and she pulled back inside the stage and tried to readjust her plumed hat. Gracious, she probably looked a mess, but she couldn't do much about that now.

Rosemary stuck her head out the window again and yelled up to the driver. "Could you just pass through town and take me on out to the house?"

The old man shook his head and yelled back," Can't do that, Miss Burke, ma'am, they're plannin' a big homecomin' for you at the bank."

Oh, of course Godfrey would do that. She leaned back against the horsehair cushions and tried to straighten her hat, mop the dust off her face, and smooth the wrinkles and early lunch crumbs from her dress.

She could almost hear Mother's disapproving voice. "You look a fright, Rosemary. Next time you buy a dress, take someone with good taste with you."

Who would I take, Mother? she thought. *I have no friends in Prairie View. You never allowed me to play with the local children or go to school here; everyone in Kansas was too low class for you.*

"I swear, you surely didn't get any of my looks, you take after your father's side of the family."

"Yes, Mother," Rosemary said without thinking and smiled. On Halloween, Rosemary would be of legal age and the first thing she intended to do was toss that handsome rascal Godfrey out into the street. He might have fooled Mother, but he hadn't fooled Rosemary.

Waco and his men had stabled their horses, had a drink at the nearest saloon to wash the dust from their throats, and presently, they were walking around inside the bank, looking up at the banners and the big cake a teller now carried into the lobby and set on a table. The crowd inside and out seemed to be growing.

"What's goin' on?" Waco asked an old man.

"Oh, ain't you heard? Banker's daughter comin' in on the noon stage. Been gone quite a while now."

"Don't say?" Waco muttered.

"Stick around," said a blue-clad soldier, "there'll be cake and punch."

"Sound good." Waco surveyed the crowd and then caught the eye of his men, nodded his head toward the outside.

The four of them ambled out onto the wooden sidewalk.

"I don't like it," Tom said. "You ever see so many Yankee soldiers? They make me as nervous as a deacon with his hand in the church collection plate."

"Gawd Almighty! Keep your voice down," Waco cautioned. "You want to be grabbed this minute? We got to keep a low profile."

"Is that the reason you ain't wearin' them silver spurs?" Tom asked.

Waco nodded. "Attract too much attention. I'll keep them in my saddlebags."

Zeb took a chaw of tobacco. "Knew it was too

good to be true about that fat bank bein' easy pickin's. Never seen so many blue-bellies; town workin' alive with them."

"I never said it was gonna be easy," Waco reminded him. Privately, he was shocked himself. When he'd been told about this bank, what he hadn't been told was that the town was a beehive of Union soldiers.

Zeke combed his fingers through his beard and took his mouth organ out of his shirt pocket. "Who's this Rosemary everyone's talkin' about?"

"The banker's daughter," Waco answered.

Zeke began to play an off-key version of "Dixie." The other three glared at him.

Waco said, "Why don't you just wave a red flag at all them Yankee soldiers?"

"I plumb forgot." Zeke looked sheepish and changed over to "Camptown Races."

"That banker must set a heap of store by her," Tom offered, "judging from all the whoop-de-do that's goin' on."

"Must," Waco agreed, shrugging wide shoulders. "Think she's been gone awhile."

A growing crowd gathered on the wooden sidewalk in front of the bank.

"Hey!" someone whooped. "I think I see the stage in the distance!"

"Somebody tell the banker!"

A short man pushed through the crowd and into the bank to carry the news.

Waco caught a freckled-face boy by the arm. "Hey, son, how come there's so many soldiers around?"

"Ain't you heard?" The boy pointed. "New fort bein' built just west a town."

"Yes siree bob," a snaggled-tooth older man said with a smile, "bringin' lots of prosperity to our little Prairie View."

The four Texans exchanged glances and moved away.

"A whole nest of soldiers guardin' that bank," Tom muttered under his breath. "So now what do we do?"

"Shh!" Waco ordered. "We got to think about this. There has to be a way."

"We don't dare go back without the money," Zeb said, putting a chaw of tobacco in his mouth.

His older brother took the mouth organ away from his lips. "You think we don't know that?"

"Hush up!" Waco drawled. "Y'all keep your minds open and your mouths shut."

"Hey," yelled a beefy Yankee sergeant, leaning against a store front.

Waco felt the sweat break out on his tanned face. "Yes, Sergeant?"

"You got the time?"

Waco relaxed and reached for his gold pocket watch. "Just about noon."

The sergeant frowned. "You sound like Texans. What you doin' so far from home?"

Tom, Zeke, and Zeb looked at each other, obviously panicked, but Waco grinned, remembering their cover story. "Up here to see if we can sell beef to the army."

The other's beefy face turned hostile. "Big, healthy bunch like you ought to be in one army or the other."

Waco gritted his teeth but forced a smile. "We

got no dog in that fight, Sergeant. We ain't about to get shot by either side."

The sergeant snorted his scorn and moved away.

Tom doubled up his fist, but Waco grabbed his arm so hard, the younger man winced.

"You're gonna get us killed for sure," Waco cautioned under his breath.

A cheer went up and people pushed forward toward the sidewalk from all the surrounding stores and out into the dusty street, looking north.

A tall, handsome man came out of the bank, smoking a cigar. From the scent, it must be an expensive one. The man wore a fine, gray pin-striped suit and his hands looked as if they had never done any work, not like Waco's big, calloused ones. People greeted the newcomer with deference and respect.

"That must be the banker," Waco muttered to his friends. The man looked a little too slick, Waco thought, more like a card sharp than a banker.

Waco pushed through the crowd to where he could look down the street. The stage raced toward them with a jingle of harness and a cloud of dust while the crowd cheered.

"Whoa, horses! Whoa!" The wiry driver pulled his lathered team to a stop, hopped down and came around to open the door while the crowd fell silent, waiting.

Inside, Rosemary took a deep breath, steeling herself for the ordeal to come. She had no social graces. Hadn't Mother told her that a million times?

The driver opened the door and Rosemary stood

up to get out. There seemed to be a sea of curious faces out there staring expectantly. She paused on the step, taking herself away from this awkward situation.

In her mind, she was Flame La Beau, the toast of New Orleans, arriving in this eager town to give a show. All the townsfolk had gathered to see the gorgeous showgirl. She wore a low-cut black gown to show off her curvacious figure. Her shiny ebony curls were done up on the back of her slender neck with a bright ribbon, and every man in the crowd was waiting for her to lift her skirt and give them a quick, heart-thudding glimpse of her dainty ankle.

Against a nearby post leaned a tall, lanky man with eyes as faded blue as his denim pants. Now as Flame favored him with a glance, he took off his Stetson and ran one tanned hand through sun-streaked hair. He looked at her with interest and she thought that when she danced tonight to a sold-out, appreciative crowd, she might throw this gent a garter from her shapely leg. No doubt he would never forget the night he met the notorious Flame of New Orleans.

Waco studied the girl poised on the step looking about. She was a tall and sturdy, softly rounded girl with pretty brown eyes in a dimpled, dust-streaked face. A plumed hat sat a bit crooked on her brown hair. She looked very hot and uncomfortable in a plum-colored dress, and her face seemed unusually florid. There was something vulnerable and unhappy in those dark eyes. The girl took the driver's outstretched hand, made a hesitant move, missed the next step, and fell in the dirt by the sidewalk.

The crowd gasped and the driver tried to help the plump girl up, but he wasn't strong enough to manage it.

Without thinking, Waco pushed through the crowd to her other side as she sat sprawled in the dust of the road with the little driver pulling vainly at her arm. Everyone gathered around, but only Waco reached down and took her arm. "Are you all right, ma'am?"

Rosemary just wanted to die from embarrassment. Tears came to her eyes.

Clumsy, clumsy, she scolded herself, not making any attempt to get up out of the dirt. Probably the crowd was laughing at her. If she could just die right here and be spared the humiliation.

Then she heard a masculine drawl and a strong hand took her arm. "Are you all right, ma'am?"

She blinked back the tears and looked up. It was that tall, handsome cowboy. How humiliating he had seen her at her clumsiest. "Gracious, I—I—"

"You must have fainted, ma'am," he said kindly, "the heat and all. Here, let me help you."

Even as she protested that he probably couldn't lift her, he swung her up in his arms, dusty plum dress and all, turning toward the bank. Oh, he was so strong. She sighed and laid her face against his chest and felt her hat fall off, but she didn't care. She'd made a fool of herself again.

But then a sympathetic murmur ran through the

crowd. "Did you hear that? Miss Rosemary swooned from the heat!"

"Well, of course, she's a lady and it so hot and all."

"Take her inside where it's cooler," a lady said.

Oh, her reputation was saved. She leaned her dusty, sweaty face against the cowboy's wide shoulder and let him carry her into the bank, followed by the curious crowd. Then she saw Godfrey pushing through the mob toward them.

"Ye Gods, dear Rosemary, are you all right?"

She closed her eyes and didn't answer.

"Get the lady a glass of water and a wet handkerchief," the cowboy drawled like he was used to ordering people around. "She fainted from the heat. Somebody pick up her hat."

"Are you sure she didn't just trip?" Godfrey asked. "I thought I saw—"

She glanced up and saw the glare in the blue eyes, aimed at Godfrey. "No, the lady fainted. She's too delicate to be out in this heat." Now the big man carried her into Godfrey's office and put her down on a crimson settee.

She smiled up at him. No one had ever called her "delicate" before. Of course, as big as this cowboy was, maybe she didn't seem plump and clumsy to him. She kept her arms at her sides so he couldn't see how damp her dress was under the arms. "Thank you, kind sir."

He grinned and stepped back, took off his hat. His eyes were a startling faded blue in his weathered, tan face. "Glad I could be of service, ma'am."

Now Godfrey was shouldering him aside. "Here, Rosemary, here's some punch. Do you feel like greeting some of my customers?"

She started to tell him they were *her* customers, but decided against it. This wasn't the time or place to confront her stepfather. "I'd really like to go to the house—"

"The customers will be disappointed," Godfrey snapped. "I've gone to a lot of trouble with the cake and all. Even got you a fine gift."

"All right." She reached out her hand to the cowboy, but he had stepped back and now Godfrey took her hand, pulled her to her feet. He yanked her toward the lobby and she turned her head and looked after the cowboy who shrugged and stepped back into the crowd. Oh, he was just being polite, she thought, crestfallen. Of course a man like that couldn't be attracted to a plain and heavy girl.

Godfrey hustled her out into the lobby. "Here she is, folks, our dear Rosemary is finally home!" Godfrey raised his voice so all could hear.

"Hurray!" the crowd shouted and surrounded her to shake her hand and wish her well.

Old Bill Wilkerson, the white-haired senior teller, gave her a warm hug. "Glad you've finally come home, Miss Rosemary, don't know why your mother sent you off to that fancy back-East school anyway after she remarried, and then that Grand Tour."

Godfrey was certainly behind all that, Rosemary thought, because Agatha Burke might not have succumbed to his oily charms if Rosemary had been around to talk some sense into her. "Hello, Bill, glad to see you."

She looked around in vain for the big cowboy, but he had disappeared. Godfrey pushed through the crowd and returned with a small box. "Here's a welcome-home gift, my dear, straight from Paris, France. Even had it monogrammed."

Bought with my daddy's money, she thought, but she only said, "Oh, Godfrey, you shouldn't have."

"Nothing too good for our dear Rosemary," he said and gave her an oily smirk.

Reluctantly, she opened it and the crowd gasped. It was a white, pure silk scarf with her initials on it, very fine and expensive. "It's lovely," she said without enthusiasm.

"Put it on," someone urged.

She tied it in a loose bow around her neck.

"Lovely as the wearer," Godfrey quipped.

She waited for God to strike him with lightning for his lying tongue, then decided God was asleep at the switch today. "If you don't mind, I'm very tired—"

"No, you can't leave yet." Godfrey put his hand on her arm and squeezed hard in warning. "Everyone will be so disappointed."

So she stayed another hour, greeting people and eating cake, too much cake because she was nervous about making a bigger fool of herself, and of course she got crumbs all over the expensive white scarf. She looked about in vain for the tall cowboy who had saved her from ridicule, but he was gone. Well, what had she expected? Hadn't Mother said that only the bank's money would get her a beau?

Finally a buggy came from the mansion to take her home.

"Oh, by the way, dear," Godfrey said as he puffed and struggled to lift her up on the seat, "I'm giving a dinner party tonight for a few select people. Be ready."

She got herself up into the buggy, thinking wistfully of the strong and virile man who had carried her. "A dinner party?" Rosemary sighed. "I'm awfully tired—"

"Be ready," he warned her, and his eyes were cold and black as marble. "I'll be home early, and oh, let Mollie help you pick out something to wear. She has such good taste."

And of course, Rosemary didn't. Hadn't her mother told her that her whole life?

"All right." She was not going to get into a fight with him right here. She would confront him later. After all, she was powerless until she was twenty-one.

The driver drove her to the imposing mansion five miles outside town that her father had built to bring his elegant, back-East bride to. Agatha Worthing had been much too good for such a country bumpkin, as she'd told her daughter so often, but her family had fallen on hard times and Noah Burke might have been a mannerless hick, but he'd gotten rich growing wheat and then began to lend money to the local farmers. He had such a sterling reputation that he soon opened a promising bank.

The household staff were lined up to greet her at the door, even Mollie, the pretty but coarse Irish maid with the crooked front teeth, whose lip seemed to curl in derision as she curtsied. Or maybe Rosemary was imagining that.

"I'm very tired," Rosemary said to all, "and I'd like to rest and clean up. Mr. St. John is planning a dinner party, I understand."

Everyone nodded.

"And I'm to help you pick out something to

wear." Mollie smirked, and her tone of importance annoyed Rosemary.

"I think I can dress myself," she snapped and went up the stairs. She didn't really like Mollie. Sometimes when she and Mother and Godfrey had been sitting before the library fire, she'd thought she'd seen her stepfather exchanging winks with the pretty maid. She dared not tell her mother, who not only wouldn't have believed it, she'd have berated Rosemary for her suspicions.

Rosemary went into her room and stared into the mirror on the dresser. Yes, she looked as big a mess as she thought she did. The big plumed hat tilted dangerously to one side and Rosemary took it off and threw it across the room. She hated hats anyway.

She fingered the white silk scarf and sighed with resignation. She didn't care much for expensive clothes, but Godfrey did. She tied it around her throat again, tucking it into the neck of the plum dress. She napped for a while, then drifted down the stairs. Everyone in the house seemed to be bustling about, getting ready for the grand dinner party.

She wished she could avoid that. Godfrey and her late mother loved to entertain with grand balls and dinners, but Rosemary found such events boring. She preferred a simpler life . . . or maybe it was because she was so clumsy; she always seemed to spill something on her clothes or trip when a young man asked her to dance.

Out of idle curiosity, she wandered out into the conservatory, Godfrey's passion. It was hot and green and steamy inside. He grew exotic, expensive plants like orchids and seemed fascinated by

plants such as fly catchers. In fact, she had seen
the gleam in his cold eyes when he fed crippled
flies to the plant.

She looked about the conservatory, admiring the
exotic flowers. Then she bumped into a small
orchid and the pot crashed to the floor with a loud
noise. Oh, gracious, she had done it again. Well, he
had so many plants, maybe he wouldn't notice one
missing. Or maybe she could repot it and save it.
She found another pot and tried to replant the
orchid, but it now sat at an angle in its pot, looking
sickly. She'd done the best she could, but if Godfrey
noticed, he'd be angry. Where could she hide it?

When she took over the estate, she promised
herself, instead of exotic plants, she'd grow no-
nonsense things like maybe some sunflowers and
some fruit trees. Maybe she could even start a
little garden here in this big glass room and grow
vegetables.

How like your father. She could almost hear mother's
scornful voice. *I've tried to turn you into a lady and you'd
rather be a farmer.*

"Yes, I would." Rosemary nodded emphatically.
"And I'll get some cows and chickens and more
horses and a dog, a big, hairy dog."

But first, what to do about the damaged orchid?
Rosemary took the pot and walked around, looking for a good place to hide it. She paused in front
of a tall, big-leafed plant. This was unusual. She hid
the little flower pot behind the big leaves. Whatever it was, some of its leaves had turned scarlet
and it seemed to have decorative cockleburrs for
flowers. Some of the cockleburrs were open and
their speckled seeds were visible. They looked a

little like pinto beans. The identifying tag on the big plant read "*Ricinus Communis*: African Origin."

Out of curiosity, she touched one of the cockle-burrs and yanked back. "Ohh! Damn it!" Then she looked around quickly to make sure no one had heard her swearing. Now she noticed the drops of blood on her fingertips.

"Clumsy me." She had pricked her fingers trying to get the seed pod. Without thinking, she wiped the blood on the white silk scarf, along with the dirty smudge from her fingers. Gracious, now God-frey would be really upset. Maybe she could rinse it out before he saw it. Rosemary hurried upstairs, took off the scarf, wondering about washing it. She couldn't give the task to Mollie, the little snit would certainly tattle on her. She heard someone coming.

"Miss Rosemary?" Mollie called, "be ye be gettin' dressed? Mr. St. John is comin' home early."

Oh, damn, damn, damn. Rosemary yanked off the bloodied scarf and tossed it under her bed. She'd figure out what to do about it later. "I'm get-ting ready if you'll pour me some bath water."

Quickly, Rosemary, stripped off the dusty plum dress and stared at herself in the mirror, then re-gretted it. She was plump, there was no doubt about it; even with her corset so tight, she could hardly breathe. She kept promising herself she'd diet, but then she'd have an ego-crushing disap-pointment and fill the void with snacks and candy. She would have given half her life to be thin and pretty, but no matter what cosmetics she bought, how she tried to starve herself, she was always going to be a tall, large girl. A man might marry her for her money, but not for love. She'd have to find that in the romantic novels she'd always hidden under her mattress.

In the next room, she could hear Mollie pouring pails of water. The Irish girl stuck her head in the door. "Would ye be wantin' my help with your bathin', miss?" Was that a hint of derision in the beauty's Irish brogue?

"No, thanks, I can take it from now on."

"Aye. Very well, then, Miss Rosemary. Mr. St. John said I should help you pick out a dress for to wear tonight."

Even Godfrey thought the maid had better taste than Rosemary did.

Remember, she is the maid and everyone expects you to be difficult. "I'll pick out my own dress, thank you."

"Ah, but Mr. St. John said—"

"You can go, Mollie." Rosemary steeled herself to be authoritative.

"All right then," the maid said in a flip tone, "but don't be ablamin' me if he's that upset." She sailed out of the room, slamming the door behind her.

He'd think upset October thirty-first when Rosemary took over and tossed him out on his handsome and well-clad posterior.

She climbed into the big copper tub and made lots of suds, then leaned back with a sigh. She was the dark and mysterious Cleopatra, Queen of the Nile. Men would give their lives to see her beautiful form bathing, but of course, only Mark Anthony and maybe some other powerful men ever would.

Then she started scrubbing herself and shook her head over just how plump the mysterious queen had become. She closed her eyes as she bathed, not wanting to be Rosemary Burke again. As she sudsed her long brown hair, she thought again of the strong, tanned man. What would he say if he could see her bathing? The thought made her shudder and she quickly finished bathing, wrapped a towel around her wet body, and went into her bedroom, avoiding the mirror. It had been a difficult day; how she wished she had a leftover piece of cake for comfort.

Mollie had laid out some underthings and a dress, despite Rosemary's orders. The arrogant servant was one of the people Rosemary intended to fire when she sent Godfrey packing. She wondered if Mollie would still find the stepfather so fascinating when he had no money?

Rosemary put on her underthings and picked up the corset with resignation. She'd like to throw it away and never wear such an uncomfortable thing again, but of course it made her appear thinner, and that was important to men. Then she looked at the dress Mollie had chosen and gritted her teeth. It was bright green, very elaborate and expensive, and Rosemary hated it. She hung the bright-colored silk back in the closet and chose a simple pale blue gown.

Mollie came into the room just then. "Ye need help with your corset, ma'am?"

Mollie was so slender, she probably never wore one.

"Yes, please." Rosemary put it on and hung on to the bedpost as Mollie struggled to lace it and pull it tight. Tiny waists and full bell skirts with hoops were the fashion now. Even when Mollie pulled the corset so tight, Rosemary felt her face turn cherry red, she knew she would never achieve the hourglass figure featured in all the ladies' magazines. "Not so tight," she gulped, "I can't breathe."

"Ah, but ye'll want to be stylish, won't ye?" Mollie scolded.

"No," Rosemary said emphatically, "I want to breathe. I don't want to swoon from lack of air."

"Gentlemen like dainty ladies who swoon," Mollie said and in the next breath, "is *that* what you're going to wear?"

Now she sounded just like Mother. Rosemary bristled. "Yes, that's what I'm going to wear."

"But Mr. St. John—"

"Enough, Mollie. I intend to wear the blue dress."

"All right, but I hope he don't blame me none that—"

"I'll deal with Godfrey." She was surprised at her own resoluteness. "You may get the curling iron and do my hair now."

The uppity Irish girl stomped out of the room and returned with a curling iron, pins, and brushes. She lit a lamp and put the curling iron to heat over it while she towel-dried her mistress's brown hair.

"Not too elaborate." Rosemary ordered.

"All fine ladies have theirs all done up fancy," Mollie reminded her.

"I don't care. I'd like it pulled to the nape of my neck and tied with blue ribbons so the curls can hang down my back."

"Yes, ma'am, it's your hair." It was evident Mollie disapproved. "Can't make a silk purse from a—"

"What was that?"

"Nuthin', ma'am," Mollie said.

No doubt Godfrey would disapprove, too.

Well, she'd deal with that when she got there, Rosemary sighed.

Below, she heard the front door open and the butler say, "Ah, good afternoon, Mr. St. John. The lady is upstairs dressing."

Then Godfrey yelled up the stairs. "Yoo-hoo, Rosemary, I'd like a word with you in the library."

Rosemary gritted her teeth. To Mollie, she said, "Tell him I'll be right down."

Mollie went to the door. "Godfrey," she called, "I mean, Mr. St. John, Miss Rosemary says she'll be right down."

The maid seemed a little too familiar, Rosemary thought, but she let it pass. She dismissed Mollie, heard her descending the stairs, and after a moment, she thought she could hear the maid and Godfrey talking.

Rosemary dreaded this evening, trying to make clever conversation with the prominent locals. No doubt someone would bring along an eligible son or nephew, hoping to marry her for her money. For a long moment, Rosemary wished there was someone out there who would be interested in her for herself.

The image of that big Texas cowboy passed through her mind. His arms had been so powerful as he picked her up out of the dirt, and he hadn't laughed behind his hand like she suspected so many others were doing. In her mind, she was Billie, the Western Queen of the Range, galloping around an arena, a tiny, spunky thing on a big black horse, roping and doing tricks while the audience applauded and the big cowboy nodded in approval from the sidelines. Then he would lift her from her saddle and—

"Rosemary, are you coming down or not?" Godfrey's annoyed voice broke into her daydream from below.

"I'm coming." She hurried toward the stairs, the big hoop skirt swaying around her as she walked. She felt like a hot air balloon about to go aloft.

Below her, Godfrey St. John looked up at his stepdaughter and frowned. He liked tiny, slender women who laughed a lot and were free with their favors; someone like Mollie. Rosemary was not his type at all, so plain and plump in that simple blue dress, and the wide hoops only made her seem heavier. Ye Gods, did he really have to marry her? Maybe it would just be easier to murder her.

Chapter Two

Rosemary came down the stairs, the hoop skirt swaying as she descended. She might as well begin practicing her resoluteness if she was going to take over the bank. Then she felt herself begin to waver. "Well, Godfrey, you're home from the bank early."

"I was so eager to see you. You've been overseas for almost a year now."

"That wasn't my idea; it was yours." She took a deep breath. She wasn't at all sure she had the courage and self-confidence to confront him.

He took her hand, frowning. "Rosemary, dear, as many clothes as you own, that's a very simple frock."

She felt herself tremble. "As a matter of fact, it is, but it suites me better than that green ornate silk. I like my clothes simple. I'm thinking about doing away with my corset and hoops entirely."

"Ah, my dear, surely you jest." He laughed without mirth. "We're people of property, and you should dress accordingly."

"I don't see why upper-class women should be more miserable than poor ones."

"Don't be difficult, Rosemary, dear. You wouldn't want to be the laughingstock of this town, now would you?" He took her elbow.

She had always felt that people snickered at her behind her back. *It's good she's rich or that poor, plump thing would never get a beau.*

"You're hurting me," she said, jerking from his grip.

He seemed to take a deep, shuddering breath for control, but she saw the muscles in his jaw working. "Ahem. Well, whatever you say, my dear. Shall we go into the library for a talk?"

"About what?"

"Do you have to be so blunt? It isn't very lady-like." He turned toward the library.

"So my mother told me over and over. It just seems honest to me." However, she steeled herself and followed him into the library. Did she have the courage to be her own woman now that she was almost of legal age? "Uh, I might as well tell you, Godfrey, I intend to take control over the assets on my birthday."

His handsome face turned pale and he rushed to close the door. "Rosemary, lower your voice. The servants will hear us and I don't want them to think we're quarreling."

"Are we quarreling? I thought I was merely making a statement." She took a seat on a straight chair, avoiding the sofa where he might sit next to her.

He sat down at his desk and took out his pocket knife, cleaning his nails. She noted his hands trembled. "Now, Rosemary, dear, let's give this a lot of thought. You are a woman and know nothing of business. I just don't think you're capable of handling the bank."

"I think I can learn." She looked him straight in the eye and it felt good.

He sighed and paused, looking at her like he'd like to stab her with the small knife. "Your mother always said you were a difficult child, but I hoped as you matured, you'd change."

She might as well be brave and plunge in. "I have changed, Godfrey. I may not be a beauty, but I think I'm smart. Besides, between Daddy's lawyer and old Mr. Wilkerson, I think I can manage."

"But you have me to look after your interests." He folded up the knife and gave her the smile he always used on her mother that had gotten him promoted from lowly teller to president of the Prairie View Bank.

"Godfrey, you have never looked after anyone's interests but your own." There, she'd said it.

He seemed to be gritting his teeth. "Dearest girl, why must you be so obstinate? I do not wish to argue with you. We'll have guests arriving in another hour."

She took a deep breath for courage. "We do have a lot to discuss. You know I'll be twenty-one at the end of the month."

He got up from his desk and came over to look down at her. "Yes, I know." He smiled. "I intend to give a ball in your honor."

"Must you? I hate balls. I always step on my partner's feet."

"Oh, but everyone will expect it. Your dear dead mother would expect it. You know she loved the social scene."

"I am not like my beautiful, vain mother, as she so often reminded me."

"Dear, must you be so stubborn and difficult? We'll talk later when you aren't so tired from your long trip."

"Why is it when I don't try to please everyone, I am being difficult?"

He hooked his fingers in his lapels and stared down at her, his lips smiling, but his cold eyes not. "I know you are lost and still grieving, my dearest child, and need both my protection and my business advice."

She was not grieving for her mother, who had always been cold and distant, but she knew to say so would only make her seem more obstinate.

She simply stared at him as he abruptly knelt down on one knee and took one of her hands in his. "Dear Rosemary, you misjudge me."

My mother might have, but not I, she thought as she tried to pull her hand from his, but he held on to it stubbornly.

"You see, my dear, I have developed feelings for you. I know there is a difference in our ages, but—"

"When did all this feeling develop?" She yanked her hand away in shock and, for once, said exactly what she was thinking. "When you discovered Mother had left the estate to me?"

He winced. "You wound me with your cold indifference. I—I have always admired you from afar, and now that dear Agatha is gone, I thought maybe someday, you might consider marrying—"

"What?" She was horrified.

"Oh, my dear, we could have such a great partnership, the two of us."

"Gracious!" She drew back, speechless. "Uh, get up off your knees, you'll wear a hole in your fine trousers." She stood up and walked toward the door. "You always treated me with cold disregard, now you want to marry me? Ridiculous!"

"Wait!" He scrambled to his feet. "Rosemary, dear, let us not be too hasty."

She trembled with outrage. "I'm not being hasty. I wouldn't marry you if you were the last man on earth. Oh, I know I'm no beauty and probably no man will ever want me, but I certainly won't settle for a man who has very questionable intentions."

He held out his hands in an entreating manner. "I swear my intentions are honorable, my dear. I admit that I have always loved you from afar. That is the reason I sent you away on tour. I didn't want to cause gossip."

"So now you think that since it's been over a year, there won't be wagging tongues?" She snorted in what Mother would have called a most unladylike manner. "There would be a great deal of gossip if you married your stepdaughter."

He smiled that oily smile that some women found so irresistible. "I had already considered that, but as you know, I am a pillar of this community. I belong to all the right clubs, I've donated a stained glass window to the church and money to the orphans' fund. I'm sure everyone would overlook it."

"Godfrey, n-o. No. You will not get control of my father's assets that way." She started out the door.

"Don't make your decision right now," he begged, following her out into the hall. "After all, this may be the only proposal you ever get."

The old hurt came back and she blinked back

tears as she paused and looked back at him. "You don't need to remind me that I'm no beauty. Perhaps my talent lies in taking over the bank, in which case, Godfrey, in less than three weeks, I will fire you."

"Rosemary, your mother would be shocked that you might actually—"

"Please stop mentioning my mother." Rosemary had never felt such freedom as she did at this moment. "I'll see you at dinner." She marched up the stairs.

Godfrey stared after her, furious, then looked around, wondering if the servants had heard. Damn that girl anyhow. She might be homely but she certainly wasn't stupid. He had hoped to charm her into marriage or at least letting him stay in control of the bank while she joined ladies' clubs, went riding, and knitted. In a few years, he could embezzle enough to last a long time as he had in St. Louis. Now there was no getting around it, he'd have to murder Rosemary.

Godfrey returned to the library and paced up and down, thinking. How to get rid of Rosemary. He paused, considered, then shook his head. No, he couldn't do the same thing twice. Maybe he could set up some kind of accident or hire someone to do the job. However, that would be setting himself up for blackmail.

That made him think about Mollie. He had certainly made a mistake getting mixed up with that little tart. Besides, when he was in Kansas City a week ago, he'd hired a new maid who was coming to work next week, one who was twice as pretty, and even a dumb Mick like Mollie would soon realize she was about to be replaced.

No, he'd have to do in Rosemary himself, make her disappear or kill her in a way that there were no suspicions about him. It wasn't as if it would be the first time.

Waco and his men had walked out of the bank to watch the buggy bearing the banker's daughter pulling away from town. "Gawd Almighty! Now that's a Texas-sized gal. I got no use for weak, skinny women. Those kind are always whinin' and helpless."

Tom rolled a smoke. "You thought she was purty?"

Waco rubbed his chin. "Wal, maybe not beautiful, but she had lots of soft curves and pretty eyes. A man could do worse."

"I've done worse," Zeb snorted, "in a saloon at closin' time when I was lookin' for a filly to go home with."

"Yep," agreed his older brother with a nod, "I've seen your women. Most are coyote bait."

Waco frowned. "This one is a lady. Don't imagine she'd ever go into a saloon."

"Speakin' of which," Tom coughed, "why don't we adjourn to that one down the street for a drink?"

"Let's get some supplies first." Waco nodded toward the general store. "Then we'll have a drink. The longer we hang around this town, the more notice we get, and this town is workin' alive with blue bellies."

"Ain't we gonna rob the bank?" Zeb put a chaw in his mouth.

His brother punched his shoulder. "Why don't you just get up on that there post office rooftop and shout?" he scolded. "There might be a few people that didn't hear you."

"Shut up, both of you," Waco snapped. "We got to decide what to do."

"Yes, sir," Tom said without thinking.

Waco glared at him.

"I mean, sure, Waco."

"That's better. A slip like that could get us all killed. We got a porcupine by the tail here, looks like. If we don't get the money, we get shot. If we try to rob this bank with all these Yankee soldiers around, we get shot."

"Yep, it's a Mexican standoff." Zeke nodded and pulled out his harmonica. He began to play "Oh, Bury Me Not on the Lone Prairie."

Zeb spat tobacco juice in the dusty street. "You know, we could just light a shuck for Californy or Canada."

Waco glared at him. "We're Texans. We gave our word. That's sacred."

"Amen." Zeke paused in playing his mouth organ. "Remember the Alamo."

"To the Alamo!" the other three echoed reverently and removed their Stetsons.

"I'll drink to that," declared Waco. "First the supplies, and then a drink in honor of the great state of Texas."

They went into the general store, got bacon, cornmeal, and coffee, then headed down the street through the swinging doors of the Velvet Lady. The place was deserted and smelled of stale beer and cigar smoke.

Waco chose a table near the window where he had his back to the wall but could watch the people and horses moving up and down the main street. An old bartender with a handlebar mustache came up to the table. "What can I get you gents?"

"Beer all around," Waco drawled.

The man paused, looking interested. "You gents ain't from around here, are you?"

"Nope, Texas," Waco said. "We're up here to sell some beef."

The bartender grinned. "That new fort will be glad to hear that. They could probably use some meat."

His partners exchanged glances but Waco said, "How long's that been there?"

"Just a few weeks. Major Mathis is in charge. It sure is bringing in a lot of business for Prairie View."

Waco nodded. "Reckon we'll go see the major. *Gracias.*"

The other man looked puzzled.

"I mean, thanks," Waco said. "Now how about those beers?"

The other man grinned and disappeared. Tom started to speak, but Waco motioned him to silence. The barkeep came back with the beers and Waco threw down the change, waited till the man had scooped it up, and headed into the back room before he muttered, "Well, now we know why it's such a fat bank."

Tom grabbed his beer, drank thirstily, wiped the foam from his lip. "But, Waco, we don't have no cows to sell."

"I got cows," Waco said, "runnin' loose on my

ranch. Reckon it will be after the war before we can round them up."

Zeke sipped his beer slowly, savoring it. "We ain't really gonna pay a social call on the major?"

"Sure we are," Waco said. He pulled out his gold watch and checked the time. "Otherwise, we'll arouse suspicion."

"What if he wants to buy cows?" Zeb asked.

Waco winked. "We'll price them too high."

Zeke grumbled, "I don't see how any of this is gonna help us get the money we need."

"Let's get outta here," Waco ordered, draining his mug. "We got to think about how to get fifty thousand dollars."

"It might as well be a million," Tom said, pulling his hat low over his big ears and red hair.

Waco motioned for them to follow him. "We'll find a place to camp and talk about it, but right now, boys, I think we ought to pay a call on the major and look over that fort, see just how many soldiers they got."

"Too many!" Zeke snorted. "And half of them standin' around in this town. We wouldn't make it half a mile with them chasin' us."

As they mounted up, Zeb suggested, "Maybe we could break into the bank at night."

"With what?" Waco challenged as he swung up into the saddle. "We didn't come equipped with dynamite or picks and shovels, and if we try to buy stuff like that, everyone would go on the alert like hound dogs sniffin' a coon scent."

Zeke wiped his beard with the back of one gnarled hand as he mounted up. "I don't like it none, this here ridin' into the fort. "You know in these clothes, we could get shot."

Waco stared at him with pale blue eyes. "You got a better plan?"

"Reckon not," the old man admitted.

"Then let's go, partners," Waco commanded.

They rode north to the fort. As they approached the new buildings and saw more and more Union troops hanging around the stables and marching on the parade grounds, Waco's heart sank to the toes of his worn boots. Yep, this was going to be a big fort, drawing in hundreds of troops and more town residents. No wonder Prairie View had such a prosperous bank. Too bad his informant had overlooked this little detail.

Tom leaned toward him and whispered, "I think we seen enough to know there's too many of them for us to give that bank another thought. Why don't we just turn around and ride out?"

Waco shook his head and kept riding. "Too many people have seen us. We got to have an excuse for comin' here."

He asked a passing private and was pointed toward Major Mathis's office. The four tied up their horses at the hitching rail and went into the new building.

A pimply faced corporal looked up from a cluttered desk. "May I help you gentlemen?"

"We'd like to see the major," Waco said.

The corporal's expression changed at the Southern drawl. "I'll see if he's in, but you'll have to leave your guns with me."

Waco felt naked without his Colt, but he said, "Sure. We're here on business."

As they were taking off their pistols and handing them over, a young officer came out of the other office. He had long blond curls. "Hanlan, I'm leaving early, got a dinner to attend—"

"Sir." The corporal scrambled to his feet, saluting. "These gentlemen are here to see you."

The pink-faced major looked annoyed. "What about?"

Waco forced a smile. "If we could just set and talk awhile, Major."

The major pulled out his pocket watch, fidgeting. "I'm in a hurry, but oh, all right, just for a few minutes."

"Won't take much of your time." Waco grinned and the others stayed behind him as they followed the officer back into his office and took seats.

"Now," said the young major in a back East accent, "I can tell you're not from around here. What do you need?"

"It's what you need, Major," Waco said. He tried to keep from staring at the blond curls. "We're up from Texas to see about sellin' the army some beef."

The officer scowled at him. "Why don't you sell that beef to your own side? I figure the Rebs need beef as much as we do."

Waco shrugged and leaned back in his chair. "We got no side, Major. We don't give diddly shit about this war. Ain't that right, fellas?"

The other cowboys nodded.

"Besides," Waco grinned, "the Rebs is broke. They got no gold to buy beef or anything else, and them paper Confederate dollars is only good to use in the outhouse. We know the Union has *real* money."

The major's frown deepened. "You men look healthy, you ought to be in the service on one side or the other."

"Like I said, Major," Waco lied, "we got no dog in this fight. We got a thousand steers we're thinkin' about drivin' up across Indian Territory to feed your troops."

"No loyalty," the major snapped. "I don't like that in a man. Very well, how much for the beef?"

"Just like that without talkin' some?" Waco asked. "In Texas, we like to have a drink and chew something over a little."

The major pulled out his watch again. "I'm due at a dinner honoring the banker's daughter. State your price so we can get on with it."

Waco glanced around at the others. He didn't want the major to say yes because he wasn't about to sell the Yanks beef. Not that he didn't own ten thousand now worthless cattle back on his ranch, but he only needed an excuse to be in Prairie View.

"Well, Major, it's a long way through hostile country, both Union and Rebel troops would try to take the steers, as well as hostile Indians along the way, so we'd probably lose half of them."

"That's not my problem." The major looked toward the door and absently twirled a yellow curl.

"I was just tryin' to explain why the price is so high," Waco said genially, "I think we'd need at least a hundred dollars a head."

"A hundred dollars!" The major's pink face looked incredulous and he stood up suddenly. "You must be insane. Why don't you just carry a gun and a mask? Go peddle your cows somewhere else, mister. They're probably stolen anyway."

"You callin' me a rustler?" Waco stood up, then remembered he had to control his temper and besides, he'd left his pistol in the outside office. He forced a laugh. "Gawd Almighty! Okay, Major. We'll find another buyer. Come on, boys." He turned back to the impatient young officer. "Enjoy your dinner, Major."

His three friends stood up and they all went out the door. They stopped to retrieve their weapons, not speaking until they were mounted and riding out.

Tom wiped the sweat off his freckled face. "Whew! Talk about waltzing' into the lion's den. I was as nervous as a rattlesnake on a hot griddle."

Zeke guffawed. "Youngster, you got no idea how close we come to a showdown when he called the sergeant a rustler."

Waco shrugged his broad shoulders. "I did come a mite close to hittin' him. Well, we had an excuse to get into the fort and now he thinks we're just rotten varmints, workin' both sides for profit."

"Did you see them curls? Who does he think he is, Custer?" Zeke took out his mouth organ and began to play "Yellow Rose of Texas."

Zeb put a chaw of tobacco in his jaw, grumbling. "We didn't find out nuthin' we didn't already know. Too many soldiers around to rob that bank. We'd never make it to the state line."

Waco watched the sun moving lower on the horizon as they rode. "Gimme time to think, boys."

"What do you mean 'think'?" Zeke complained. "Ain't we now hightailin' it back to Texas?"

"You know what's waitin' for us there." Waco frowned. "I thought I saw an old cabin down past the town a few miles as we came up the trail. That might be a good place."

"That place on the river?" Tom nodded. "Looked deserted."

"Just a place to rest and think," Waco said, "let's go."

He didn't dare tell them yet the idea that had just occurred to him. The banker obviously adored his daughter. *What if we cowboys kidnapped Miss Rosemary and held her for ransom?*

Chapter Three

Rosemary didn't want to deal with Godfrey again, so she waited until she heard the dinner guests arriving in the front hall before she left her room and paused on the landing.

She was Queen Victoria, standing at the head of the grand staircase of her castle, about to go downstairs for a state dinner with the prime minister and a bevy of her most important, adoring subjects. She wore the crown jewels, of course, and a small diamond tiara. As always, she was regal and dignified.

Rosemary descended the stairs carefully and only caught her foot on the next-to-the-last step. She managed to right herself and grabbed for the imaginary tiara as the gentlemen rushed forward to assist her.

"Miss Burke," said a young, pink-faced Union officer, taking her arm, "are you all right?"

"Of course," she said. "I—I was merely feeling—feeling a bit faint." She couldn't stop staring at his yellow curls. "Good evening, gentlemen." She sighed as she looked over her guests. The only one she didn't know was the young major, who introduced himself. The others were the pastor, the doctor, and Mr. Simms, the owner of the biggest farm in the area, and his dull son.

They all murmured appropriate things about how happy they were at her return, and she managed to curtsey without falling. In the following moment of silence, her tummy rumbled like a bear because she hadn't had a snack. Probably Queen Victoria's tummy never rumbled. Godfrey glared at her and sighed.

"Perhaps," offered old Dr. Graham, "the lady might benefit from a sherry? I know I could use one."

Does the old man never draw a sober breath? Rosemary suspected the doctor had not been sober the night her mother died, but then he probably couldn't have saved Agatha from acute appendicitis anyway.

Evidently Godfrey took the hint. "Of course." He smiled broadly and ran his finger over his penciled mustache. "We'll have a drink before dinner."

He gestured the group into the library.

The major took Rosemary's arm and escorted her toward a small love seat. She was several inches taller and probably outweighed him, she thought with a sigh. She didn't want him sitting next to her, so she maneuvered so that she took a single chair, leaving him standing beside her awkwardly.

"I'll pour," Godfrey said with a flourish, "since the butler is busy with dinner. Sherry, my dear?"

She decided to be difficult. He couldn't do anything about it with company in the room. "No, I—I'll have a whiskey, if you please."

"You mean sherry, don't you, my dear?" His mouth smiled, but his eyes glared.

"I said whiskey," she said in an unmistakable tone that caused the other gentlemen to shift their weight uneasily.

Godfrey forced a laugh. "Oh, these young ladies who have been on the Grand Tour, they do get some naughty ideas."

That broke the ice and the other men laughed, too.

"I'm sure the lady was only joking," the major said.

"If the men are having whiskey, that's what I'll have, too." Oh, she was so brave tonight, just like one of her story heroines. In her own mind, she tossed her pretty head carelessly and all the men hung on her every word.

"All right, Rosemary, dear," Godfrey said and there was an edge to his voice, "but don't blame me if you're sick in the morning."

"Yes," Doc chuckled, "whiskey and a lady's delicate constitution just don't mesh."

The other men laughed as if dismissing her. Evidently they saw it as a rebellious, childish whim. Godfrey served the whiskey. "You know, it's a good thing I have a storeroom. The best whiskey comes from the South, and the war has stopped the supply."

"Oh, must he talk about the war?" young Mr. Simms protested. "I think it might upset Miss Rosemary." His big Adam's apple bobbed as he looked toward her.

"Actually it doesn't," she returned, sipping her drink. It burned all the way down into her empty stomach and she was already regretting her choice. "You're all profiting off the war, aren't you?"

The men looked at each other as if not quite sure what to say.

Old Mr. Simms stuttered, "Well, of course I'm selling a lot of horses and grain to the army."

"And the bank is doing well, too," she said and gave Godfrey a questioning look.

Godfrey blinked and sipped his drink. "Well, yes, my dear, the army needs payroll, and we have all these new people moving to town."

The butler came to the door of the library. "Dinner is served," he announced grandly.

"I hope we have a good wine?" Doc Graham asked.

"Of course. I knew you would appreciate a new vintage I just had shipped in," Godfrey said.

Rosemary stood up, but before the major could move to her side, young Simms rushed to take her arm. His big Adam's apple looked like a fist in his long neck.

She was suddenly queasy, thinking she might throw up. Ladies never did such a thing. Well, it wouldn't be the first time she'd made a fool of herself. She swallowed hard and allowed young Mr. Simms to escort her toward the dining room. They trooped in to dinner and Rosemary managed to take her seat at the end of the table as hostess without tripping over her hoops and stumbling. She felt her face pale as her stomach seemed to rock. Maybe she could faint in a ladylike manner before she threw up. She grabbed a piece of bread and stuffed it in her mouth while the gentlemen stared at her. If she could just get a little food in her stomach, she'd be okay.

Godfrey, at the other end of the table, glowered

at her and said, "I'd like to ask Reverend Post to say grace."

She had never thought Godfrey religious, but the pastor said a blessing and then the arrogant butler began to serve the food out of silver dishes. In the meantime, she was choking on the dry bread. She grabbed her goblet of water and gulped it in a most unladylike way. Godfrey glared at her again and turned his attention to his guests.

The food looked excellent. Among other items were pinto beans, a favorite of her father's.

"When did we hire a butler?" she asked as she helped herself to rare roast beef the servant offered.

"While you were in Europe, my dear. All the best homes have one."

"Well, we may be the only house in Kansas with a butler." She snorted and accepted a deviled egg from a silver tray.

"Oh my! Asparagus," the pastor said. "I do love them, and is that roasted quail?"

"Yes, and do try these new potatoes and gravy," Godfrey urged, "and wait till you taste the wine."

The butler was now working his way around the long dining table, pouring the wine. She waved him away. With the whiskey in her stomach just beginning to settle down, she wasn't about to chance the wine. The candles in the big candelabra flickered and Rosemary sighed as she ate. It was going to be a long, boring evening, she was certain.

She retreated into herself and concentrated on her crystal goblet. She was Lady Georgiana at her country estate and now hosting a dinner for a group of eager swains. All were here just to court her because she was pretty, graceful and knew how to flirt. Each handsome gentleman was holding his breath, waiting for Lady Georgiana's next witty remark.

". . . don't you think so, my dear?"

Rosemary jerked out of her fantasy and stared at Godfrey. "What?"

He frowned at her. "I said you were pleased with the improvements I had made to the bank, aren't you, my dear?"

She must not sputter, but she had been caught by surprise. "Uh, possibly. I—I haven't had a chance to think about it."

All the men laughed and the major said, "Well, ladies shouldn't bother their pretty heads about business anyway."

She squelched the urge to splash her glass of water all over his fine uniform. "Tell us about news of the war, Major?"

"Oh, I don't think you'd be interested." He demurred modestly.

"Oh, but I'm sure everyone would like to know the latest," she encouraged him.

"Uh, well." The young man's thin chest puffed out now that he was the center of attention. "We are winning on all fronts. Of course, I'm disappointed not to have been sent into the thick of battle, and I'm afraid it will all be over before I can get to the front and earn my medals. I don't see why George Custer should get all the glory."

"So brave," she murmured and his face brightened. Maybe he was after the bank fortune, too.

"Yes, indeed," he blustered, evidently encouraged by her comment. "He's my hero. Reports from Washington say the Rebs are out of money to the point of melting down wedding rings and silverware. You know those blockade runners don't want any of their worthless Confederate dollars."

"Is that the reason the Rebs tried to invade California and Nevada?" the doctor asked and motioned to the butler to pour him more wine.

"Certainly," the major nodded, "hoped to capture those gold and silver mines, but of course, were defeated. I hear they're desperate for boots, overcoats, and food with winter coming on."

Rosemary pictured hungry men shivering in the coming cold, wet and sick. She felt sympathy for them even though they were the enemy.

"And," said the major, "they've been trying to rob our banks."

"What?" That seemed to catch Godfrey's attention.

"Oh, you needn't worry," the major joked. "Not around here. A group of them came down from Canada and tried to rob a bank in Vermont, and only this past August, a small group of their cavalry hit a bank in Kentucky. Didn't get anything, I hear."

"Kentucky?" asked young Simms, and his Adam's apple bobbled up and down as he sipped his wine. "But Kentucky's a Union state."

"Exactly!" said the major. "Very daring of the devils, I'd say. Worse yet, they burned a Union barge on the river in that town and executed the black soldiers guarding it."

"Oh dear," said Reverend Post nervously, "I don't think this is fit conversation for a young lady—"

"You're quite right, Reverend," Godfrey said. "We don't want to shock Rosemary."

"Oh, I apologize," gulped the young officer, "I didn't mean—"

"It's all right," Rosemary said. "After all, I asked. Anything that affects the war will affect banking even here in Kansas."

"Quite right." Godfrey beamed at her. "We must all remember to pray for all the poor souls being lost in the horrors of this terrible war."

Everyone murmured agreement while Rosemary waited for lightning to come through the ceiling and strike the hypocrite.

Mr. Simms smiled at her. "I'm sure that with stalwart young men about like the major and my son, you needn't worry your pretty little head about those dirty Rebs attacking this town."

At least he had said "pretty." Obviously Mr. Simms and his son had designs on the bank's assets, too.

"Oh, I'm not worried," she said, cutting up her roast beef. "I'm quite convinced Kansas has seen the last of the action. Indeed, as I was telling Godfrey this afternoon, I intend to take charge of the bank myself on my birthday per my mother's will."

"Halloween," she heard Godfrey mutter under his breath, "how very appropriate."

The other men looked shocked and the major said, "Surely you jest, Miss Burke?"

"Not at all."

Godfrey laid down his fork and cleared his throat. His expression told her he'd like to stick that fork in her heart. "Don't take my stepdaughter seriously, gentlemen. Perhaps she's had too much to drink."

"I have not," she snapped and the other men looked at each other, uncertain what to say in the awkward silence.

Doc Graham drained his glass and looked about. "I could use another glass of wine. Excellent vintage."

"Me, too," said the other gentlemen to cover the awkward pause.

The butler went about the table, filling goblets. Rosemary waved him away again. She didn't want any more of her conversation dismissed because the men thought she'd had too much to drink.

Doc Graham already looked drunker than a boiled owl, she thought, and wouldn't know an excellent wine from moonshine, but he was the only doctor in town.

Doc Graham drained his wine without tasting it and looked down at his plate. "Oh, pinto beans, I see. I don't think I've eaten those since the night I was here for dinner and Agatha . . ." His voice trailed off. "I'm sorry," he said. "Miss Rosemary, I didn't mean to bring back sad memories."

It's quite all right," Rosemary said. "I understand you did everything you could to save my mother."

"Yes, he did." Godfrey sighed and the others nodded. "You were away at school and we'd had such a lovely dinner party and were all still having coffee in the library when my dear wife was stricken with acute appendicitis."

"There just didn't seem to be anything to be done." Mr. Simms shook his head. "She lingered on for three days in terrible pain."

"I heard," Rosemary said. "I'm sorry I couldn't get here before she died."

"I prayed over her," Reverend Post said, "and your stepfather held her hand all night. Never saw such devotion."

Godfrey pulled out a handkerchief and wiped

his eyes. "I'm sorry, my dear, you didn't get home in time for the funeral. My poor darling Agatha. I miss her still."

"Uh, perhaps we should talk of lighter matters," young Mr. Simms said uncomfortably.

There was an awkward silence before young Mr. Simms talked again of business.

Was there any way she could bring this dull evening to a close as the conversation dragged on?

Finally she said, "Godfrey, why don't you take the gentlemen to the drawing room? I think I may retire early so I can ride early in the morning, and I'm not feeling well."

Both young men jumped up to jostle each other about who got to pull out her chair as she stood up.

"No, no, gentlemen. You all retire to the drawing room for cigars and brandy. I'm going upstairs."

Godfrey looked relieved. "Very well, my dear. Good night."

All the men said good night and offered concern for her health, but she assured them she was only tired, nodded and left the dining room, attempted to make a graceful exit, but her hoop caught on a potted fern in the door and she had to stop to pull it free before leaving. She paused at the foot of the stairs, listening. The men were moving toward the drawing room, talking business as usual.

She ought to go upstairs and try washing the blood out of the white silk scarf. Godfrey would be so cross when he saw it. Worse yet, she didn't want him asking questions and discovering she had wrecked one of his pet orchids.

She knew Godfrey was already furious with her for the small fuss at the table before his guests. She was powerless for less than three weeks and then she would take over everything. It was all hers unless she met with an accident, and though she was clumsy, she didn't expect anything fatal. She went upstairs, got Mollie to help her out of her corset, and dismissed the sour girl. There was a small lamp burning on her bedside table and while Rosemary dug through her lingerie drawer for a nightgown, she found a large peppermint stick left over from at least two Christmases ago and a romantic novel she hadn't read: *Lady Cavendish and Her Secret Love or Carried Off by a Highwayman*. She tasted the peppermint as she crawled into bed. No candy was ever too stale to eat, and the romantic novel looked promising.

It was a long time before she turned off her light, dreaming of being the beautiful, desirable Lady Cavendish.

The tumbledown cabin by the river seemed to be a good hiding place, and now Waco sat on a rock in the darkness overlooking the river. They were many miles from town and well hidden in a grove of cottonwoods. He rolled a cigarette, thinking. He was responsible for his men, and that weighed heavily on him. There was only one way to get the money they needed, yet he didn't like the idea. It didn't seem too chivalrous, certainly not to a Texan, to kidnap a sweet little lady like that banker's daughter and hold her for ransom, but nobody had a better idea. After all, it was so evident that the banker adored her and surely would pay anything to get her back. Of course her father wouldn't call in the law or the army; he'd be too afraid something would happen to sweet Miss Rosemary. Why, in a day or two, three at the most, the quartet would be headed back to Texas with all the gold they needed.

Yep, tomorrow, Waco was gonna find the banker's mansion and scout things out to see when would be a good time to snatch her. He'd try not to scare her or make her cry, but like most women, she'd surely be terrified. Of course, he would see that not one hair on her head was harmed. No Texan would treat a lady that way. Of course, true Texans probably wouldn't kidnap a lady neither, but he was desperate and running out of time.

He tossed away his smoke and went back into the tumbledown cabin to spread his blankets on the sagging floor. Tomorrow early, he'd tell the boys the details.

Rosemary was awake before dawn and dragged the sleepy, protesting Mollie out of bed to help her into her corset and a blue wool riding outfit complete with a jaunty hat with feathers on the side. Then she let the sleepy maid go back to bed while she rummaged around in the kitchen for a bit of breakfast. She didn't want to get the cook up or wake that snooty new butler. She would have loved a cup of coffee, but she had no idea how to accomplish that. The cook always made her muffins and jam or coddled eggs, but Rosemary didn't even know how to work the wood stove. Finally she settled for some cold milk and half a cake from last night, which made her very happy. She sliced some crusty bread and cold roast beef for a picnic lunch, wrapped it up in a napkin with a dozen cookies. Then she got an apple for her horse.

The house was still quiet and dark. She wished she could get some evidence on Godfrey St. John; she'd always been suspicious of his handling the bank's money. Thinking that, she tiptoed into the library, crashed into a table, but managed to catch the lamp before it fell. She lit it and quietly rummaged through his desk. She had no idea what she was looking for and she didn't find anything except a handful of speckled pinto beans, some of them cut up into tiny pieces. That puzzled her. Well, beans didn't belong in a desk anyway. She picked up several and stuffed them into her pocket as she dug through the drawers. Nothing of importance. She thought she heard people stirring about upstairs, hurriedly closed the drawers, and blew out the lamp. She didn't want to get caught snooping in Godfrey's desk, so she'd look again when she had more time.

Now she went outside into the coming dawn. This early morn of October was going to be a crisp, sunny day. Around her, leaves had turned gold and scarlet. They swirled about her as she walked to the stable. Her favorite thoroughbred mare, Lady Be Good, whinnied when she saw Rosemary coming.

Rosemary rubbed the sorrel's velvet nose. "I brought you an apple. Would you like to go for a ride?"

The mare snorted as she took the apple, and Rosemary looked about for the light sidesaddle. She could wake a groom, but she was perfectly capable of saddling a horse and she was an excellent rider. Did she dare ride astride? She thought about it a moment, decided that Lady Cavendish would use a sidesaddle as she rode about her English estate, and got that one down. She could hardly wait to be away from the house and Godfrey. She could lose her worries for an hour or so at least.

Rosemary felt almost dizzy with her freedom and the anticipation of a good lunch. Food had always comforted her when she was a sad little girl, and it still did. Her mother had always nagged her about her eating and never allowed her to ride unescorted or very far from the house. Since she'd spent so much time away at school, Rosemary was a stranger in her own area. Well, that was about to change. She would ride as far as she wanted to, and she hadn't even left a note. Not that anyone would care where a lonely fat girl had gone riding.

Chapter Four

Zeb was up making coffee and the other men were stirring as Waco slipped on his boots.

"Well, boys, I've wrestled with this all night, and I don't see no other way out. We've got to kidnap the gal."

"What gal?" Zeb wiped tobacco juice off his straggly beard. "Have you gone plumb loco?"

Waco shook his head at his three surprised compadres. "The banker's daughter. Look, we can't rob the bank with the town crawlin' with Yankee soldiers, and we got to have the money."

Tom ran his hand through his unkempt red hair. "And suppose them same soldiers come lookin' for the kidnappers?"

"The banker will keep his mouth shut, afraid we'll kill his darlin' daughter. You saw how much he adores her when we was in the bank."

"It ain't right." Zeb shook his gray head and poured Waco a cup of coffee. "It just ain't gentlemanly to scare a lady like that."

"Well, you are right about that," Waco admitted

and sipped the coffee, savoring it. Coffee had been scarce in Kentucky. "It ain't something a Texan ought to do, but we're desperate."

"And suppose the banker won't pay?" Zeke got up, scratching himself.

"Oh, he'll pay plenty," Waco promised, "and fast. You saw how much he loved her, with the big celebration and all. We probably won't have to keep her but a day or two until he quietly hands over the money to get her back."

"Won't he then send the soldiers and law after us?" Tom leaned back in his chair and reached for his boots.

"Not if we hold her until we reach the state line. Then we turn her loose and skedaddle back to Texas with the loot."

"Sounds too easy," Zeke grumbled. "If there's a woman involved, there's bound to be trouble."

"It ain't like we got lots of choices on gettin' cash," Waco reminded him. "Would you rather ride into town and try to rob the bank? Besides, you saw the lady. She seemed as purty and sweet as apple pie."

"Apples sometimes have worms in 'em." Zeb spat again. "Suppose the lady turns out to be as much trouble as a barrel of rattlesnakes?"

"That sweet-lookin' little thing?" Waco shook his head. "Naw. Why just think, fellas, for the day or two we'll have to keep her, she can clean up the cabin and cook us some good vittles."

Tom nodded. "Yeah, that's right. This dump could use a woman's touch." He looked around the tumbledown cabin. "And I'm hungry for some home-cooked meals. I say Waco's got a good idea."

"How you gonna manage this?" Zeke sighed.

"We find this big fine house they live in. Shouldn't be hard to do, there ain't that many rich folks around. Then we watch it and see if she goes to town or ridin' or whatever. After that, we'll have a plan to grab her."

"You know," Zeb sliced bacon, "I got a bad feelin' about this. Women is always trouble. I say we just try to knock over the bank and risk gettin' shot."

The other two looked to Waco.

Waco rubbed his chin for a long moment. "Gawd Almighty! It's damned if we do and damned if we don't. Ransom should be a hellova lot easier, sweet little thing that she was, and mighty purty, too."

"A little plump for my taste," said Tom. "And anyway, I prefer yeller hair."

Waco laughed. "You must be blind. I thought she was sturdy and had such soft, generous curves; mighty comfortin' on a cold night. None of them scrawny, whinin' women for me."

"That don't matter no never-mind," Zeke said. "Who cares if she's purty or ugly as a mud fence? We only got to put up with her a day or two til her adorin' daddy hands over the money, right?"

"Right!" Waco said.

In truth, his Southern heart balked at scaring a lady, but the four had to get some big cash or they dared not go back to Texas, and they sure couldn't stay long in Yankee country dressed as they were. They didn't mean to harm that sweet miss none, even though she might be terrified for a few hours until her dear daddy handed over the cash.

He wolfed down the bacon and biscuits Zeb

cooked. It was none too good, but soon, they'd have a woman to cook some tasty grub.

Before dawn, he saddled up and rode out the direction Major Mathis had indicated. The other three wanted to go, but since he was just looking things over, he ordered them to stay at the cabin and keep alert for Yankee patrols. He followed yesterday's buggy tracks west from town until he saw the imposing Victorian mansion on a far hill. By damn, the banker really was rich.

Now how will I manage to kidnap the daughter? He didn't want to invade the home, that would put him and his men at major risk. Maybe she would come out in her buggy today, headed toward town. All he would have to do was wait. He reined in the shadows of a tree and checked his watch. Soon people should be stirring about in that big mansion. He settled in to wait. It was a crisp dawn with falling leaves swirling across the pastures.

After a while, he saw a rider come out of the stable on a fine sorrel horse. For a minute, he thought it might be the banker, then he realized by the long blue skirt and perky hat that the rider was female and she was headed south. Whoever she was, she was an excellent rider. He took a deep breath when he recognized by the full, soft curves and long brown curls that it was the banker's daughter. He grinned. Lady luck must be looking out for him today. All he had to do was trail the lady and, in some isolated spot, grab her.

"Miss Rosemary, I hope I don't scare you too bad," he said and he nudged Amigo forward, following the lady as she rode south.

That sorrel was a mighty skittish animal for a lady

rider, he thought. However, as Waco watched, the girl gave the mare her head and galloped so fast, her long brown hair came unpinned and blew out behind her as she rode.

He had to admire her. She rode as well as any Texas ranch gal. Sweet, purty, and a good rider besides. If it weren't for the circumstances, she was the kind of girl that this Texas cowboy could fall for. Well, there was no chance of that; and besides, he didn't trust any woman as far as he could throw an iron anvil.

He followed her at a distance and watched her enjoy her ride. She rode to a little pond, stopped to get a drink and water her horse. Then she mounted up and rode on.

She was now some miles from her house, Waco thought as he followed her. He didn't think a lady ought to ride out so far alone. If she'd been his sweetheart, he would have insisted she wait for him to accompany her. She was either foolhardy or had a lot of grit for a Northern girl. Texans admired grit and high spirit in a woman, just like in a fine horse.

He allowed her to stay far enough ahead of him so that she wouldn't know she was being followed. He could have followed her by her tracks anyhow since he had been a part-time tracker for the Texas Rangers against the Comanche raiders long before the war started. He watched for other people along the trail, but the area seemed deserted. He decided that all he needed to do was ride up beside her, engage her in conversation, and then grab her. She'd probably be so frightened she'd swoon, but he couldn't help that.

* * *

Rosemary was enjoying her morning. Horseback riding was one of the few things she knew she did really well, and out here on her fine-blooded mare, Lady Be Good, she quit worrying about what she was going to do about Godfrey and all the responsibilities of the bank.

As she rode, she was Lady Cavendish, trotting along a bridle path at Hyde Park. Perhaps handsome Sir Trevor Cunningham would seek her out to ride with her and beg her to attend the hunt ball. Or more daring, perhaps she was on her way to Windsor Castle for a fox hunt and might be waylaid by a dangerous highwayman wearing a mask who would steal a kiss and beg her to give up her title and run away with him.

Not likely. She sighed as she dismounted at a little stream and let Lady drink again. Handsome highwaymen only existed in the books she read and her dreams. Besides, even in stories, the virile heroes always wanted the slender, graceful heroines. She heard a sound in the bushes and turned. A yellowish, nondescript dog walked out of the brush. His ribs showed and he wagged his long tail as he stopped to drink.

"You poor, starving thing," she said and held out her hand. The yellow mutt hesitated, then approached, cowering as if he expected to be beaten. She patted him and the stray licked her hand gratefully. All she had with her was a roast beef sandwich and a dozen cookies for an early lunch. She hesitated, then decided the starving dog needed the food worse than she did. Rosemary unwrapped the napkin and fed it all to the stray. "I wish I had more to give you. I know what, I'll take you home with me."

The dog licked her hand again, happy for a kind word. "I'll call you Prince," she decided, thinking of the graceful greyhounds or shepherds that would accompany Lady Cavendish.

That sent her mood soaring as she mounted again and rode on, the new Prince following after. So now she owned a dog. "Well, in a few days, Prince, the house will be mine and you can have your own rug in front of the fireplace."

The straggly yellow dog wagged his tail and stayed beside her horse.

After a few minutes, she heard the sound of hoofbeats behind her and looked back. A tall rider was coming, but he was too far away to recognize. She only knew he was a big man and sat easy in the saddle, riding as well as she did herself. Smiling to herself, she nudged Lady into a canter. Ah, suppose it was Sir Trevor Cunningham or the dashing highwayman coming to steal a kiss from beautiful, willowy Lady Cavendish?

Well, she could dream, couldn't she? Would she rather go to the Hunt Ball or be carried off to Sherwood Forest? Such a difficult choice between the two virile, handsome males.

Lost in her daydreams, she didn't realize for a long moment that the rider was gaining on her. She moved over to let him pass, but he reined in next to her.

"Good day, ma'am." She recognized the Texas drawl as he smiled and touched the brim of his cowboy hat.

"Oh, it's you." She smiled and tried not to sound too flustered. "I—I thought you might have gone back to Texas by now. I never did properly thank you for helping me when I got off the stagecoach."

"Any gentleman would have done the same, ma'am." He looked embarrassed.

Oh, handsome, virile, and modest, too. She liked that. He was even better than Sir Cunningham or the highwayman. Once she had read a romantic novel about a cowboy named Two Gun Pete who rode bucking horses and made love to the rancher's beautiful, graceful daughter. Of course this cowboy wouldn't be interested in her, but she gave him her best smile anyway. "Well, thank you again. My name is Rosemary." She held out her hand.

Waco took it, staring into those wide brown eyes. "That's the purtiest name I ever heard, but then, you're a mighty purty lady."

He watched her as she pulled her hand back, coloring and laughing as if unsure of herself. "Nobody ever said anything like that to me before. Tell me, might you be a Texas Ranger or an outlaw with a price on your head?"

"Ma'am?" *She isn't far wrong,* he thought. He hated that he was going to have to scare her, she was so sweet and shy. For a moment, he almost backed out, then thought about the trouble awaiting him back in Texas and decided there was no other way.

"Never mind," she smiled and ducked her head, "it was just one of my silly daydreams. You want to ride a ways with me?"

"Miss Rosemary, I'd like that just fine."

"Then I'll race you!" Before he knew what she was up to, she nudged her startled mare and took off at a gallop, the yellow dog running to keep up with her.

Waco mustn't let her get away. He spurred Amigo and took off after her at a gallop. She and her horse were worthy competitors, he thought as he caught up with her and they rode neck and neck for a few moments before she reined in.

She threw back her head and laughed and he loved the sound of it, not a silly giggle like most girls', but a hearty laugh. "I say, that bay of yours has some speed."

"Quarterhorse." He grinned. "Use em for ropin' down in Texas. That mare of yours would be a good match for him." He took off his bandana.

"Well." She seemed almost hesitant to leave. "It's been fun, but I suppose I have to go back now."

He looked around, making sure there were no witnesses. "I'd—I'd rather you wouldn't."

"Oh, but I must. What are you doing in Prairie View anyhow?"

"Uh, we had business with the bank."

She remembered then that the first time she had seen him was in front of the bank. Was he a friend or employee of Godfrey's?

He reached over and put his big, calloused hand over hers. "Miss Rosemary, I want you should go with me."

"What?" She looked a bit startled, but smiled and shook her head slowly. One brown curl fell across her round face. "I wish I could, but you see—"

"Missy, I'm afraid I must insist."

"Insist? What kind of joke is this?" For just a split second, confusion crossed her face, but not fear.

"Now don't be afraid, but I'm kidnappin' you."

"What? You can't do that!" She drew back her hand and hit him hard, hard as any scrappy boy.

"Gawd Almighty!" The blow stung and he blinked and grabbed for both her hands. The two struggled as the two horses did a slow dance under them and the yellow dog ran in circles, barking. She was supposed to be terrified and screaming by now, but instead, she was fighting like a bobcat, all teeth and sharp nails. "Now don't be scared, Miss Rosemary, but you've got to go along with me."

"The hell I do!" She clawed his face and tried to gallop away, but he was stronger and bigger than most men and he lifted her bodily from her horse while she fought him.

Waco had been caught by surprise, having expected the genteel girl to weep and sob and beg, but she was biting and clawing and kicking. Even as he struggled to turn her across his saddle so he could tie her hands behind her, she sank her teeth into his thigh, while he howled and tried to escape her teeth. "Ow! You bite like a coyote bitch!"

"You'll think coyote bitch if I can get my teeth into your—"

Oh, hell, surely she wouldn't try to bite him there, but yes, she was trying. What had happened to the delicate lady? Both horses danced about as the two struggled, neighing and stomping. In the meantime, the yellow dog ran in circles, barking and jumping about.

"Stop it, gal, you're supposed to swoon away, but don't worry, I ain't gonna hurt you none."

"Damn right!" And she sank her teeth higher on his thigh.

"Ow! Missy, don't do that now. You're about to turn me into a steer."

"That's my intention, you—you—" She couldn't think of anything bad enough to call him, but she intended to get away. No doubt Godfrey had hired him to kidnap her. He was going to make sure she didn't get control of the estate, and that thought made her furious. She had underestimated her stepfather. She bit the cowboy's thigh as hard as she could while he struggled to get her hands behind her. Somehow, this wasn't how it was done in the stories she read. He was supposed to charm her into going with him, and this was not only uncomfortable, it was downright ridiculous.

He was a big man and very strong. "Gawd Almighty, gal, now you hold still while I get my piggin' string."

"Are you calling me a pig?" And she tried to bite and kick him in the belly and groin.

"No, ma'am, a piggin' string is used to tie up cows after we rope them and—"

"I've never been so insulted!"

"You ain't supposed to be insulted, lady, you're supposed to be scart—"

"Like hell!"

While she fought, he managed to get her hands tied behind her and lay her across his saddle before him. Then he took his bandana and wrapped it around her eyes so she couldn't see where she was going. While he was tying it, she sank her teeth into his hand.

"Damn, missy, that's my gun hand! You tryin' to chomp it off?"

"You betcha!"

Waco sighed and surveyed his bitten hand. While he had to admire her gumption, he was beginning to think Zeke was right; she was going to be a lot more trouble than he had thought. She was still kicking and trying to bite as he reached to grab her mare's reins. Then he took off at a lope for the cabin, the barking yellow dog following behind.

It seemed like a long trip with her fighting every inch of the way and yelling in protest. If he hadn't been as big as he was, she might have managed to push him out of his saddle and steal his horse. She'd lost her hat, and her long brown hair was flying loose and pretty as a filly's tail. What had happened to the shy, timid lady he'd planned on kidnapping? This fiesty bitch was more sassy than most Texas gals.

Well, they'd only have to deal with her one day, two at most. When her adoring papa got the ransom note, he'd come up with that money quick as a scalded hound. And then they could give this wildcat back and light a shuck for Texas.

Rosemary took a deep breath and tried to think as she bounced along on the galloping horse. Oh, that damned Godfrey had outsmarted her. October thirty-first, she'd have plenty of money and Godfrey would be penniless, but that was almost three weeks away. She must not panic. What would Lady Cavendish do? What would Flame La Rouge do? Forget about Queen Victoria, she was known to be so staid, she probably wouldn't do anything but call out the palace guards.

If Godfrey had told the Texan to murder her, he'd have probably have done that back in the grove rather than subdue her and carry her off. As she bounced along, she overcame her panic and tried to think. She'd make this kidnapping so miserable and difficult, the cowboy would rue the day he made this bargain. If that failed, maybe she could seduce or entice him with her charms. Rosemary almost snorted with laughter at that thought. She wasn't certain what was going on in her stories when the print said, "and so the lady decided to seduce the virile hero into letting her escape, so now, dear reader, let us draw a curtain of privacy around the two lovers behind which we dare not peek."

At that point, Rosemary had always sighed and smiled, imagining being in the lady's place. However, she didn't know the first thing about seduction, and this Texan seemed to be too smart to fall for that trick anyway.

Waco galloped back toward the cabin, the girl lying across his saddle before him. He had his hand on her back to keep her from falling, and he could see a bit of white lace peeking out from under her blue skirt. That sent his temperature up and then he was ashamed of himself. This was a lady, after all, even though she was acting a bit more like a wild Injun. A bit more? Hell, that was an understatement.

Less than an hour later, he reined in before the tumbledown cabin, the two horses lathered, the yellow dog dancing about and barking, and the girl still trying to take a major bite out of his leg.

At the noise, his three men came out of the cabin.

"Well, I see you got her." Zeb spat tobacco juice to one side.

"I hope you didn't scare the pore little thing to death," Tom said.

"Hardly," Waco said, and about that time, his victim came to life again and sank her teeth in his thigh. "Ohh! Get her off me!"

The dog's barking unnerved the horses, and the three men watched helplessly while the bay stallion danced about and Waco tried to remove his thigh from Rosemary's mouth. He finally managed to dismount and reached up to lift her down. She sank her teeth into his hand as he did so.

"By damn, stop it, missy. A lady ain't supposed to act like this!"

"Don't tell me how a lady should act, you—you dastardly villian!" She managed to get one foot up and kicked him hard in the groin.

Waco groaned and went down, leaving her standing awkwardly, looking about with her blindfolded eyes. The yellow dog ran over and licked his face, his tail wagging hard.

"I think," Tom advanced cautiously to help Waco to his feet, "you must have got the wrong girl."

"He sure as hell did!" Rosemary shrieked.

Zeke circled her as carefully as if she were a *loco* mustang. "What happened to that shy little gal what wouldn't be no trouble?"

Waco moaned and managed to stand up. "I might could have underestimated her a mite. Now, missy," he limped over and pulled the blindfold off, "you just take it easy and everything will be all right."

Rosemary looked around, blinking in the sudden light. There were four of them. Why would Godfrey hire four men to kill her? He must be up to something else. For a moment, she was shaken and scared, then remembered she was Flame de Rouge, the naughty toast of New Orleans. She tossed her head in what she hoped was a coquettish way. "Whatever he's paying you, I'll pay double, but you'll have to wait till Halloween."

All four looked at each other and then her, evidently puzzled. One of the grizzled old ones grimaced. "I'd think Halloween would be appropriate for a witch like this one."

"Now, Zeke, you'll hurt the lady's feelin's," the big one said soothingly as he approached her. "Ma'am, we're awful sorry, but you see, we're desperate men."

She let him take her arm and lead her toward the cabin. "You mean, like outlaws?"

"Well, I reckon you Yankees would call us that. We don't aim to hurt you none, you're just gonna have to stay with us awhile."

So they didn't intend to kill her; at least, not yet. She breathed a little easier as he steered her into the cabin. "What do you mean?"

He paused in front of the cabin, looked down at her, so big and virile and those eyes, so full of soul and the color of faded denim. "Why, until you adorin' daddy pays the ransom to get you back."

She began to laugh then, threw back her head and laughed. The cowboy looked puzzled. "Ma'am, there's no need to get hysterical. You ain't in any danger. Why, your daddy will probably get that ransom by tomorrow night and you can go home and we'll head for Texas."

She managed to stop laughing. They couldn't fool her. She knew Godfrey had hired them because they had been coming out of the bank when the stage arrived. Okay, she'd play along for a while until she saw her chance. Of course, that might not be till her birthday. That was a long time to stay out here, but she could be so difficult, they'd wish they hadn't made a deal with her crooked stepfather.

The dog continued to dance around her legs. "Prince, get down," she said.

"What'd you call him?" said one of the old geezers, the one with the harmonica.

"Prince," she replied haughtily.

Prince promptly sat down in the dirt and scratched a flea.

All four men broke up in guffaws.

"You could at least untie me," she snapped at the big man.

"Yes, ma'am." He strode over, towering above her as he whirled her around and untied the little rope. "I'll have to have your promise you won't try to run away."

"I promise." She watched all four visibly relax. Then she ran madly toward her horse. She might have made it, too, but being as clumsy as she was, she caught her foot on a rock and stumbled as she ran to her horse and tried to mount up. However, Lady was nervous and kept sidestepping while the dog began to bark again and the big cowboy cursed and yanked her from her horse. She stumbled backward and they both went down, whereupon Prince licked both their faces.

"You promised, you little liar!" he snapped as he came up on top.

"I had my fingers crossed, you—you outlaw!" She glared up at him, thinking he was so strong and his jaw so square, just like one of her romantic heroes.

"I told you so, Waco," grumbled one of the old men.

She kept fighting but the big one called Waco stood up and yanked her to her feet.

"I should have known better than ask a Yankee for a promise."

"What are you?" she shrieked and tried to kick him again as he retied her hands behind her. "Are you bandits? Are you with Quantrill's guerillas? You can't be Rebel soldiers, you don't have uniforms."

The men exchanged looks while Waco took her arm. "All right, Miss Rosie, you'd best stop fightin' now before I forget I'm a Texan."

"Don't call me Rosie! And what are you doing up here in Kansas?" she yelled at him, but he didn't let her go.

"It's a long story, but I ain't got the time or incli- nation to tell it," he drawled. "Now make the dog stop barkin' and let's all go inside, missy. You may be stayin' a day or two with us."

One of the bearded old men led the horses off to a tumbledown barn while the others and her dog started through the door of the log cabin.

Maybe this would turn out to be a great adven- ture in her boring life, she thought. In her mind, she was Frontier Fanny, riding with a wild gang of outlaws, and the lover of this most wanted of all the desperados, Texas . . . "what'd you say your name was?"

He pull up a chair for her, looking baffled. "Now, little lady, why would you want to know that?"

"Well, it isn't as if I could do anything about it."

"That's right. Well, if it makes any difference, my name's Will, but everyone calls me Waco cause that's where my ranch is, near Waco."

The most wanted of all desperadoes, Texas Waco, leader of these outlaws.

She looked about the dusty cabin. There was almost no furniture, and she could see sky through the holes in the roof. Surely Godfrey could have found a better place than this. No, how like him to put her in a miserable dump. "Is this the best you can do? I wouldn't stable my horse in a pigpen like this."

Waco sighed and leaned against the rock fireplace. "It ain't as though we had a lot of choices, Miss Rosie."

"My name is not Rosie, it's Rosemary."

He shrugged. "Suit yourself. Now if you'll behave yourself, I'll untie you."

She nodded, trying to look meek. She'd wait until later to make her escape. He stood up and strode over to her. His tall, muscular frame molded against hers as he reached around her to untie her hands.

For a moment, she closed her eyes, pretending she was in a romantic embrace. Flame would have kissed him, Lady Cavendish would have fainted so he could catch her. Queen Victoria would probably slap his tanned face and call her guards to cut off his head.

Waco struggled with the knot as he reached around her. She was soft and yielding against him as he tried to untie her hands. Her hair felt soft and it smelled good. When he untied her, he didn't want to pull away. *Waco, are you* loco? *This is a business deal. The lady is for sale like a heifer on the auction block. Tomorrow or the next day at the latest, she'll be back in her adoring daddy's mansion and you'll be headed for Texas with his money.*

He watched her rub her chafed wrists. "I'm mighty sorry, Miss Rosemary, I didn't mean to hurt you."

"I can't say the same," she snapped and walked over to a pitcher of water, poured herself a tin cup full, then knelt and gave Prince a drink from the cup.

"Well," said the young red-headed man, "I've drunk after worse than dogs before."

"I found him along the road and he's hungry. I'm hungry, too. Can't you feed us?"

The old one who chewed tobacco wiped his mouth and looked toward Waco. "We ain't long on grub."

"Feed 'em," Waco snapped. "I can't stand to see anything hungry."

"Yes, sir." The old one shrugged. "All I got is cornbread. You think a pooch with a name like Prince will eat cornbread?"

"You can try," Waco said.

"Cornbread?" the lady sniffed. "Really now, I'm not that hungry."

"Then don't eat it." The old man put the pan on the rickety floor and Prince attacked the pan of stale bread like he was empty as a barrel. Then he sat down in the middle of the floor and scratched a flea.

"It's gettin' late," Waco said and rubbed his thigh where she had bitten him. "Let's try writin' a ransom note."

She smirked at the men. "You can continue this charade if you wish, but I'm wise to your subterfuge."

The men exchanged puzzled looks.

"Ma'am?" Waco said.

"Never mind." If they were determined to pretend they weren't in cahoots with Godfrey, she wasn't going to dignify this tomfoolery by acting scared. She was getting hungry and a little panicky because she always kept a little stash of food to comfort herself and she didn't have so much as a cookie.

"Anybody got any paper?" Waco said.

"I got the brown paper our supplies were wrapped in," Tom volunteered.

Zeke said, "I got a stub of a pencil and I can write some."

"All right." Waco stared into the fireplace. "Write this: *Dear Banker, we got your daughter*—"

"Wait a minute, how do you spell that?" Zeke had his tongue at the corner of his mouth as he labored over the letter.

"Uh," Waco said, "I ain't sure."

"I think it's d-o-t-t-er," Tom said.

Rosemary sighed. "Really, now."

Tom said, "We ain't got much book learnin'."

"We can't help that." Waco shrugged. "Our ancestors came out of the mountains to Texas, but we can handle a gun and a rope, and that's what's important to cowboys."

"What else, Waco?" Zeke asked.

"Tell him if he don't give us fifty thousand dollars, we'll murder her."

"How do you spell 'murder'?" Zeke paused.

"Use 'kill'," Waco suggested. "I can spell that: k-i-l."

Rosemary threw back her head and laughed. This was carrying Godfrey's joke too far. He might be trying to scare her into leaving the country and forfeiting the inheritance. "Surely you jest with this chicanery," she said.

"What?" Said Zeb, spitting tobacco juice into the fireplace.

Waco shrugged his wide shoulders. "You'll have to get used to her talkin' like that. She don't always speak English."

"It *is* English," she protested. "It means you are joking or bluffing."

"Oh," said Waco, "you mean like when you only got a worthless hand and you make out like you got a royal flush?"

"I have no idea what you are talking about," she admitted.

"Well, then, I reckon that makes two of us." Waco grinned. "Now write that we'll get back to him later about where to bring the money."

"This is absurd and ridiculous," Rosemary sneered.

All four men looked at her again, puzzled.

"I told you she don't always speak English so's you can understand it." Waco shrugged.

"Gracious! You aren't going to send that note with all those misspelled words, are you? I'll be humiliated if it gets passed around town."

"Well, if you're so smart, why don't you write it?" Zeke challenged, evidently insulted.

"Of course I will. I'll go along with the joke."

"What joke?" asked Tom, scratching his ear.

"Surely you jest."

"I told you not to trade words with her, it's like gettin' a knot out of a lariat," Waco said.

Zeke snorted and handed over the paper and pencil stub.

"If you're going to do it, you might as well do it right." Rosemary took the stub of pencil and scratched out the writing. This was all a big joke and she'd let Godfrey know she was in on it by writing the note herself. After a minute, she handed it to Waco, who read it and nodded.

Then he handed it to the red-headed man. "Now, Tom, you ride into town and get some kid to deliver that. He'll no doubt send a note back that he'll pay anything. In the meantime, we'll decide where is a good place to trade the gal for the money."

"This is all so ridiculous," Rosemary said, "but you can't scare me."

"We ain't aimin' to. Now little lady, you just keep quiet and let men handle this," Waco ordered. He sounded as if he were used to taking charge.

"Oh, shut up!" She swished across the room.

"What happened to shy and timid?" Zeke snorted.

The young redhead took the note and went out the door.

"I'm sorry' ma'am," the big cowboy said again and took off his hat, "I know you must be so scared, you're *loco* with your words."

She had no idea what *loco* meant, so she said nothing as they all listened to the horse galloping away. "This is worse than a stable," she snapped. "You surely don't expect me to stay here?"

"Not if your adorin' papa sends the money."

"Ha! You must think I'm a damned fool."

The three men looked at her and then at each other. Waco reached to pat the dog and Prince wagged his tail and licked the cowboy's hand.

"That's *my* dog," she said. "Bite him, Prince!"

Prince looked at her, wagging his tail, then licked Waco's hand again.

Well, so much for her guard dog.

Old Zeke began to play his harmonica.

The other one, the one with the tobacco stains on his beard, said "I'm so hungry, my belly thinks my throat's been cut."

Waco grinned. "Maybe the little lady will cook us some grub."

"Grub? What's grub?" she asked.

"This Yankee gal don't speak very good English," Zeb complained.

"I told you that." Waco rolled a cigarette.

"I'll have you know I made high grades in English composition. I also write poetry."

"Imagine that." Waco nodded. "Purty and smart, too."

Did he say she was pretty? For a moment, she was flustered, then remembered he worked for Godfrey.

"I am hungry," she admitted. "Where is the cook?"

All three looked at her.

Waco said "We was hopin' you could throw something tasty on the table."

"Me?" She touched her chest. "Me?"

In truth, Rosemary didn't know a thing about

cooking; she'd always had servants to take care of every need.

"Well," Waco grinned, and she noticed it was an engaging grin, "you're the only gal here."

"So for that reason, you jumped to the conclusion I could cook?"

"Can't you?" Zeke paused in playing his harmonica.

"I've always had servants," she answered loftily.

Waco sighed. "Does that mean you can't clean, either?"

"Of course not."

"Useless as a fifth leg on a hoss," Zeb said. "Just what are you good for, miss?"

The way Waco was looking at her made her nervous. "I could think of something if she weren't a lady."

In her romantic novels, this was always where the virile hero "had his way" with the heroine. Rosemary had never even been kissed. Too bad the author always drew a curtain over the characters' privacy so Rosemary wasn't sure what happened between them.

She walked across the wooden floor and sat down on a dusty chair. Prince ambled over and sat down next to her and she rubbed his ears.

The one spitting tobacco sighed. "Well then, I reckon we'd better open up some beans and make some coffee."

Beans. That reminded her. She reached in her pocket and felt the pinto beans there.

"Lady, what you hidin'?" the old one asked. "You got a knife?"

Waco crossed the floor in three giant strides and grabbed her hand. "I didn't check for a derringer."

She let him wrestle her hand open. "See? It's pinto beans, just like I said."

"The hell it is!" Waco swore and took the beans from her hand, stared at them. "Where'd you get these?"

Rosemary was mystified as to why he'd be so interested in plain old pinto beans. "None of your business."

Waco took them from her hand, showed them to the old men. All three glared at her, then Waco strode to the door and tossed them outside.

"Now what was that all about?" she asked.

"Oh, you know full well, missy. I underestimated you. You're underhanded and crafty as a coyote," Waco scowled at her. "You got any more?"

She shook her head.

"Now, missy, you lied to me before. Maybe I ought to feel through your pockets and clothes myself."

"You wouldn't dare!"

"Don't try my patience, missy."

He didn't seem like a man to be trifled with. "I—I swear to God I have no more pinto beans."

"I reckon I'll take your word for it, Miss Rosie. I'm a Texas gentleman and I don't cotton to runnin' my hands all over a real lady, although you tempt me."

You tempt me. Of course he was joking. She felt her face flush and she gasped, imagining him running those big hands inside her dress and under her lace petticoats.

Waco turned to one of the old men. "Zeb, you best open up some canned beans and make some cornbread."

Zeb frowned at her. "What happened to that good, home-cooked meal?"

"You heard her, you ain't gettin' it. Zeke, put away that mouth organ and make some coffee. I'll get some water."

"I'll do it," Rosemary broke in. Maybe she'd get a look outside and figure out where they were.

"You think I'm dumb as a stump?" Waco asked. "You can go along with me, but don't get any ideas."

She stood up, thinking fast. Oh hell, what would Flame La Rouge do?

Chapter Five

It was midafternoon, Rosemary noted as she walked out of the cabin carrying the bucket, Waco trailing along behind, Prince running ahead. The October day had turned unseasonably warm. Her corset, under the blue velvet dress, was killing her and she was hot in all these petticoats. She couldn't take the corset off without some help, and she certainly wasn't going to ask one of these rascals to unlace it.

She paused and looked around, hoping to recognize some landmark. They must be quite a few miles from town because she didn't recognize anything, but then, she'd hardly ever been more than a mile or two from the mansion when she was home from Miss Pickett's Female Academy. That must be the Arkansas River down the hill, but it meandered so much, she couldn't get her directions from it. The cabin was well hidden by bush and a grove of cottonwood trees. She saw her mare hobbled and out on the prairie contentedly munching grass with the other horses.

"You can quit lookin' at your horse, ma'am," Waco said, "you ain't goin' anywhere."

"I was seeing if she had grass and water. I love that horse."

"I love horses, too, miss, and I wouldn't mistreat one."

She whirled. "But you don't mind mistreating women?"

He looked shame-faced. "I do apologize for that, miss, but it couldn't be helped. We're desperate for money."

"Yes, and working for Godfrey is a low-down way to get it."

"Ma'am?" He took off his hat and ran one big hand through his sun-streaked hair.

"Oh, I see through this charade." She snorted.

"I beg your pardon, ma'am, but I don't quite understand the word—"

"You must think I'm a fool." She wanted to slap his face for his duplicity.

"No, ma'am, but you might have a touch of the sun. Your face is turnin' a mite red."

She must look a sight, she thought, but indeed she was too hot and feeling a bit faint from hunger as they walked toward the river. She paused on the bank and leaned over to dip her bucket.

"Watch out, Miss Rosemary, that river's runnin' purty fast. You fall in, we might never find your body."

She turned and looked at him, feeling her face go ashen. *Is that what Godfrey paid these outlaws to do to me?*

"Didn't mean to scare you, missy," he said softly. "I just reckoned you can't swim, and with all them

petticoats, you might get swept away while I was
tryin' to save you."

"You'd try to save me?" Maybe Godfrey hadn't
told him to drown her. Or maybe this tall Texan
was a Noble Outlaw like Robin Hood.

"Reckon so." He shrugged broad shoulders. "We
can't collect ransom on a dead body."

"Thanks a lot!" So he was determined to carry on
with this tomfoolery. She filled her bucket and
struggled to lift it.

"Let me carry that," he drawled.

"No!" She slapped at his hand, angry with him.
"If I'm supposed to be a captive, I guess I might as
well act the part."

"Ma'am?" He took off his hat and scratched his
head.

"Will you stop saying that?" She struggled to take
a step with the bucket and the water splashed on
her fine riding boots.

"Let me have that bucket, damn it!" He took it
away from her as they walked. "No Texan worth his
salt is gonna stand by and let a little thing like you
struggle with a big load like that."

Nobody had ever called her a "little thing." Beside
him, of course, she was almost small. She was way
too warm and her vision seemed to blur a little. She
took an uncertain step as he strode on ahead with
the bucket. Prince bounded ahead of him, barking
and wagging his tail. She hadn't realized how hot
the day was or how uphill the cabin sat from the
river. She tried to breathe deeply, but the tight corset
constricted her rib cage. She stopped walking.

Ahead of her, the big Texan paused and looked
back at her. "Are you all right?"

"Of course I am," she said, then keeled over on the grass.

"Oh, damn!" She heard the Texan's agonized drawl as he strode down the hill and leaned over her. "Miss Rosie?"

She kept her eyes closed, enjoying the tension in his voice. He must be scared that if she died on them, they wouldn't collect from Godfrey. Now was when the hero always leaned over and kissed the heroine and she came back to life. Should she let this outlaw kiss her, even if it was all part of her imagination? Or maybe he would take her hand and rub it gently or hold a linen hankie with smelling salts under her nose while she roused and coughed genteelly.

"Gawd Almighty, missy, I told you you was too hot in all that gear."

Her eyes opened and saw his agonized face even as he threw the bucket of water over her.

She came up sputtering and shrieking. "Are you crazy? You trying to drown me?"

He shrugged and knelt down. "I figured I'd better cool you off fast."

"It's my corset," she seethed. "Ladies can't breathe in them." She struggled to get to her feet.

"Why didn't you say so?" Before she could move, he leaned over, flipped her on her belly, and undid the hooks on the back of the blue dress. "Take the thing off."

"You—you masher! Unhand me!"

Instead, she felt him touch her. "Hold on a minute, missy. I got a Bowie knife."

While she sputtered in protest, he cut the laces

on her corset, reached under her, and yanked it off. She had never felt so naked. "Why, you—you—"

"And while you're at it, missy, all them petticoats will just get dirty anyhow."

"What?" Even as she tried to get up, he reached under her, caught the hem of the lace petticoats, and yanked them off, leaving her lying there in her blue riding dress and lace drawers. "Unhand me, you brute!"

"Here, get up, Miss Rosie, and I'll hook your dress up."

"Don't you touch me!" she seethed, retreating from him, feeling the cool breeze on the bare skin of her back. "You've destroyed my corset. You know what I paid for that in New York City?"

He grinned. "I reckon you must be recovered from your swoon, your jaw is workin' again. You could at least say 'much obliged.'"

"What?" She wanted to hit him with both fists. This stupid joke had gone far enough.

"*Much obliged* is what folks in Texas say for *thank you.*"

"Thank you?" she shrieked. "I should thank you for what you've put me through? I ought to be home in a bubble bath right now, enjoying iced tea and sugar cookies."

"You could swim in the river," he suggested, "but I reckon you're cooled off enough now?" He spun her around to hook her dress. He saw her bare back and how pale and soft it was. He had a sudden desire to run his hands around her waist and then up the front until he could cup those fine, big breasts. His manhood rose at the thought of pulling the dress off. Then he scolded himself.

Will, are you loco? *This is a lady, not some tart you can throw down on the grass and take. Besides, her daddy will expect her to be returned untouched if he's to pay the ransom.*

Oh, but she was so much woman and so spirited. *Remember, this is all about the ransom,* he reminded himself. Still, his hands trembled as he hooked her dress up.

She felt the heat of his hands on her bare skin and she stood still, goose bumps rising on her skin from the touch of his fingers. It seemed to her he was hooking the loops very slowly and he stood so close, she could feel the warmth of his breath on her bare skin. No man had ever touched her body so intimately before. She wanted him to stroke her back and then maybe he would turn her around and—

"You cold, Miss Rosie?"

She came out of her fantasy with a jerk. "No, I am not cold, you villain."

"I got it all hooked now."

Prince had swum out a few feet into the river and now he came out of the water and shook hard all over both of them.

"Oh, you're a lot of help," she said to the dog and it licked her hand. She stood there dripping water while the blue velvet clung to her curves. She tried to wring on her hair and when she took a step, her sodden riding boots squished. She didn't even want to imagine what she must look like now.

"Let me get another bucket of water and we'll start over," the cowboy drawled and took long strides back to the river.

Whatever trick Godfrey had up his sleeve, it wasn't funny anymore.

"Hey," Zeke stuck his grizzled face out the door of the cabin and yelled, "what about that water?"

"We're comin'!" Waco called from the river and started up the hill.

"What about my corset? Ladies have to wear a corset!" she snapped, falling in step with him, water dripping off her drenched hair and dress.

"You don't need a corset." He grinned at her as they walked, the wet dog bounding ahead of them. "You're beautiful without it."

She didn't know what to say. Was he joking? She'd always laced herself tightly, her mother despairing of getting Rosemary's waist down to a dainty size. Well, there wasn't anything to be done about it now. The corset was useless, but she had to admit she felt a lot cooler without it or the petticoats.

They reached the cabin and the old man stared at her. "Miss, you fall in the river?"

Waco held up one big hand. "Zeke, don't even ask!"

It was Mollie who first noticed that Rosemary hadn't returned. She got the buggy and went to town and walked into the bank.

She saw St. John sitting at his office desk cleaning his nails with his pocket knife. He looked up and frowned as she came in. "What are you doing here?" he muttered. "I told you never to come to the bank."

She could sense he was annoyed with her, no,

more than annoyed, he was bored with her. Things had changed in the time he'd been sneaking into her bed at night after his wife was asleep and again now that Mrs. Burke had died so suddenly. She suspected she was about to be replaced, and it scared her. "I just thought ye should know Miss Rosemary ain't returned from her mornin' ride."

His dark eyes lit up. "Suppose she's been in an accident and been killed?"

Mollie was horrified. "You ain't done nuthin' to her, have ye? I ain't plannin' on gettin' mixed up in murder."

"Oh, of course not. I was just joking." He leaned back in his chair and ran his hand over his penciled mustache. "I'm not lucky enough to have her break her neck. Go on home and if she doesn't turn up by suppertime, we'll think about organizing a search party."

"*Think* about it?" Mollie felt a chill go down her back. She was beginning to be afraid of Godfrey, feeling that he was capable of more evil than she knew.

"I didn't mean it that way." He shrugged. "She's an expert horsewoman, I'm sure she's just fine. Look, I'm busy. Go back to the house. It doesn't look good to have the maid hanging around my office. People might suspect there's something between us."

The maid. That's all she'd ever really been to him, that and a bed partner when the cold Mrs. Burke wasn't willing. He'd promised to marry Mollie after the woman had died, but that hadn't happened either. Now she suspected it never would. Mollie didn't quite know what to do. She didn't really like the plump, clumsy Rosemary, but she felt an obligation as an employee. Too bad there wasn't a Catholic church in this town where a Irish girl could confess her sins to a priest. Maybe Godfrey was right; maybe Rosemary was still out riding. Not knowing what to do, Mollie got in the buggy and went home.

Godfrey stared after her as the buggy drove away. He was more than weary of the ignorant serving wench. Except for her crooked teeth, she was pretty, and she'd been good in bed. However, now she was trying to get possessive and he had higher ambitions than some low-class Irish baggage after all the trouble he'd gone to to get rid of Agatha. Was Rosemary really missing? He smiled at the thought and leaned back in his chair. He couldn't be that lucky. No doubt she'd turn up later in the day. Plain and plump as she was, Rosemary was excellent with horses. He couldn't imagine her in a riding accident. Maybe there might be bandits or wild Indians out there who'd grabbed her. He thought about it, felt sorry for the hapless bandits or wild Indians. Godfrey shrugged and returned to his paperwork.

"I'm getting hungry," Rosemary said. "Is there any food?"

"I thought we'd try to catch some fish in the river," Waco said. "Miss, you ever do any fishin'?"

"Of course not. Ladies don't fish."

"You better try," Zeb spat tobacco juice to one side, "or else you might go hungry tonight."

She was determined to make their job as difficult

as possible. They'd rue the day they ever hired on with Godfrey. "Since I'm your captive, I expect to be fed. Right now, a trout broiled in butter or a flounder stuffed with shrimp sounds good."

"It does, don't it?" Waco grinned. "I'm feared we don't got those in the river, ma'am. We might get a catfish or a perch, though, awful good fried with some potatoes."

"All right," she sniffed, "that sounds edible. Catch me some of that."

The three men looked at her.

The old one who chewed tobacco said, "Waco, remind me again about how handy it would be to have a woman around the cabin."

"She can't help it she's a bit spoiled," Waco apologized.

"I am not! I simply don't know anything about work, and I see no reason to help you."

"Missy, you might oughta learn," Waco said. "I'll get you a pole."

"I won't do it."

"We can't leave you up at the cabin by yourself. You might get into stuff or work on a plan to get away."

Damn, that was what she'd been hoping for. The big cowboy might not be well educated, but he was smart as a fox. "All right, I'll go along and watch."

The four of them walked to the river and sat down under the shade of a big cottonwood.

"I haven't the least idea what to do with this," she complained when the big Texan handed her a pole with a string on it.

Waco picked up an old can. "Zeke dug some worms. Put one on your hook."

She withdrew in horror. "Surely you don't expect me to do that?"

Waco sighed with infinite patience. "I reckon I could bait your hook for you." He leaned over and put a worm on her hook.

Rosemary made a face. "Eww. Now what?"

"Hang it over in the water and maybe you'll get a bite."

"Of course," Zeke said with smug authority, "since you never done this before, don't be disappointed if you don't catch nothin.' We been doin' this all our lives."

In about an hour, Rosemary had caught a whole stringer full of fish and the men had caught none at all.

"I thought you said this was difficult?" she said with a smug smile. "Looks like I eat tonight. I don't know what the rest of you are going to do."

The old men frowned at her. "You wasn't plannin' to share?"

"I don't see why I should. I caught them."

The old brothers grunted in disgust and headed toward the cabin.

"Okay, Miss Rosemary," Waco said, "I was gonna offer to clean those fish for you, but if you're not gonna share them, you can clean 'em yourself."

She looked at the dead fish. They seemed to be staring back at her with accusing eyes. "I can probably clean them."

"Okay." Waco shrugged.

She hesitated. "You—you might have to give me a hint."

"Well, you start by cutting the head off and guttin' em. Then you got to rake the scales off."

She swallowed hard, picturing this procedure as the dead fish stared back at her with unblinking eyes. "What—what do I use?"

"A knife." He reached to pull the biggest knife she'd ever seen out of his belt.

It was big enough to kill a man. She held out her hand.

Waco seemed to hesitate. "On second thought, maybe I better clean the fish."

She snorted. "Don't you trust me?"

"Missy, I don't trust any woman." He put the knife back in his belt.

"Why not?" He was more complicated than she had thought.

"Now, I don't see that's any business of a little Yankee gal's."

Little. He had called her "little" again. That was better than a fistful of candy. Well, almost.

"On second thought, there seems to be plenty of fish to go around if you'll clean them." She handed them over and fled into the cabin.

The two old men had already gone inside. The taller one said, "Lady, can you peel some potatoes?"

"No." She didn't intend to cooperate at all.

"Then we ain't gonna have much for supper." They both eyed her. "I ain't never heard of a gal who can't peel potatoes."

"I didn't say I couldn't, I just won't." As a matter of fact, she had never peeled a potato or handled a kitchen knife in her whole sheltered life.

"I do hope your papa hurries with the money," Zeb said, "otherwise, this is gonna be a long, long ordeal."

"I'm already feeling that," she said.

"I didn't mean for *you*, lady, I meant for *us*," Zeb said with a resigned sigh. "Wonder when Tom will get back? The sun is purty far on the horizon."

Godfrey smiled as he went over his bookwork. He was in the midst of foreclosing on a poor widow and her brood of brats. Yes, this was a very prosperous bank, and he could enjoy a lot more of its income if that eagle-eyed Bill Wilkerson didn't keep such a sharp eye on the books. When Godfrey owned the bank, the first thing he intended to do was fire the old teller.

It was nearly three o'clock and almost time for the bank to close. Godfrey lit a fine cigar and wondered idly if Rosemary had ever shown up at the house.

A small, freckled-faced boy walked past the bank window and came inside. Godfrey scowled. He hated children, and it was a labor to teach a Sunday school class of the brats, but it was expected of a pillar of the community.

The boy came into his office. "Good afternoon, sir."

This was a ragged street kid, not any of his customers' children, so he didn't have to be polite. "What do you want, kid?"

"A man give me this note, said don't give it to anyone but the banker."

"Well?" Godfrey held out his hand.

"The other man give me some money, said you'd give me some, too." The boy held on to the note.

"You young whippersnapper. Here, here's a penny." He held out the coin grudgingly.

"He said you'd give me a dime."

"Oh, he did, did he? Okay, you brat, here's your dime. Now get out of here." He almost threw it at the boy and grabbed the note from the grubby hand, settled back in his chair, and read.

It was Rosemary's left-handed, hard-to-read scrawl all right. Godfrey read it three times and almost laughed. "Fifty thousand dollars? Why, you rich snot, didn't you think I'd recognize your handwriting? I don't know what kind of trick you're trying to pull, but I'm not about to hand over that kind of money to extortion."

He couldn't figure out what she was up to. If she was going to get the bank at the end of the month anyway, why would she try to extort money from him? Was she smart enough to suspect he'd kill her if he had to, to inherit the estate? Maybe she figured on taking fifty thousand and fleeing before he could do that?

He leaned back in his chair and lit a cigar, thinking. He didn't believe for a moment that Rosemary had been kidnapped and held for ransom. She was trying to get money out of him the easy way, that was all, rather than wait for her birthday or fight him in court. Besides, if she was held captive, the perpetrators would live to regret it. "She can just go suck an egg."

Gray-haired old Bill Wilkerson stuck his head in the door. "We're gonna close now, sir. The books are balanced."

"Fine. Have my buggy brought around. You finish taking care of things here."

The old man nodded and left the office. Old Bill, dependable, honest. Rosemary was right; between the two of them, they could run the bank and cut Godfrey out. He wasn't about to let that happen. He read the note again. He was supposed to pull the window shade halfway down to show he agreed with the ransom demands.

"Don't hold your breath, stepdaughter, dear." He grinned and smoked his cigar. He was not even curious enough to go to the window and see if he could figure out who might be watching for the signal.

Rosemary's partner was going to be very disappointed. Godfrey wondered how much she had promised the poor dolt to help her. Well, when she finally realized Godfrey wasn't going to fall for her trick, she'd give up and come home. As spoiled as she was, he couldn't imagine she'd be willing to rough it more than a day. And if she still wouldn't marry Godfrey, he'd have to murder her. He'd done it several times before when someone got in the way of his plans.

He wondered for a moment if she might really be kidnapped? "No, I couldn't be that lucky. If somebody really took the wench, they have my sympathy."

And with that, he struck a match and burned the note in his ashtray. Then he went out and got into his waiting buggy, while behind him, old Bill Wilkerson began closing the bank.

Chapter Six

Godfrey left his office and headed home in the late afternoon shadows. Back at the mansion, he walked inside to be met by Mollie. Why was it all he could see now were her crooked teeth? "Has Rosemary turned up yet?"

The tart shook her head. "No, and all the servants are whispering."

He lowered his voice. "Well, come into the library and I'll tell you about the note she sent me. The dull-witted thing thinks she's going to trick me out of a lot of money."

Mollie looked relieved. "Oh, she's alive, then? Aye, and I feared—"

"Of course she's fine," he snorted as he sat down behind his desk and poured himself a whiskey. "She's hiding out, trying to extort money from me. You pack up a little carpet bag and hide it and I'll tell everyone she's ridden over to visit friends. I'll try to figure out what to do next."

"And when this is over and you've got the bank, we'll get married, won't we?"

"Huh?" He stared at her blankly. Why had he ever thought she was pretty? Those crooked front teeth seemed to dominate her face. "Uh, yes, of course. Now go take care of that." He shooed her away, wondering what to do about Mollie. A prettier new servant was due here in a few days, and Mollie wasn't such a stupid Mick that she wouldn't see the handwriting on the wall. Well, that wasn't today's problem.

Later, as Godfrey sat down to dinner, the portly butler said, "Miss Rosemary will not be here for dinner?"

Godfrey shook his head. "Tell the others Miss Rosemary has ridden over to Thackerville to spend a few nights with a friend. I'm sure she's having a lovely time."

"Yes, sir. Shall I serve, then?"

"Of course." Godfrey sat back and surveyed his empire of fine furniture and silver with satisfaction. Not bad for a poor boy on the run from the Cincinnati law. His name wasn't Godfrey St. John, of course; he'd chosen that name himself. To him, Elmo Croppett sounded too common.

He'd start out as a lowly servant in a fine home, so he had learned how to act as if he was to the manor born. The little old spinster had belonged to a garden club and had a passion for exotic plants. He'd learned to care for them himself while he plotted how to get her money. Owning a glass conservatory and expensive plants was considered definitely upper class.

In the end, she had written him into her will and he'd used his pocket knife to pry up the tacks holding the stair carpet. When she had tripped and fallen all the way down, her friends had become suspicious and he'd had to move on before he could collect his inheritance. He discovered he could make a good living with his charm and good looks. There were always rich, lonely women in every town eager to share his company while he stole their money.

When he decided his face was on too many wanted posters back East, he had come to Prairie View and ended up working as a bank teller. The widowed Mrs. Burke had been a pushover, but somehow, he'd never fooled Rosemary. She must think she was smart, trying to scare him into fleeing. No, he'd worked too hard to get where he was and he didn't intend to start over.

"Yes, Watson, you may serve the beef now. Make sure it's rare like I like it. And I believe I'll have some mushrooms and a good red wine with that."

"Yes, sir."

Ah, life was good and Godfrey didn't intend to give all this up, no matter what he had to do.

It was near dusk when Tom walked back into the tumbledown cabin. "Something's gone wrong."

"Shh!" Waco motioned for him to go outside and the brothers followed. Rosemary was left sitting on the floor patting the dog. "I don't want to scare the lady none."

They all hunkered down in the yard and looked at Tom.

"He never did give the signal." Tom took off his hat and ran his hand through his red hair.

Waco said, "Are you sure he got the note?"

"Yeah." Tom nodded. "I even watched through the window and saw the kid hand it to him."

"He see you?" Zeb asked.

Tom shook his head. "You know what he did with the note after he read it? He burned it in his ashtray."

Waco shook his head. "I reckon he's so shocked and worried about his precious daughter, he hasn't quite figured out what to do."

"Poor devil," the others muttered.

"I reckon," Waco said, "you'll have to ride in again in the mornin'. By then, he'll be over his shock and will be runnin' that window shade up and down like a flag on a flagpole."

Zeb scowled and spat tobacco juice in the grass. "I thought this was supposed to be over in a day, fast and easy."

"Well," Waco rubbed his chin, "maybe there's a problem."

Zeb turned and looked through the open door of the cabin. "Yep, and her name's Miss Rosemary."

Tom sighed. "I'm as nervous as a long-tailed cat in a roomful of rockin' chairs about ridin' into that town again. Might could, he'd have the law and a whole platoon of soldiers waitin' to grab me."

"Naw, he won't do that." Waco shook his head. "He's got to keep this secret. He'll be afraid we might harm his dear daughter if he brings in the law."

"Don't tempt me," Zeke snorted. "She pigged most of the fish, threw a plate of beans at me, and said, 'Is this all you got?'"

Tom stared at him. "I thought she was gonna cook some good homemade meals for us?"

Waco rolled a cigarette with a resigned sigh. "It seems she can't cook."

"What?" Tom's expression was incredulous. "All women can cook. They's born knowin' that, so they can take care of men."

"This one can't or won't," Zeb said. "She's a real handful."

"Well, give *me* a plate of beans," Tom said, "and I'll be glad to get it."

"I could go into town myself," Waco said.

"Naw, you can't do that," the other three protested.

"Somepen' happen to you, we're leaderless," said Zeb.

"Besides which," scowled his brother, "then we'd have to deal with Miss Sweetness, and I might kill her."

Waco said, "Now, you know a Southerner, especially a Texan, can't harm a lady."

"Keep remindin' me of that," Zeke answered. "Besides, if she's so sweet, what was she doin' with them castor beans?"

Waco rubbed his chin, mystified. "That I don't know. It ain't as though they're plentiful up north."

"Let's go inside," Tom urged. "I'm hungrier than a coyote out in the Panhandle."

They trooped back into the cabin.

The girl looked up. "Well, did he give you the money?"

Waco hesitated. He didn't want to alarm her.

However, she laughed. "Of course not. Now why don't you cowboys forget about this prank and let me go home?"

He took off his Stetson and scratched his head. She might be a bit touched in the head. He knew

Indians wouldn't harm a *loco* person, they thought the crazy one had been taken over by spirits. "Miss Rosie, I'm sorry, but we can't let you go home tonight."

She looked about the cabin in horror. "You don't expect me to spend the night in this shack?"

"We at least got a roof over our heads, even if it leaks," Zeke said. "As cowboys, we've slept out under the stars many a night."

"Besides that, my dress is still wet and I don't have a nightdress."

"You could sleep in your long handles like the rest of us," Tom said.

The others mumbled agreement as Zeb gestured toward the beans and cornbread. Tom helped himself to a plate and a cup of coffee. Prince promptly left the girl's side and went over to sit next to Tom, licking his chops repeatedly. Tom relented and shared with the dog. The other men settled down around the fireplace to drink coffee.

"I don't wear long handles." She kept her voice cold enough to cut steel.

"You could sleep jaybird nekkid," Zeb suggested.

She only snorted, miserable in her damp dress.

Waco said, "Miss Rosie, wouldn't you like a cup of coffee?"

"Be careful," Zeke grumbled, "she might throw it at you."

She wanted a cup, but she wasn't about to admit it. "No, thank you."

"It's mighty good," Tom said.

"No, thank you. I'll just starve myself to death and then we'll see if Godfrey pays you." She stuck her nose in the air and tried not to smell the hot coffee. It smelled delicious.

"Ma'am?" Waco asked and looked puzzled.

"Small chance of her starvin'," Zeke muttered as he sipped his coffee, "she et most of the fish."

"Well, I caught it." She kept her tone haughty.

"Huh! Beginner's luck," Zeb said.

Zeke got out his harmonica and began to play "Streets of Laredo."

"Stop it, Zeke," Waco commanded, "that's too sad." To her, he said, "Now, miss, there's a loft upstairs and even an old bed. Can you climb a ladder?"

"I'm not going to," she said stubbornly. "Gracious, you expect me to sleep in this dump? It's insulting that I wasn't provided a nice hotel and a change of clothes. You might as well let me go now. I'm not scared, and tell your boss I won't give up the inheritance."

The men looked baffled but they weren't fooling her.

"Fifty thousand," Tom scoffed. "Why, I wouldn't pay a dollar for her, when for five, I could get one of the girls at the Golden Horseshoe back in Austin—"

"Don't talk like that in front of a lady," Waco growled. He paced up and down, thinking. "Maybe it's just gonna take a lot more time." He turned and looked toward Rosemary.

She smirked at him. "I thought you said you were in a hurry and don't have time to stick around here for weeks?"

"I vote with the lady," Zeb said. "Puttin' up with her for even another day ain't somethin' I want to do."

"I beg your pardon!" she snapped.

"Gawd Almighty!" Waco sighed. "This is gettin' confusin'. Well, Miss Rosie, I reckon you're gonna be here awhile longer. You gonna go up the ladder?"

"No."

"Okay then, you can have a blanket on the floor with the rest of us, but I warn you, we all snore."

She seemed to think it over. "I changed my mind." She stood up. "I'll sleep in the loft."

Prince had helped Tom finish his plate and now ambled over and curled up by the fire.

"I reckon," Zeb said, "that is the most useless yeller mutt I ever saw. He ain't worth the powder and lead to blow him up."

"Don't you touch my dog," she snapped.

"Nobody's gonna bother your dog, miss," Waco said. "Now go up to the loft."

She took a step toward the ladder. "I don't know; I'm a little afraid of heights."

"And she's clumsy as a cow on locoweed," Zeke said.

"I resent that!" Of course, it was true, but it was only because she was so unsure of herself.

"Now that ain't the way Texans talk about ladies," Waco defended her. "Here, miss, let me help you." He came to her side. "Now you just hang on and start climbin', I won't let you fall."

She felt his strong hands on her waist, and for a moment, she lost herself in a romantic fantasy about Two Gun Tex.

"Take a step, ma'am," Waco murmured against her ear as he helped her.

It felt good to have the virile cowboy's hands on her waist. She stood there a moment more, enjoying it, forgetting how annoyed she was with him for working for Godfrey. She took a tentative step, and now he had his hands under her bottom, pushing her up the ladder.

"Excuse me, ma'am, I don't mean to be rude, but could you help by movin' your foot up to the next step?"

Embarrassed, she went on up the steps and disappeared into the loft. There were a few holes in the roof, but at least there was a bed. Some of the windowpanes were broken, but the night was not that cold. After a moment's hesitation, she took off her damp clothes and hung them over an old chair to dry. Naked, she got into bed and pulled the blanket up over her. Her indignation knew no bounds. Damn that Godfrey anyway. None of this made any sense unless he was trying to scare her into running away so he could claim the estate. For all she knew, he had told the cowboys to kill her. Surely if they had been going to do that, they would have already done it.

The next day, Tom rode out and the others watched him go.

Rosemary said, "Is he going in to confer with the bank?"

"You might say that." Waco turned away abruptly. He didn't want to scare the girl by any hint that there was a hitch in the negotiations.

They passed the long day playing with the dog and fishing. Much to the old brothers' disgust, Rosemary again caught most of the fish.

She saw Tom ride in late in the afternoon and Waco went out to meet him. She couldn't hear what was being said, but there was a lot of head shaking and disgusted looks.

Then the three others went off to feed the horses and Waco came into the cabin. "Wal, I reckon it's my turn to cook supper."

"You mean I'm stuck in this hog pen for another night?"

"Looks like it." Waco nodded. "Things ain't workin' out."

"I want to leave," she demanded.

"So do we, missy," Waco said, "but none of us can yet."

With an exasperated sigh, Rosemary sat on her bench and watched Waco build up the fire on the old cookstove and get a big skillet off the wall. In a minute he had grease sizzling and fish frying. "That smells good."

"You know, if you'd get some potatoes peeled, I'd make some coffee," Waco said.

"I caught the fish, that ought to be enough."

"I don't think the boys will feel that way."

"You mean, you'd all eat in front of me and not share?"

"I'll have to ask them," Waco said, measuring coffee into the big pot.

"Never mind, I'll make a stab at it." She marched over to the counter, picked up the small knife and a potato, stared at it doubtfully. In her mind, she was Little Nell, fighting off the dangerous bandit who lusted for her so, he would risk her dagger to accomplish it.

"If you're thinkin' about stickin' that little knife in me, I wouldn't if I was you." He grinned at her. "It ain't big enough to do much damage."

"It would if I cut your throat!" she snapped.

"Now, missy, you don't think I'd stand still and let you do that?"

She looked at the size of him. "I suppose not." She picked up a potato uncertainly, stared at it. Being left-handed, she was awkward with almost any tool. She began hacking at the potato.

"Hold it, missy, you're wastin' most of the potato. Peel it thinner."

She tried, cut her hand, and howled. "Now see what you made me do!"

He took the knife from her, held her bloody hand in his big paw. "Here, missy." His voice was soft, gentle. "Let me get that wrapped up in a rag."

Her hand hurt and she couldn't help it, she started to cry.

"I'm sorry," he said, "I never saw anyone handle a knife so poorly before. Here, you set on the bench and I'll peel the potatoes."

He took her hand in his and led her off to the fireplace.

"I meant to stab you with the knife," she gulped.

"Well, missy, the way you handle a knife, you're more danger to yourself than anyone. Why didn't you tell me you was left-handed?"

"It didn't exactly come up, with the kidnapping and all."

He went back to the counter, looked at the mess, and sighed. "Well, I can throw this one away and do some more."

She watched him as he peeled potatoes expertly. "Where'd you learn that?"

"My ma was the ranchhouse cook when I was

growin' up. I had to help her to keep a roof over our heads after dad was killed in that stampede."

He seemed more human to her now. She could imagine a poor child struggling with buckets and heavy skillets, helping his mother. "I bet she's really proud that you became an outlaw."

His face grew somber. "She's been gone more'n fifteen years; I sorta raised myself. Besides, I ain't no outlaw."

"Ha! Kidnapping women and holding them for ransom?"

"I'm real sorry about that, ma'am, but our first plan didn't work out."

"What was the first plan?"

He grinned. "Robbin' your daddy's bank."

He seemed so honest and sincere. Maybe he wasn't working for Godfrey if they had planned to rob the bank. Of course he had to be lying.

"What'll you do with all that money if you get it?"

"Now that's hardly a little Yankee girl's concern, is it?" He returned to peeling potatoes.

Little. He had called her little twice now. Nobody had ever called her that before. Of course, next to this big Texan, she did feel small. As she watched, he threw the potatoes into the hot grease and they popped as they fried.

"Missy, will you check the coffee?"

She didn't know how one made coffee. For all her education, she was feeling ignorant. She flounced over and stared at the pot. "Uh, I think it's fine."

He chuckled. "You don't have the least idea what to do next, do you?"

"I didn't say that."

"I could tell by lookin' at your face. Ain't you

ever done a lick of work in your whole life, or are you just for decoration?"

"What?" Was he making fun of her? She'd been called plump, plain, and clumsy, but never decorative.

"Never mind. I reckon rich, pretty gals don't have to be able to cook or anything."

"Don't make fun of me, I get enough of that at home."

"Ma'am?" He looked truly puzzled. "Could you scare up some tin plates and maybe some cups so we can eat?"

"I guess I can do that. Where's the napkins?"

He looked at her blankly. "Mostly, we just wipe our mouths on our sleeves."

She shuddered visibly. "Never mind." She found some tin plates and cups, most of them scratched or dented, and put them on the table.

"Now, missy, go tell the boys we're ready to eat."

"I'm not your servant, do it yourself!" she snapped.

"Okay." He sauntered to the door and leaned out. "Slop's on. Come eat it quick or I'll throw it out!"

Rosemary sat down at the end of the old rickety table. She was Lady DuBarry hosting a fine banquet. A servant was announcing dinner to the four young blades who were invited. She sat at the end of a long, long table with all its silver, china, and candles. They would have at least three kinds of wine, squab, and lobster while the young noblemen vied with each other to sit close to her, hoping to receive a smile, and maybe later, one might be bold enough to steal a kiss in the shadows of the formal gardens. That would be after the chocolate mousse, of course, and several kinds of cake.

The cowboys came in from the yard.

Waco slammed a tin plate down before her and piled fried fish and potatoes on it. "Here you are, missy, eat up before one of the boys takes your share."

Tom scowled. "Is she just gonna sit there like a princess while you wait on her?"

"Of course I am," she snapped. "And before you sit down, you can pour the coffee."

"Yes, Princess." Tom looked like he might argue, shrugged, and got the big coffeepot. "You want some, lady?"

His manners were deplorable. "I would suggest," she said coldly, "that you say, 'my lady, may I pour the coffee now?'"

"Ain't that what I said?" Tom looked puzzled.

She sighed. "Just pour it. Where's the cream and sugar?"

All four paused and looked at her.

"Don't look so idiotic," she said. "It's a perfectly reasonable request."

Waco finished piling fish and potatoes on everyone's plate. "I'm sorry, Rosie, but we don't got no cream and sugar."

"Don't have any," she corrected.

"That's what he said," Zeb barked. "You deaf, lady?"

They were hopeless. She took a sip of the coffee and coughed. That's—that's too strong."

The others took a sip of theirs.

"No, it ain't," said Zeke. "Just like Texans like it, strong enough to float a horseshoe."

"I am not a Texan," she reminded him.

"Well, you don't need to apologize," Waco said, "you can't help that. Lots of folks have that shame, but it ain't your fault. Might you be Scotch-Irish?"

"I have no idea."

"You don't know your own kin?" Tom asked, staring at her.

"It never seemed important."

"It is to us." Waco nodded. "We're proud of our ancestors who helped create the Republic of Texas."

"Hear! Hear!" All four men placed their hands over their hearts and murmured "Amen!"

Then they all took their forks and began gobbling like someone might take their plates away from them.

She tried to imagine the table as the banquet hall at Versailles with her as Madame DuBarry or Marie Antoinette with four young nobles nibbling the squab and delicate cakes, but it was impossible with the way they were all chewing and burping.

The food was good, or maybe she was just hungry. She decided on giving up on the manners lesson for tonight and just enjoying eating.

Later that night, Rosemary lay on her small bed in the darkness, looking up at the moon shining through holes in the roof. There was a crispness of frost in the air that spoke of autumn. Below her, she heard all four men and the dog snoring. Now what would happen? If this was one of her romantic novels, the handsome cowboy would sneak up the ladder in the middle of the night.

"I know I should stay away, but I can't help

myself," he would whisper, "Lillibelle, I must have my way with you!"

She would toss her yellow curls. "No! No! A thousand times no! I will not surrender my virtue to you, even though my heart longs to."

He would sit down on the edge of the bed. "Lillibelle, you are so thin and so beautiful, I cannot overcome my desire. I must have you tonight."

He would take her in his arms and kiss her deeply, thoroughly, while she slipped her delicate little arms about his neck. "Two Gun Tex, I've longed for your kisses, but I cannot let you have your way with me."

He fell to his knees beside the bed. "I will shoot myself with my own pistol if you do not let me spend this one night in your bed. Let me love you, and if it's as wonderful as I expect, tomorrow, I will release you."

"One night in my bed buys my freedom?" She looked into his pale blue eyes with her own smoldering ones. "All right, then, I will seduce you and make such passionate love to you that you will never forget this night."

He kissed her fingertips, her throat, her lips. "Lillibelle, would you run away to Texas with me, you willowy slip of a girl?"

"I'll have to think it over," she yawned as he groveled. "There's Sir Cunningham and Robin Hood and the Marquis—oh, wait a minute, that's another novel entirely."

She sighed and listened. No one was climbing the ladder. All the men were snoring. Prince woke up to scratch a flea, his foot pounding rhythmically on the floor, then he too returned to slumber. No one loved a chubby girl except in her romantic stories. What she needed to comfort her was some cookies; a big sackful of cookies. Funny, she hadn't even been thinking about food much with everything else that was going on.

She should try to escape. However, if she did, dared she go back to the mansion if Godfrey was this desperate to get rid of her? He was such a pillar of the community now that she didn't think the sheriff would believe her. She didn't trust the young major, either—he seemed to be after her money. Was there anyone she could trust to help her?

Chapter Seven

Before dawn, Waco got up and started some coffee, put the skillet full of bacon on the fire. He heard stirring around upstairs. He went to the foot of the ladder. "Miss Rosie, are you ready to come down?"

"My name is Rosemary," she corrected in a voice sharp enough to cut glass. "I'll be down in a minute."

"You ain't buck nekkid, are you?" He'd like to see that.

"Now, that's hardly your concern." Her head appeared at the top of the ladder. "I can get down by myself, thank you." She started down the ladder. He didn't move, and one of her feet slipped and she slid all the way down and into his arms.

"Good thing I was here to catch you." He grinned. He swung her around easily and set her on her feet.

"Unhand me, you blackguard," she ordered.

"I never know what you're talkin' about," he grumbled and returned to his coffee. "I don't reckon you know how to fry eggs?"

"You must be joking."

"I was afraid of that." He shrugged. "Most Texas gals can at least fry eggs."

She took a sniff of the coffee and bacon frying. "I—I suppose I could try peeling potatoes again."

"I don't think so." He looked at her bandaged hand doubtfully.

"I'm not completely helpless." She took his big knife off the table. "Good gracious, this looks like a sword."

"Bowie knife," he explained, "right handy. Be careful, Miss Rosie, you ain't too good with a knife."

"Don't give me orders." She picked up a potato.

The dog and the other three men slept on peacefully.

"So much for your guard dog." He grinned and returned to the old cook stove.

"He must be good for something," she excused Prince. "We just don't know what it is yet."

Waco grunted and moved to the fireplace, squatting to poke the logs.

She held up the big knife and looked at Waco's broad back. It would be easy to stab him and run out of the cabin before the others woke up. She hesitated.

"I wouldn't if I was you, missy," he said without turning around. "Before the war, I had to fight Comanches and rustlers. Nobody can steal up on me without me hearin' the tread of a moccasin."

"I wasn't thinking about that," she lied.

"Of course you weren't." He turned and grinned up at her. "You got a lot of grit, I'll say that. Don't expect that from Northern gals."

For a moment, she thought he was ridiculing her, then she saw the admiration in his pale blue eyes. At that, she felt a little more sure of herself. Rosemary turned back to the pile of potatoes. She didn't have the least idea how to peel one, but it couldn't be that hard. She put her tongue between her lips and concentrated on it, hacking with the Bowie knife.

"Watch it," Waco warned from the fireplace, "you're wastin' half the potato, don't peel it so thick."

She tried again and this time she sliced into her thumb. With a yelp, she dropped both the knife and the potato. "I'm bleeding."

"Again? Oh, Gawd Almighty, give me patience." He got up from the fireplace with a resigned sigh and came over to her. "Oh, you did cut it pretty bad."

She didn't mean to, but she could feel the tears gathering in her eyes.

The other men were stirring.

"What's goin' on?" Zeke demanded.

"If I'd been a Yankee patrol, you three would be tied up and headed to a Northern prison by now, sleepyheads."

Tom viewed the knife with alarm. "She try to stab you?"

"No, she cut her hand again peelin' potatoes. Anybody got any liniment?"

"I got some horse salve in my saddle bags," Zeb said, putting a wad of tobacco in his mouth.

"Horse salve?" She was indignant. "Now see here—"

"Oh, hush, missy," Waco ordered. "Get it, Zeb, and see if you can find a scrap of cloth for a bandage. Her petticoat is still on the grass outside, tear it in strips."

"That's a fine petticoat," she protested, but Waco held her hand in his big one.

"Missy, you don't need a petticoat, but you do need a bandage."

She was furious as she heard Zeb out in the yard ripping up her best petticoat while the other men stood around, watching and waiting.

Zeke handed Waco a small tin of salve.

"This stuff any good?" Waco asked.

"Don't know," Zeke said, "horse ain't complained."

"I need to go into town to see a *real* doctor," she protested as Waco spread the salve on her hand. His touch was gentle as a woman's.

"Sorry, Miss Rosie, this will have to do." Waco began to wrap the rag around her hand.

"Suppose it gets worse?" she asked.

"Well," said Tom, "if you was a horse, we'd have to shoot you."

"You wouldn't dare."

"In the field hospital," Zeb drawled, "they'd just saw your arm off."

"What's a 'field hospital'?" she asked.

"Oh hush, all of you," Waco commanded. "Jaws flappin' and tellin' too much. Zeke, see about the bacon, I think it's burnin', and Zeb, you peel us some potatoes. Miss Rosemary won't be doin' anything to help with that hurt hand."

"She ain't been doin' anything anyways but eatin' up our grub," Zeb griped, but he picked up the knife.

Waco frowned at him. "That's no way to talk about a lady. Now, Tom, get a move on. Remember you got to go back to town."

"Are you going to continue this ridiculous charade?" she snapped.

The men all looked at each other.

"Don't this gal ever speak plain English?" Tom asked.

"Got the bacon and eggs ready," Zeke yelled. "Gimme them spuds."

In a few minutes, everyone sat down to a big plate of bacon, eggs, and fried potatoes, washed down by strong coffee.

Rosemary looked around. "I'll have some cream and sugar, please."

"Sorry, señorita," Waco mumbled, his mouth full, "you'll have to drink it like a Texan, strong and black."

"That's not even civilized," she said and began to eat.

"Never claimed to be," Waco said and poured his coffee in his saucer, blew on it. "Hotter than Texas in July," he said.

She had never seen a man drink his coffee from a saucer before. "Nobody gave me a napkin."

The men all looked up.

"Wipe your mouth on your sleeve like the rest of us," Waco suggested.

"Gracious, such barbarians," she snapped and began to eat. Fried potatoes and bacon tasted pretty good, or maybe she was just hungry.

Waco finished up and put his plate on the floor for the dog, then he leaned back in his chair and rolled a smoke. "Damned good, if I do say so myself."

The other three burped and wiped their greasy mouths on their sleeves.

Waco said, "Missy, you can clean up the kitchen now."

"What?" Her indignation knew no bounds. "I don't know how to do that."

"Ain't she and her dog good for nuthin'?" Zeb snorted.

"Well, she's decorative." Waco smiled at her. "Anyway, I reckon with that cut hand, she can't wash dishes."

"Does that mean it's my job?" Zeb griped.

"Pleased you volunteered," Waco said and lit his cigarette. "Tom, let's you and me go outside and talk."

Rosemary and the dog started out the door with them, but Waco caught her arm. "Sorry, Miss Rosie, this ain't for your ears."

"Oh, you're not fooling me with all this secrecy."

"Go back inside anyhow."

"I'm not used to being ordered around." She glared up at him.

"You want I should spank your bottom?" He towered over her.

"You wouldn't dare!"

"Missy, don't try my patience. I ain't used to people buckin' me."

There was something masculine and authoritative about him. She retreated back into the cabin.

Waco squatted down in the dirt and pulled out his gold watch. "Tom, ride into town and see if he's thought it over, pulled that window shade. He's had some time to get over his shock and ought to be ready to bargain."

"Suppose he ain't?"

"You jokin'?" Waco blew a puff of smoke. "He's

crazy about his daughter; you saw how he acted that day in the bank."

"If the window shade is down, then what?"

"Get a note to him that we'll pick the time and place to drop off the money. I don't want us to walk into no trap with the whole Union army and the law waitin' for us."

"Yes, sir." Tom snapped him a salute without thinking.

"Gawd Almighty, boy, you're gonna get us all shot yet."

"Oh, Waco, I'm sorry. I plumb forgot." His consternation was evident.

"Just don't do it again," Waco said. "Yankee firin' squads don't appeal to me. Now get ridin'."

He watched Tom stride out to grab his hobbled horse and lead it to the barn.

He walked back into the cabin.

The girl stared at him from the doorway. "Did I see him salute you?"

"What? Naw, he was slappin' a fly on his forehead, that's all." He turned away. This gal was becoming more trouble than he'd expected. She might figure out enough to get them all shot if she should escape and get back to town or to the major.

The day passed and finally Tom rode in. "Nuthin'," he said to Waco as he dismounted.

"What? I can't believe that."

"Believe it," Tom said as he began to unsaddle his horse.

The two old men came out of the cabin. "What's up?"

"Nuthin'." Waco frowned. "I just can't figure it out." He turned and looked at the girl in the cabin. "Maybe," he said, "the bank don't keep that much money around."

"It's a mighty fat bank." Zeb spat tobacco juice.

"Yep, but that's a whole lot of money," his brother argued. "I know there ain't that much in Texas right now."

Waco rubbed his chin. "That must be it. He'd like to ransom her, but he just can't lay hands on that much cash."

Everyone agreed that was probably the reason the banker hadn't tried to deal yet for his precious daughter.

"Well," Waco said, "could we get by with less?"

"I don't know, Waco. You could talk a cow into givin' up her calf," Zeke said. "Maybe you can convince him to part with thirty-five thousand."

Everyone nodded.

Waco said, "Thirty-five is a powerful lot of money, sure more than might have been in that Kentucky bank. Okay, we'll make her write another note and lower the ante."

Thus agreed, they all ambled down to the river to smoke and watch the sun set. Leaves fell from some of the trees and there was a chill in the air.

"It's cold than a whore's kiss up here in Kansas," Waco complained. "I can hardly wait to get back to Texas."

He turned and looked toward the cabin. The girl, with her hand all bandaged, and the dog came out on the step. Then she tripped over the yellow dog and went down.

"Clumsiest woman I ever did see. It's a wonder

she ain't killed herself with the way she handles a knife," Tom said.

"You ain't bein' Texas gentlemen. She ain't used to doin' things around a house, but she could learn." Waco jumped up and strode toward her. "You all right, missy?"

"I just tripped, that's all. Can I come join you? It's boring here in the cabin."

"Sure." He caught her good hand and pulled her to her feet.

She stood there in the dusk, only aware of the fireflies and the closeness of this big man. She looked up at him, wondering if he would kiss her. He looked down at her, his hand tightening on her arm. He stood so close, she could feel the warmth and the strength of him.

"I need you to do something for me." His voice was a soft drawl.

"If you're asking to have your way with me—"

"What?" He blinked.

"Uh, what is it you want?" This wasn't one of her romantic stories, she reminded herself, stepping away from him in confusion.

"I don't mean to scare you none," he assured her, taking her hand, and they followed the dog down to the river.

"What is it?"

He took off his denim jacket and spread it on the grass for her. "We need you to write us another note."

"What?"

"Well, I don't mean to upset you, Miss Rosemary, but it appears the bank don't have that much money."

She didn't understand where this was leading. "Oh?"

"So we need you to write and lower the amount to thirty-five."

She threw back her head and laughed. "I don't know what the point of this crazy game is, but you aren't fooling me."

The four looked at her, evidently confused. She wondered what was going on here. What was the point in Godfrey having them kidnap her and then go through all this? It must be to scare her. "Look, I'm tired of this silliness. I'd like to go home."

"Not as much as we'd like you to," Zeb grumbled.

"Zeb," Waco snapped, "that ain't no way for a Texan to talk to a lady."

He was coming to her defense like Sir Galahad. She shivered with the thrill of the thought.

"You cold, ma'am?" Waco put his arm around her and drew her close in the darkness. She could feel his muscles ripple against her. Such virility, such power. She almost leaned against him, then she remembered he worked for Godfrey.

"I'm fine. Let's go back to the cabin."

"The lady's right; it's late," Waco said and stood up. They all walked back to the cabin, the dog loping ahead of them.

Zeb lit a coal oil lamp and Tom found another scrap of paper.

"Here," Waco said, "write us a note askin' for thirty- five thousand."

"This is foolishness," she snapped. "And I won't take any part in it."

She got up and marched to the ladder, climbed up to the loft.

The four men looked at each other.

"Now what do we do?" Tom asked.

Zeke took out his mouth organ and began to play "Jeannie with the Light Brown Hair."

Waco reached for the paper and stub of pencil. "I'll write the note, and Tom, you take it into town first thing in the morning. He wrote very laboriously: *Deer Banker: We still have ur darling dotter, but we no u may not have $50,000 dollars. We will settle for $35,000. If u agree, pull your window shade down so we can see it and we will plan a meeting. Pay the monny or we will kil her.* He thought about how to sign it, finally added: *Desperate min.* "That ought to do it."

Tom took the note and folded it, then put it in his shirt pocket.

Waco smiled. "By tomorrow night, he'll have ransomed her and we'll be on our way back to Texas."

"He might send the army to overtake us."

"Not if we hold the girl until we reach the Kansas border," Waco said. "My mama didn't raise no fools."

The four men lay down on their blankets and soon three of them were asleep. The dog snored the loudest, Waco thought as he turned over restlessly. He kept remembering how warm and soft she had felt when he had put his arm around her. He was a virile man and he'd been a long time without a woman. If he should climb that ladder and sneak into her bed, would she welcome him with hot kisses and open arms?

"Are you loco?" he whispered to himself. "She's a lady, she'd scream and try to throw you down the ladder. The other men would laugh like yappin' coyotes over that."

After a while, he too slept, ever alert for the slightest sound. He hadn't dealt with Comanches and Yankee raiding parties all this time without learning something.

The next morning, Tom rode into town.

It was such a long, boring day that Rosemary tried to clean up the cabin for want of something to pass the time. Of course all the dust made her sneeze, so Waco ended up taking her outside to blow her nose and told her Zeb and Zeke would do it, which didn't endear her to the old men.

Again, late in the afternoon, Tom rode in, shaking his head as he dismounted. Rosemary was both annoyed and disgusted. She couldn't quite figure out what Godfrey's game was if he didn't want her killed and he wouldn't let her come back to town. What did he expect his men to do with her?

Zeke made a tasty hash out of a fat rabbit and some potatoes and onions, then later, the men all went outside to sit on the porch steps and smoke.

"Miss Rosemary, you are welcome to join us after you clean up the kitchen," Waco yelled.

"What?" She couldn't believe her ears.

He shrugged. "Somebody's got to do it."

"Yes," said Tom, "and you're the woman."

She thought about throwing the coffeepot at him, then decided it wouldn't do any good. "I don't know anything about cleaning kitchens."

Zeke looked at her in disbelief. "Women are

born knowin' how to do female things like cook and wash dishes."

"Who says?"

"Everybody knows that," the other old man said and the four of them went off down to the river to sit and smoke.

Now what to do? She pondered that thought. It was dusk dark and fireflies began flitting about. She looked toward the horses, but they grazed a long distance away and they were all hobbled. She'd never get the hobbles off Lady and manage to ride her away bareback without the Texans catching her.

She didn't know what would happen tomorrow, except she was sure Godfrey wouldn't send the ransom money, if indeed that was part of the plot. Would these outlaws actually kill her? The other three might, but she didn't think their leader would. He was handsome in a rough-hewn sort of way. Maybe she could bribe him with a kiss. She was Little Nell being held by the villain, but the villain was handsome. "You," he said in a Texas accent, "if you'll let me have my way with you, I'll release you."

"No, no, a thousand times no!"

"Well, maybe for one kiss?"

She imagined kissing Waco. "Maybe one kiss," she whispered, thinking if she could seduce the Texan, she might escape.

"What?"

She looked up to see the tall Texan stooping to come through the door. "Nothing." She felt foolish.

"I thought I heard you talkin' to someone." He looked around.

"No." She held up her bandaged hand. "You

don't expect me to wash dishes with my hand like this? Besides, I don't know how."

"You don't know how to wash dishes? All women know how to wash dishes."

"I never had to."

"I forgot you was born with a silver spoon in your mouth." He paused in the dusk dark and she saw his silhouette and how tall he was. In the darkness, he could be a romantic highwayman ready to trade a kiss for her freedom.

"Yes!" she sighed.

"What?"

"I mean, hadn't you better light a lamp? It's getting dark in here."

She heard him sigh. "I reckon you don't know how to do that, either?"

"No." For once, she felt utterly useless. Texas women were evidently more accomplished.

"All right, then." He pulled out a small match safe, lifted the glass globe on the old lamp, and lit it, then adjusted the flame. He paused, looking at her. "I do apologize for stealin' you, ma'am. My mama would turn over in her grave at a Texan doin' this."

"Then why don't you let me go?"

He shook his head. "Can't do it, we need the money."

"What for?"

"Not inclined to tell you, missy."

"I guess you intend to spend it on wine, women, and song?"

He grinned. "Or spend it foolishly? Here, I'll show you how to wash dishes."

"Suppose I don't want to learn?"

"Then we got no clean cups for in the morning. Of course, we could just wipe everything off with a dirty rag and forget it, or let the dog lick 'em clean. I'm sure the boys won't mind." He filled the kettle from the bucket of water in the corner and put it on the stove.

"You wouldn't."

He shrugged and looked down at her. "Don't try my patience, missy. I think we got a sliver of soap, and I saw a big pan hangin' on the wall by the back door."

A big pan. She wondered if she banged on it really hard, would the sound carry a long way? Rosemary glanced over her shoulder as she walked toward the door. Waco seemed to be concentrating on stacking the dishes. She still had the big spoon in her hand. She stepped outside and got down the big metal pan. The other three cowboys were loafing by the river. She took a deep breath and banged on the pan as hard as she could. The sound reverberated across the plains. The trio by the water looked up, startled.

From inside, she heard Waco's sudden, angry voice. "What the hell?"

In a split second, he had crossed the floor and grabbed at her. Rosemary ducked and whirled away, banging hard on the pan.

"Damn it! Stop that racket!" Waco tussled with her and they struggled for possession of the big pan. With his great strength, he yanked it from her hand. She gave him a hard whack on the head with the spoon and he stumbled backward, bleeding.

"Good God, she's killed Waco!" The trio were

running toward her now as she tried to make a run for it.

Rosemary stumbled and Tom grabbed the spoon away from her.

Waco half lay, half sat on the grass with the cowboys gathering around him. She saw the blood on his face and it scared her. She had never done anything half so daring before, but she hadn't meant to hurt him. Hurt him? He had kidnapped her. This was her chance to get away. But as she turned to run, Waco reached out and grabbed her ankle. "No, you don't, missy."

She fell in a heap on top of him. "Let me go! Let me go!"

"Gosh, sir," Tom babbled, "are you hurt?"

Waco managed to sit up, let go of her. "No, I'm okay. I should have known better than trust this fiesty little wench."

Zeb frowned at her. "Okay, sister, you hurt him, you patch him up."

"I will not!"

She saw a cut on his forehead and blood ran down his weathered face into his light blue eyes.

"Hell, I wouldn't let her touch me," Waco swore. "She'd probably kill me."

She did feel bad even though he deserved what he got, she thought. He looked so shocked and disappointed.

Zeke went inside and came out with her white petticoat. "Here, we can use this for bandages." He tore off the white lace.

"Stop!" she shrieked. "I'll have you know that fancy petticoat is imported from France."

"Oh, shut up!" Waco groaned.

Zeb took a critical look. "It ought to be stitched and there'll probably be a scar."

"Won't be the first one," Waco said. "Forget stitchin' it up, just bandage it."

Zeke tore more strips off her fancy petticoat.

This time she didn't object. Instead, she watched the men's clumsy efforts to bandage the big man's head. "Oh, here, let me do that. You're making a mess of it. You got any salve?"

"Maybe a little kerosene," Tom said. "We used up the horse liniment on you."

"That'll sting," she said.

"Then that should make you happy, missy." Waco scowled.

She shook her head. "How about some whiskey?"

"Thanks." Waco smiled. "I'd love some."

"I meant for your head, cowboy."

"Oh." He looked disappointed.

It was getting so dark, she couldn't see very well. "Haul him back inside and one of you get the whiskey."

Zeb and Tom lifted him and stood him on his feet, draping his arms across their shoulders.

"Heavier than a bull," Zeb complained as they half walked, half carried him inside.

"Sit him in that chair and bring the light a little closer," Rosemary ordered. She was Florence Nightingale, angel of mercy, treating a wounded British officer in the Crimean War. Sir Rodney would be saved by her diligent care and would want to marry her and take her back to his family's vast estate in the English countryside.

"Ow!" Waco complained, wincing. "You're wiping that cut like you're scrubbing a floor."

"I do not know anything about scrubbing floors," she sniffed.

"Well, I wouldn't let you doctor a sick cow," Waco groused.

"Oh, shut up. Where's that whiskey?"

Zeke produced the bottle. "It might do a little more good if you'd pour it in him rather than on him."

"I'd drink to that," Waco said.

"Oh, shut up and tilt your head back or you'll get it in your eyes," she snapped.

She poured a little in the wound and Waco howled like a wounded coyote.

"I thought Texans were supposed to be strong and resilient?" she scoffed.

"You been readin' too many dime novels," Waco complained.

She wiped the blood off his face and took a strip of her petticoat. "Mother would faint at the waste of this."

"I wonder what she would think of her sweet little daughter tryin' to beat a man to death with a spoon?" Waco said and grabbed the whiskey from her hand, took a swig.

"Oh, shut up." She was clumsy with her own hand bandaged but she wrapped the bandage around his head and tied it to one side. Then she looked toward the open door.

"No, you don't, missy," Waco said. "Tom, close that door and then you sleep in front of it. I ain't hankerin' to go chasin' her in the middle of the night."

"Probably the whole army and the law are looking for me right now."

"I almost wish they would find you," Waco complained.

"Oh, God," Zeke said, "we got to keep her all night again?"

"Well, what would you suggest?" Waco said. "Her daddy probably won't be able to get the money together until at least morning."

"What a charade," Rosemary snorted. If Godfrey wanted her killed or scared away, why was he going to all this trouble? She didn't believe for an instant that these cowboys were kidnappers. They seemed too bumbling and naive.

"There you go with them big words again," Waco complained.

"Oh, shut up and have a drink of whiskey." A plan began to form in her mind: turning the tables on Godfrey. *In less than two weeks*, she'd be able to legally take over the estate. If Godfrey was willing to pay these Texans, maybe she could offer them more to help her. It was worth the chance.

Chapter Eight

"I reckon we'd better bed down for the night." Waco gingerly touched the bandage on his head. "Tom, you seen to the horses?"

The younger man nodded. "What are you supposed to do with her all night?"

All four men look at her.

She backed away. "If any of you think my father would pay good money to get me back after you have had your way with me, you're sadly mistaken."

Zeke said, "Is she speakin' English?"

Waco snorted. "Look, lady, if you think any of us would want to pull your drawers off, you're mistook."

"Don't be crude." She felt her face flame.

Waco said, "Missy, go up to your loft." He nodded toward the ladder. "You'll be safe enough."

"The blanket up there is ragged."

Waco sighed. "Zeke, give the lady another blanket."

Zeke handed her a blanket and she looked it over critically.

"This isn't very clean."

"Don't be so snotty, little gal," Zeke said. "It was maybe washed last summer, so it's clean enough."

"Eww!" She made a face but took the blanket and went up the ladder, peering over the edge of the loft at the men in the semidarkness. "You're sure none of you will—?"

"Tom," Waco ordered, "now take the ladder away so she can't get down."

"You tricked me!" She peered over the edge as Tom pulled the ladder away.

"I don't want to be beat to death with a spoon while I sleep." Waco smiled up at her. "Okay, boys, turn out the lamp and let's get some shut-eye. Tomorrow will probably be a long day."

She saw the men unrolling blankets and then Zeke blew out the lamp. She spread out her blanket, and after a tentative sniff, put it on the old bed. Moonlight filtered through the holes in the old roof. She needed to keep track of time so she'd know when her birthday came and she'd see if she could convince these cowboys to come over to her side. She didn't seem to be in any immediate danger and it would be a while before they figured out that Godfrey would probably trick them out of whatever money he had promised them. That would give her time to plan an escape.

Tiptoeing to the broken window, she got a piece of broken glass and made marks on a beam. In about two weeks, she would be twenty-one years old.

Waco woke stiff and sore. Around him in the coming daylight, the other three snored. Above him, he heard the gentle snoring of the girl. He smiled in spite of himself. She was fiesty, but spoiled. Well, what could he expect from a rich, privileged girl like a banker's daughter? She had pretty brown eyes, he thought.

"Rise and shine, boys," he said as he stretched and got up. "We're burnin' daylight."

The other three groaned and began to stir. Above him, the girl still snored. "Hey, missy," he yelled, "how about some coffee?"

"I'd love some!" came her sleepy answer. "And I'd like a muffin and some jam with it, too."

Waco blinked and looked at old Zeke, who scratched his whiskers.

"Ain't she a spoiled one?" the old man said.

"Never mind. The way she makes coffee, I'd rather drink shoe polish," Waco groused.

"I heard that!" came the retort from the loft.

Zeb scratched himself all over. "I'll make it."

Zeke and Tom went out the door.

The girl peered over the edge of the loft in the coming light. Waco thought she looked tousled and desirable with her brown hair loose. God, he'd been without a woman too long.

"Gracious," she gulped, "I need to get down. Well, you know."

"You better wait till the men come back in," he cautioned, "I'd hate for you to be embarrassed."

She went to the little window and looked out. Tom and Zeke stood out by the woodpile peeing. Quickly, she turned away.

Waco grinned up at her. "I told you, but you just had to look, didn't you?"

"Oh, shut up and put up the ladder."

He obliged and she started down, but felt the ladder slip. "Would you hold it please?"

"Okay, missy, come on down." She began backing down the ladder. When she paused halfway and looked down at him, he grinned. It occurred to her then he was looking up her skirt.

"You are incorrigible," she scolded.

"Now, missy, I don't know what that big word means, but if it means I'm thinkin' like a man, yep, I reckon I'm guilty."

She came down quickly and he reached out and put his hands on her waist, then lifted her down the last step. His hands were big and strong and she felt the power of his arms as he set her on her feet. She was only shoulder high on him.

"No banging on pans this mornin'," he admonished, "'cept there ain't anyone for miles anyway."

"Just where are we?" she asked.

"Far enough away from town you can stop thinkin' about being rescued," Waco said.

She wished now she had gotten out more so she would know the landscape, but her mother had thought ladies ought to stay in the parlor and do needlework and write poetry except for the occasional horseback ride.

The men came inside then and she went out and looked around. The horses grazed quite a distance away and they were hobbled. She thought she could ride bareback, but trying to get a bridle on Lady and get those hobbles off would be difficult before the cowboys noticed. Instead, she went behind a bush and relieved herself. Mother would be shocked, but there was no help for it. She only hoped there were no spiders or poison ivy out here.

She returned to the cabin where Waco was cutting up bacon. He looked up. "You like bacon and eggs?"

"I like mine coddled in butter, please, and a scone would be nice." She sat down at the table.

The men laughed.

Tom asked, "What the hell is a scone?"

"It ain't polite to cuss in front of ladies," Waco scolded him. "Here, missy, get over here and I'll show you how to fry an egg."

"I don't want to know how to fry an egg. Besides, my hand is hurt, remember?" She held up her bandaged hand.

He looked at her out from under his bandage. "Never mind, you'd probably burn them anyway, and we don't have but one apiece."

"Is there coffee?" she asked.

"Yes, your royal highness." Zeke bowed low. "Sorry we ain't got cream for it."

"Don't be rude," she snapped and poured herself a tin cup. "I hope you all have thought it over and realized by now how futile this effort is. If you will return my horse and point me in the direction of town, I will consider not filing charges."

"Huh?" said the trio at the table.

"Now, missy," Waco said patiently as if talking to a small child, "you know we can't do that. Tom, after breakfast, you ride into town and see if there's any signal from the banker or any talk around the saloon about us snatchin' her."

"I'm sure the law and the soldiers are scouring every inch of the county," she said as she sat down and sipped the strong brew. "They will probably lynch you before you can say a word, so you'd do well to head for the border."

"They're ready to lynch us back in Texas, too," Waco grinned, "so I don't reckon it matters which side gets the rope on first."

"You're wanted in Texas? Just as I thought!" she snapped. "Robbing banks or shooting people down in the streets?"

"No," Zeb said, "it's 'cause we wouldn't shoot—"

"Zeb!" Waco snapped. "Now, the lady don't need to know all our business."

"Well, if it wasn't for that, we wouldn't need the money," Zeb said.

"Hush up anyway," Waco said. "Here, lady, I cooked some for the men, but you'll have to cook your own."

"I don't know how." She was indignant. "I never had to do this before."

"Then it's about time you learned," Waco said, carrying tin plates of bacon and eggs to the table.

It all smelled delicious. She pretended not to watch them eat. "It's adding insult to injury to kidnap a lady and then not feed her."

"We ain't your servants, missy," Waco said, his mouth full, "and God willin' we'll be rid of you by afternoon."

"Amen to that!" said the others.

Tom finished gobbling, gulped his coffee and wiped his mouth on his sleeve. "What time is it?"

Waco pulled out his watch. "About seven."

"Okay, I'll head into town now."

"Be sure and circle some so the lady can't figure out the directions."

"I don't need to," she snapped. "I'm sure the army will be out here by afternoon and they'll shoot you down like dogs."

"Maybe," Waco said and sipped his coffee.

"That's a fine watch for an outlaw," she said. "Did you steal it?"

"For your information, missy, my grandpa left this watch. Only thing of value I own besides a pair of silver spurs and a tumbledown ranch. I set a heap of store by this watch."

Tom had left and Zeb and Zeke went outside to sit under a tree.

"Missy," Waco said, "you can cook yourself something and then clean up the dishes."

She was hungry enough to swallow her pride and try. She got up, went to the counter, and tried to slice some bacon. She wasn't having much luck.

"Gawd Almighty, gal, you're gonna cut your hand off," Waco said and got up from the table, came over, took the knife away from her.

"I can't help it, I'm left-handed."

"I know." He began to slice bacon off the slab expertly. "Now you drop it in the skillet, see? There's some biscuits left over."

"Any jam?"

He sighed. "No, missy, this ain't some fancy back-East hotel. Here, let me show you how to crack an egg."

As she watched, he got her breakfast cooking. "I feel sorry for you, Miss Rosemary, you must have lived a very sheltered life."

"I've got servants to do all this," she said haughtily.

"Not here, you don't." He grabbed a tin plate and shoveled the bacon and eggs out on it. "This ain't fancy, maybe, but it'll keep you from starvin'."

"Are you making fun of my weight?"

He looked genuinely puzzled as he handed her

the plate. "No, ma'am, I like a gal who ain't so thin, she'd blow away in a west Texas wind."

"Oh." She was so used to people making gibes about her weight that she had become defensive.

"I'm used to women cookin' for me," he said, "not the other way around."

"And I'll bet there's been a lot of them!" she snapped and sat down to eat.

He frowned. "There was a gal, but she run away with a rich Yankee blockade runner."

"Oh, I'm sorry."

"Forget it. I have." His expression told her he had not.

"You don't trust women, do you?"

"Missy, this conversation is over. I don't like people diggin' into my personal life."

"If you keep living like you have so far, you'll get hanged before you ever settle down," she said and began to eat.

"Don't you wish!" He grinned and poured himself another cup of coffee, then he went out and sat on the steps, rolled a smoke.

Now what was she supposed to do? If someone didn't wash up these dishes, there wouldn't be any clean ones for later. She stuck her head out the door. "I don't intend to clean up this mess."

"That's okay, missy." He shrugged. "We'll just let the dog lick 'em clean or wipe them with dry grass and use 'em again."

"You wouldn't!"

"Done it before. Men ain't as fussy as ladies."

"I'll bet you never met any ladies."

"Just you," he said and grinned.

She brushed past him and picked up the dishpan still lying in the yard.

"Don't bang on that," he warned as she went back in. "There's no one out here to hear it anyhow."

"I know." She stuck her nose in the air so high, she tripped going back into the cabin and nearly fell. They were all probably laughing at her. She glanced around, but none of the men seemed to be noticing.

She stood in the middle of the floor with the dishpan, trying to decide just how one went about washing dishes. She knew she had to have hot water and some soap. Where would she get the hot water?

Waco came in the door behind her. "What's the matter?"

"Nothing. I—I'm not used to being a slave, that's all."

"Miss Rosemary, you are spoiled, you know that?"

"It's not my fault. Upper-class girls know how to embroidery and play the piano, and maybe speak a little French, that's all."

"Don't seem too practical."

"We aren't supposed to be useful, we just decorate rich men's parlors."

"That seems purty dull to me. You got a young man?"

She hadn't realized how boring her life had been, and every young man she had met was after her money. "My personal life is none of your business." She looked around, puzzling.

"You heat a kettle of water," Waco said patiently, "and you pour it in the pan. Then you take that sliver of soap and suds the water up some."

"I knew that," she said, but she didn't. "I don't

think there's any water." She looked toward the pail in the corner.

"It's out in the river," Waco said.

"I knew that." She got the pail and went outside. She walked down to the water and leaned over to fill it.

"Here, let me help before you fall in." Waco came up behind her, reached past her to grab the bucket. His body was warm against hers as he lifted it. She attempted to take it from him.

"Here," he said, "I'll do it. Women oughtn't to carry heavy things when there's a man around."

"I'm perfectly capable of carrying a bucket of water," she snapped, but she let him carry it while she followed along back to the cabin.

Somehow she managed to wash the dishes with one hand and even felt a little pride in it, although she was determined not to do it again.

Later in the day, Waco started removing the bandage from his head, but it was stuck on the bloody cut.

"Here, let me," she said.

"Do you promise not to kill me?" he asked.

"Oh, don't be silly. Here, sit down here and I'll get some water to loosen it up." She took off the bandage and looked at the wound critically. "Worse than I thought. Maybe you'll get lockjaw and die."

"Don't be so cheerful, missy. If a Yankee shell couldn't kill me, I don't reckon a little bump on the head will."

"You were in the Rebel army?"

"The Confederate Forces," he corrected.

"Are you all deserters?"

"I beg your pardon!" He seemed genuinely insulted.

"Gracious, I just asked. The war is still on, but you aren't in it."

"I don't care to discuss this with a little slip of a Yankee girl."

Nobody had ever called her a "little slip" before. It made her feel dainty and feminine.

At midday, Tom rode in. "Window shade not down and folks in town not talkin' about her bein' gone," he announced as he dismounted.

"That's strange." Waco looked at her. "You'd think the whole town would be on the alert by now."

"Maybe," Zeke opined, "her adorin' papa is so afraid she'll be killed, he's keepin' it quiet while he tries to raise the money."

"This is all so silly," Rosemary said. They stared at her, and they weren't smiling. Suppose her kidnappers weren't in league with Godfrey? Suppose they were *real* kidnappers? The thought chilled her.

"You," Waco gestured to her, "you go in the cabin while we figure this out."

"You might as well let me go," she said as she went into the cabin.

"Reckon maybe she's right," Waco said as the four huddled together. "Could be he ain't got it or he'd use it to save his precious girl. Maybe if we'll settle for less, Daddy will come up with it."

"But we need the full amount." Zeb spat to one side.

"Well, half a loaf is better than none," Waco said. "I figure the colonel will feel that way, too. There might not have been that much in the Kentucky bank."

"Now how do we know that when we never got into the vault?" Tom pointed out.

Waco sighed. "We'll do the best we can, and if it ain't enough, they can shoot us. Tom, I'll write a note and lower the amount to twenty-five thousand. Tomorrow mornin' you can ride into town."

"I was hopin' we'd be gettin' rid of that female pest today," Zeke grumbled.

"Oh, hush up," Waco said, "I'm kinda gettin' used to her. She's spunky and she's got grit."

"And she never shuts up," Zeb said. "Females, bah!"

Waco had a scrap of greasy paper off the bacon. He licked the tip of the pencil stub and began to write: *Dear Banker, we thot to giv u a bargin and sel ur purty gal back to u for $25,000. If u agree, pull ur window shade down and well tel u wher to meet us. Otherwise, we may kil her. Signed yours truly, Desperate Min.*

"She gets much more annoyin', that'll be a real temptation," Tom said.

"She ain't pretty," Zeb protested, "you'll have him thinkin' we took another one of his daughters."

"Does he have more than one?" Zeke asked.

"She is *to* pretty," Waco said.

"Wal, each to his own taste," Zeb said. "She's plump and plain."

"She ain't," Waco protested, "she's got the purtiest brown eyes."

"So does your prize Jersey cow back in Texas," Zeke reminded him.

"Well, I think she's purty," Waco said. "You know, if we didn't have to have that money, I might ask her to go back to Texas with me."

"You trust her?" Tom asked.

Waco scowled. "You know I don't trust any woman now. But she'd be mighty good company on a cold winter night."

"That yeller dog would keep you just as warm," Zeke pointed out.

"But not as much fun," Waco said.

"I believe he's fallin' for her." Tom's eyebrows went up. "We need to get her back to her daddy quick."

Zeb took the note and tried to read it. "I don't think you should put 'yours truly' on a kidnap note."

"We're Texans, ain't we?" Waco said. "Mama said I should always be polite."

"Even to damned Yankees?" Zeke snorted. "I don't think so."

Waco looked up at the setting sun. "It don't make no never-mind because by tomorrow night, we'll have the money and she'll be back home. Let's go see if we can rustle up some grub."

"We're runnin' low." Zeb spat tobacco juice. "That gal eats as much as two men."

The next morning, Tom rode out again.

The three of them watched Tom ride out. Then they went into the cabin.

"Missy," Waco said, "I reckon by tonight, you'll be back in your feather bed and we'll be headed to Texas."

"You lowered the ransom, didn't you?" she asked.

"Now don't get alarmed none," Waco assured her. "We just figured that he didn't have that much money in the vault."

So they really were kidnappers. Now what was she going to do when Godfrey wouldn't pay that either? She didn't think he'd give two cents to save her life. There was no way around it, she was going to have to escape.

Godfrey St. John looked up to see the snotty-nosed little urchin coming in his office door again. "What is it this time?"

"I got another note, but you got to give me a dime."

"A dime? That's highway robbery, you young whippersnapper."

"Then you don't get the note." The freckled-face boy turned to go.

"Wait a minute. Come here." He motioned impatiently.

"Gimme the dime first."

"All right, here." Godfrey opened his coin purse and handed over the dime, then grabbed the note.

He waited until the boy left and opened the greasy paper. So again this time she'd had her part-ner write it. He laughed. He wasn't about to give Rosemary twenty-five thousand dollars. Maybe her partner in crime would get mad and kill her. He smiled at the thought. So they wanted him to lower the window shade as a signal that he agreed to the terms.

"It'll be a cold day in hell," he vowed. He could play poker with the best of them. Rosemary could just stay wherever she was hiding out and rot or get tired of this silly game and come home. As clumsy as she was, maybe she'd fall or trip or something and never return. He could only hope.

Chapter Nine

Tom waited all day until the bank closed, then rode back to the cabin. "Nuthin'," he said to the three men coming out to meet him as he dismounted.

"Nuthin'?" Waco stared in disbelief. "Are you sure the banker got the note?"

Tom nodded. "Sure as I'm a Texan. Kinda stood where I could watch the kid hand it to him from outside. He seemed to read it, laughed, and then burned it in his ashtray."

"Laughed?" Waco shook his head.

"Well, his face crinkled up and he threw his head back. I could see his body shakin'."

"He was cryin'," Waco decided. "I'd feel sorry for him if he weren't a Yankee and us in the mess we're in. He's brokenhearted that she's been kidnapped, and maybe he don't have twenty-five thousand to give us."

"That mean we're stuck with her?" Zeke and Zeb registered horror on their weathered faces as they looked toward the cabin.

"You two stop it," Waco ordered. "She ain't that bad once you get used to her."

"No, she ain't bad," Tom said, "about like dealin' with a case of smallpox."

The girl came out of the cabin just then, accompanied by the straggly yellow dog.

Waco lowered his voice. "Let's not upset her none by tellin' her about her daddy cryin'. We'll give him a day or so to come up with the money. We might have to lower it some more."

"Lower it some more?" Zeb griped. "We already lowered it twice."

"You want to be stuck with her longer?" his brother asked.

Zeb nodded. "You're right. Get rid of her if you have to take a thousand for her. Let's cut our losses and head south."

"If we go back with just a thousand, the colonel will have us shot for sure."

"In the meantime, we're runnin' out of time." Tom ran his hand through his red hair. "We're expected in Austin by mid-November."

"You think I don't know that?" Waco tipped his Stetson back on his sun-streaked hair. "I just don't know what to do next."

Rosemary called, "What are you men talking about?"

"Nuthin'!" they all yelled. "Just talkin', that's all."

It was apparent from her expression that she didn't believe them as she walked over and patted Tom's horse. "Did he give you the money?"

"Now, Miss Rosemary, don't be alarmed." Tom made a soothing gesture. "It might could be it's takin' him a while to raise it, that's all."

Now she looked worried. "What are you going to do with me if he doesn't pay?"

Waco patted her shoulder. "Don't worry your pretty little head about that, Rosie. I'm sure your lovin' papa will come through for you."

She started to say something, then seemed to think better of it.

The day had turned warm and Waco took out his bandana and wiped his sweaty face. "A mite warm. Miss, why don't you go back to the cabin? Tom, you put away your horse and maybe we'll go swimmin'."

Tom walked away with his horse and Rosemary said, "I might like to go swimming, too."

"Can you swim?" Waco asked.

"No," she crossed her arms stubbornly, "but I can learn."

"If she drowns, the banker won't pay," Zeb reminded Waco.

"Yeah," said his brother, "can't you go back to the cabin and darn some socks or whatever it is that ladies do while men have fun?"

"No. I'm hot, too."

Waco sighed. "Look, Rosie, you can't go with us. We swim buck nekkid."

She felt her face flame. "Oh. Why didn't you say so?" She went back inside while Prince ran to join the men in the river. From all the barking and splashing, it sounded as if they were having a great time. Maybe she could at least climb to the loft and look out the windows. If she could see a house or a road in the distance, maybe she could figure out where she was.

She climbed up into the loft, but the terrain gave her no clue. She stared out and saw no houses or anything else except rolling plains. She might be five miles or twenty miles from Prairie View; there was no way to tell. Behind her, the men splashed and laughed. Curious, she went to the other window and looked out. They were buck naked, all right. She knew a lady shouldn't be looking, but she had never seen a naked man before.

Funny, their arms and faces were tan, but their other skin was pale. My gracious, that Waco was a big man, wide shouldered and narrow hipped. She didn't mean to, but her gaze swept lower. He certainly had a much bigger . . .

She felt the blood rush to her face when she realized he had paused on the river bank and had turned in time to see her watching him. His face turned red and he dove into the water.

She felt her own face flame as she ducked away from the window. A lady probably shouldn't be spying on naked men swimming. But again, she wouldn't have been in a position to watch them if they hadn't kidnapped her in the first place.

Righteously indignant, she started down the ladder, caught her skirt on a nail, and ripped it. The fine blue riding dress was beginning to look faded and ragged. She doubted there was a needle and thread anywhere in this old cabin.

In a minute, Waco came back to the cabin wearing only his pants. Water still clung in droplets to his muscular frame and his sun-streaked hair was wet. "Ma'am, you shouldn't have been watchin' us."

"I beg your pardon!" She whirled on him. "I—I was looking to see if I recognized anything in the landscape so I could escape."

"Uh-huh." He paused in front of her, looking

into her eyes, and for a split second, she thought he might be thinking about kissing her. Nobody had ever kissed her before. She closed her eyes and held her breath. She was Maid Marian and Robin Hood had carried her deep into his forest hideout, and now the dashing outlaw might want to steal a kiss . . .

"Is there any coffee?" Waco said, padding over to the stove.

"What?" She opened her eyes and saw that dashing Robin Hood had been replaced by an indifferent Texan. Why was she disappointed? She knew men didn't like plump girls. "Coffee? How should I know?"

"What happened to your dress?" He seemed to be staring at her bare legs.

He was probably thinking how chubby they were. She pulled the torn edges together. "I ripped it getting down the ladder."

He smiled approvingly. "You've got dimpled knees."

Was he making fun of her? "It isn't polite to comment on a lady's limbs."

"Hard not to, ma'am, when your dress is ripped halfway to your waist."

"May I remind you that you didn't give me a chance to bring along any other clothes? This is all I've got."

The other three had come into the cabin and were listening.

"Hey," Tom said, "when I was comin' back from town, I saw a field with a new scarecrow not far from here. Maybe she could wear that outfit."

"What?" She drew herself up to her full height.

"You must be joking! Me wear the leftovers from a scarecrow?"

Waco leaned against the stove. "Well, you could just wear what you've got and let us men look at those dimpled knees."

She yanked her torn skirt closed. "I'll take the scarecrow's clothes," she said with as much dignity as she could muster.

"Good. Then after dark, we'll go get them," Waco said.

"I could go get them by myself," Tom suggested.

"Naw, we'll take the lady along," Waco said. "If they don't suit her, we'll rob another scarecrow somewhere else."

"I hope this never gets back to Prairie View," she said, "I'm supposed to be a fashion leader."

Zeb put a chaw of tobacco in his mouth. "What's a fashion leader?"

"I reckon it's a rich girl who's got nuthin' else to do but sashay around town in fancy clothes," Waco said.

Zeke played a note or two on his mouth organ. "You know, we could use some supplies. I'm gettin' tired of bacon and beans."

Waco looked toward Tom. "There a farmhouse with that scarecrow?"

Tom nodded. "Yep, big, rich Yankee farm. Probably won't miss a few punkins or melons or anything else left in the fields."

Rosemary drew herself up haughtily. "I will not be a party to stealing produce."

"All right," Waco put on his shirt, "but if you ain't willin' to help, we may not share the food."

"I am your prisoner," she reminded him. "You aren't allowed to starve me."

"Make up your mind," he said. "The only thing gonna keep us from starvin' is takin' a few leftovers the harvest didn't get."

So it was that after dark, they started on foot for the cornfield, the dog bounding ahead of them.

"Why don't we ride horses?" Rosemary asked.

"Because we can sneak in and out easier on foot," Waco said. "Besides, it'd be easier for you to get away if you were on horseback."

They walked maybe a mile, but the night had turned cloudy and Rosemary wasn't good at directions anyway, so she didn't have the least idea where they were.

They lay on their bellies on the edge of a field, watching the horizon. Prince flopped down next to her and licked her face. Rosemary was certain she could feel ants or spiders crawling on her skin but when she tried to get up, Waco reached out and yanked her back down.

"Watch it, missy, you never know who's out there."

"I think there's something crawling on me."

"A snake?"

"A snake?" she yelped and scrambled to her feet, but Waco yanked her down again.

"Did it feel like a snake?"

"Now how in the hell would I know? Rich girls don't usually lie down in farm fields at night, I don't know what a snake feels like."

"If it was a rattler, I'd think you'd know," Waco said. "Oh my God, it isn't bad enough that I'm kidnapped and running around in a torn, dirty dress, I've got to worry about rattlesnakes? I don't know what the girls at Miss Pickett's Academy would think about all this."

"Will you keep her quiet?" one of the old men complained. "Reckon you can hear her for a mile."

"How dare you—?"

Waco reached out and clapped his hand over her mouth, pulled her close to him. "Zeb's right," he whispered. "Missy, you're makin' too much noise."

His arm was around her shoulders and across her mouth. She could feel the warmth and the power of his big body next to hers. She thought about biting his fingers, but then she liked the feeling of his arm around her. She remembered one of her romantic novels, *Captured by a Handsome Rebel*. Now she thought of that plot. She was a farmer's daughter and had gone out at night to check on a barking dog. A handsome rebel officer had grabbed her. *Missy, keep quiet. And suppose I don't? I'll keep you quiet if I have to kiss you to do it. General Grant is in the area, and we aim to capture him.*

His mouth came down on hers as he held her close and she forgot about warning General Grant or anything except this handsome officer's torrid kisses.

"Okay." Waco took his hand off her mouth. "Rosie, take a look at that scarecrow out there. Do those clothes look like they might fit you?"

"Now how am I supposed to know that?" she complained in a hoarse whisper. "I can barely see the damned thing."

"I'm not used to ladies cussin'," he said in a shocked tone.

"I think I've earned it, after all you outlaws have put me through."

"We're not outlaws," Tom protested. "We're—"

"Hush, Tom!" Waco snapped. "Crawl out there and take those pants and shirt off that scarecrow."

"You want I should put her dress on it?"

"And leave me here almost naked in my lace drawers and corset cover? Don't you dare!" she snapped.

"She's right," Waco said. "Besides, someone might recognize the dress. We'll bury it later."

"This was an expensive riding outfit I bought in New York City—"

"Well, it's rags now," Waco said. "Now hush up, would you, missy?"

"I am not used to people giving me orders, and I—"

He clapped his arm around her and put his hand over her mouth again. "Tom, go get the clothes."

Tom was back in a couple of minutes with the faded shirt and denim pants and a straw hat.

Rosemary pulled away from Waco and examined them in the moonlight when Tom tossed them to her. "These have holes in them and are kind of ripped."

"Not as bad as your dress," Waco said. "Folks don't usually put new clothes on scarecrows."

"You expect me to pull my dress off in front of everybody, or can I wait till we get back to the cabin?"

"Suit yourself," Waco shrugged, "but we're gonna be crawlin' through a corn field and a melon patch."

She considered. There was really no place to

hide and change. "All right, but you men must close your eyes."

"Now how do you know we'll close 'em?" She saw Waco's white teeth gleaming in the darkness.

"Well, if you're gentlemen, you will. What am I thinking? I'm dealing with outlaws here."

Tom said, "we ain't outlaws, we're—"

"Hush, Tom," Waco sighed. "All right, men, close your eyes. The lady is modest."

"She's also mouthy," Zeke complained.

Rosemary didn't know if they would peek, but there was no help for it. She shimmied out of the torn blue dress and stood there a moment in her drawers and corset cover. Then she pulled on the faded pants and plaid shirt. "These are terrible. Even a self-respecting scarecrow wouldn't—"

"Oh hush," Waco said. "I'll find you a piece of rope to hold your pants up." He plopped the torn straw hat on her head.

"I am so glad the citizens of Prairie View can't see one of their most important ladies crawling around in a cornfield wearing a scarecrow's cast-offs—"

"Stop yammerin'," Waco ordered.

"Are you telling me to shut up? I never—"

"Oh Lordy," Zeke sighed, "that's sure the God's truth!"

Waco said, "Now let's stoop down and crawl between the rows. Here and there, we should find a few ears of corn the pickers missed."

Fresh corn did sound good to Rosemary. She crept down the rows checking for overlooked ears. Her castoff pants were much too big and sliding down as she crawled on all fours. Prince suddenly stuck his cold wet nose on her bare side and licked her skin. She squealed.

"Rosie, you find a snake?"

"Never mind. I can't believe I'm doing this."

In a few minutes, Waco called in a hoarse whisper, "Everyone get some?"

Affirmative mutters from everyone.

"All right, let's take what we got and pile it back on the other side of the fence. Then we'll go lookin' for melons and maybe punkins."

Rosemary did as she was told, holding on to her too-big pants with her other hand. She felt naughty. Never in her sheltered life had she done anything that was questionable, like stealing a scarecrow's clothes or taking corn and melons out of a farmer's field. It was kind of fun.

The thought shocked her. What was she thinking? She ought to be in her own parlor right now doing needlework or practicing the piano. Of course, she didn't have any talent there either.

"Tom, where's the melon field?" Waco asked.

"Up close to the farmhouse," Tom whispered.

Aha. She might get close enough to call for help.

"Now, missy," Waco commanded, "you don't get any fancy ideas, you hear? You be as quiet as a little mouse."

"You can't tell me what to do."

"I'm tellin' you." He sounded like he was used to giving orders. "Besides, we wake up that farmer, he might have a shotgun and shoot first, ask questions later."

Uh-oh. In her mind she saw headlines in the Prairie View Gazette: *NOTED SOCIAL LEADER SHOT DEAD STEALING MELONS. Local women's club ladies shocked at such skullduggery. Worse yet, Miss Burke was not dressed in the height of fashion, and unspeakably, was not wearing a corset.*

"Come on," Waco snapped.

She could barely see the four men crouching down between the rows. With Prince following her, she looked around for melons. Most of them had been harvested, but here and there, one had been overlooked. Way ahead of her, she saw a big melon. That looked good to her. She crept closer.

Abruptly a dog began barking at the distant farmhouse. It sounded like a very big dog. Prince's ears went up and he began barking, too.

"Oh, hell," Waco muttered behind her, "we've woke up the watchdog. Let's get out of here."

Prince seemed to need no coaxing, he was already running toward the fence. The farm dog's barking sounded closer and more frantic, but she was determined to get that big melon.

"Rosemary!" he yelled in a hoarse whisper. "Come on, let's go afore that dog gets here."

The melon was only a few steps away, although the barking seemed closer. It sounded angry. She ignored Waco and scrambled over to grab the melon.

"Rosemary! Come on afore the dog gets you!" She turned to see the other three running for the fence behind Prince with Waco standing up now, motioning frantically.

She wasn't going to let go of that melon. She had it now and turned. "Here I come."

Behind her, the dog sounded closer. She stumbled, began to run. She could feel her pants slid-

ing down around her ankles. Ahead of her, Waco
dived through the fence.

"Missy, drop that damned melon and come on!"

She wasn't about to give up this prize. She kept
running but glanced back over her shoulder. It was
a big white dog and it was coming hard. From
here, she could see the flash of its teeth. At that
point, she tossed the melon to Waco and dived for
the fence just as the pants tangled around her
ankles. She felt the dog snap the leg of her pants.

Waco reached out and grabbed her, dragging
her under the wire, pants and all. The dog hit the
fence and reared up on it, barking and growling.
He tried to get under the wire, but he was too big.

"I—I think he got me!" It was the most exciting,
scariest thing she'd ever done in her whole life.

Waco inspected her. "Naw, but he tore your
pants. You little idiot! Why didn't you drop the
melon first thing?"

"I thought I could outrun him."

They all crept away in the darkness with the dog
barking behind them. Prince gamboled along
beside her, licking her hand. "Fine brave dog you
are," she scolded.

"He ain't good for nuthin'," Zeke complained.

"Oh, hush up," Waco muttered as they fled. To
Rosemary, he said, "I'll carry your melon. You got
a lotta grit for a gal, especially a Yankee gal." There
was a hint of admiration in his voice.

"What's grit?"

He shrugged. "Hard to explain. All Texans got it.
It means you don't quit when the goin' gets tough.
I thought you was just a whiney rich gal."

She held up her pants with both hands as they

crept along in the darkness. "Good gracious, if you're gonna turn me into a thief, I figure I can steal with the best of them."

"Ma'am," Zeb said, "we don't ordinarily steal, it's just that under these circumstances, we ain't got a lot of choice."

"Shut up, Zeb," Waco said.

"Yes, sir. I just didn't want her to think we was common crooks—"

"Well, now," Zeke complained as they walked through the darkness and gathered up their corn, "who cares what that uppity Yankee gal thinks?"

"The little gal got more'n her share of the loot," Tom defended her.

"Yes, I did," she crowed. Holding up her pants with one hand and some ears of corn in the other, Rosemary followed the men back to the cabin. They carried their booty inside and piled it on the table, lit the lamp.

Prince flopped down in front of the fireplace, panting hard. He looked at the people and wagged his tail.

"Like I said," Zeke muttered, "most worthless dog I ever did see."

"Well, men," Waco surveyed the pile, "looks like we got enough food to make it awhile longer. Any day now, the banker will send the money, and we'll be headed back to Texas."

Rosemary felt her face blanch. They were serious. Why had she not realized that? And what would happen to her when these Texans found out Godfrey wouldn't pay a nickel to get her back?

Chapter Ten

Waco looked her up and down. "Missy, your pants is torn."

She felt her backside. "Good gracious, I wasn't about to lose that melon to that dog."

"The lady is almost as gritty as a Texas gal," Tom said with admiration. "That's a good melon, too."

She tried not to smile at the compliment. After all, since when did the admiration of a bunch of Texas outlaws matter to a rich society girl?"

"Rosie," Waco said, "if you can find a needle or some pins, we can fix that for you."

She held on to her pants. "You'd better find me a belt or something first."

"I got a piggin' string."

"I beg your pardon!"

"I ain't insultin' you," he explained. "Cowboys use it in tyin' a steer's legs when they're brandin'." He handed it to her. "I don't know if you look any better than you did, but at least your pants won't fall down and show those dimpled knees."

Was he making fun of her? He looked serious.

She found a handful of rusty pins in an old bureau and handed them to him. Waco knelt behind her. "You fellas get some water boilin' for that corn and cut up some melons while I protect the lady's modesty."

"I could pin her up," Tom offered with a smile.

Waco scowled. "I believe I'm in charge here. I'll do it. Stand still, Rosie."

She started to protest that she didn't like that name, but coming from him, it sounded different. Besides, with him now putting his hands on her bottom and pinning her pants, they were more than better acquainted.

"I believe you're losin' some weight," he said. "We got to feed you better."

He must be making fun of her. But on the other hand, she had been too busy and preoccupied to stuff food in her face.

He got her ragged pants pinned, then stood back and looked at her, grinning. "Well, it may not be high fashion, missy, but I do declare it looks better on you than it did on the scarecrow."

"Thanks, I think."

The men had the corn cooked and some melons sliced. It smelled delicious. They all sat down at the table and dived in.

"I wish we had some butter for the corn," she said.

"Now, Rosemary," Waco said, "I don't think I could get away with stealin' a cow just so you could have butter."

"It'd be fun to try," she said before she thought.

All the men looked at her in surprise and she was horrified at herself. "I meant," she stammered, "I really do like butter."

"If we was back in Texas," Waco said wistfully, "I've got the sweetest little Jersey cow that gives the best milk and butter. Got a garden, too, with all sorts of vegetables."

She paused in eating the melon. "Outlaws have gardens?"

"Missy," he said softly, "I had another life before the war; nice little ranch, lots of beef cattle, too."

"That's right." Zeke wiped juice off his gray beard. "We was all his hired hands."

"Then what are you doing in Kansas robbing banks?"

The other three looked at Waco.

"Never mind," he sighed. "The war changed everything. Sometimes things happen and you just got to play the hand Fate deals you."

"What does that mean?"

"You're curious as a possum," he said abruptly, "and you've asked too many questions already. I'm goin' out for a smoke." He got up and went outside.

Rosemary looked around at the other three. "What'd I say that upset him?"

"You made him long for Texas," Tom said. "We all do. It's purty country around Waco; God's country. If it weren't for this dad-blamed war, we wouldn't be up here—"

"Shut up, Tom," Zeb cautioned.

"What's the war got to do with outlaws?" she asked.

No one answered her.

"Miss," Zeke said gently. "Waco ain't a bad 'un. He's not what you think he is."

"Well, he's holding me for ransom, I'd say that makes him an outlaw."

Nobody said anything for a long moment. Finally Zeke said, "We got to have that money, miss. Our lives depend on it because of what happened in Kentucky."

Now it was Tom's turn to say, "Zeke, you got a loose lip. Shut your face."

"What happened in Kentucky and why were you there?" She had to know the answer to this whole puzzle. However, the men looked at her in stony silence, then Zeke got his mouth organ out of his shirt and began to play "Jeannie with the Light Brown Hair."

She waited a minute, then decided no one was going to tell her anything else. She got up from the table and went outside into the moonlight. The night was cool but not crisp.

Waco sat a few yards from the cabin, leaning against the trunk of a big tree. She walked toward him. Behind her, she could hear the lonesome sounds of Zeke's music. ". . . borne like a vapor on the summer air . . ."

Waco looked up. "What do you want?"

What did she want? "It—it's dull in the cabin. May I join you?"

He shrugged those wide shoulders. "Reckon so."

She sat down next to him, watching his profile. He was a handsome man, more handsome than any man she had ever met except Godfrey, but this was a man's man, masculine, virile, capable of handling anything the world threw at him. "I didn't mean to upset you by getting you talking about Texas."

"That's okay. We just got more trouble than a barrel of snakes, that's all."

"And that's why you need the money?"

He nodded.

"What if—what if you don't get it?"

He looked at her with those eyes the color of faded denim. "Your adorin' daddy will come through, missy, don't worry."

"What if he doesn't?"

"Now why wouldn't he? You sayin' he ain't got it?"

She didn't dare tell him the truth. "He—he might not have it right there in the vault. He might have to wait for a shipment from back East."

"God, I hope not." He tossed his cigarette away. "We only got till the middle of November or—" He paused and shrugged. "Well, little gal, what happens to us ain't your problem."

She leaned against the tree trunk. "I guess it is if my ransom is all that stands between you and disaster. Otherwise, would you go back to your ranch?"

He nodded, too aware of her warmth against his arm. "I wish I could, Rosie. 'Course it's probably all tumbled down, take a lot of work and some money to rebuild it. I reckon my cattle are scattered all over three counties by now." He sounded tired, almost defeated.

"On that ranch of yours, is there a Mrs. Waco?"

He laughed. "My real name is Will; Will McClain, Scotch-Irish, you know."

"So is there a Mrs. McClain?"

"No, not since my mama died. The gal I was gonna marry—well, never mind."

"You said she ran off with a Yankee blockade runner."

"Sometimes I run off at the mouth. I haven't trusted a woman since her."

"Was she pretty?" She knew the answer, but she had to ask.

"Beautiful. Long yellow hair."

"Oh." And of course Rosemary wasn't. She was plain and plump with ordinary brown hair. No man, especially one like Waco, would be drawn to her. Well, she had money. "If I could get that gold for you, would you trust me?" Without thinking, she reached out and put her hand on his strong arm. She could feel the muscles and sinews underneath that faded denim shirt.

"Now why would you want to do that?" He turned and looked into her eyes.

"I—I don't know. You seem to be in such a mess. If you'd trust me, I might be able to get you more money than this ransom plot will." Their faces were so close, her heart almost seemed to stop. She could hear him breathing and for a moment, she thought he would kiss her. He reached out and brushed a wisp of hair away from her face.

"Missy, I wish I could trust you."

There was something so sad, so earnest about him that she put her small hand over his big one. Abruptly she wanted to help him, in spite of him being an outlaw and a kidnapper. He sounded so lonely and sad, and she had always been lonely and sad. "Will, what I haven't told you is on Halloween, I could give you the money. All you got to do is let me go and—"

"Nice try, missy." He laughed and leaned back against the tree. "All I've got to do is let you go and you'll get me the money? You think I'd believe that?"

"I didn't mean I could get it right away, I could get it at the end of October."

"And you'd just give me a few thousand?" She could see the disbelieving smirk on his rugged face.

"Yes."

"Missy, my mama didn't raise no fools. You think I'm stupid enough to trust you? All I got to do is turn you loose and you'll get me the money?"

"Yes."

He shook his head and laughed again. "And I reckon you'd want to bring it out to me with an escort of lawmen and a platoon of Union soldiers?"

"No, I wouldn't do that."

"Like hell you wouldn't!"

"Are you calling me a liar?" She started to withdraw her hand, but about that time, he reached out and covered her hand with one of his big ones. It was warm and calloused and powerful.

"I can't trust women anymore. You're a great gal, Miss Rosemary," he said gently. "I'm sorry we had to kidnap you, but we're desperate. Our lives are on the line."

"Who's after you?"

He shook his head and turned to look at her with those honest, faded blue eyes. "Can't tell you, ma'am; wish I could."

What on earth was he mixed up in? She couldn't imagine. Was it a gambling debt? Was there a mortgage on his ranch?

"You've only got a couple of weeks to raise the money?"

He nodded, squeezing her hand. "That's why every day your dear daddy delays puts us in deeper trouble."

She took a deep breath. "What—what if I told you I don't think my father will pay?"

He laughed gently and removed his hand from hers. "Oh, he wants you back for sure, and we've run out of other ideas. We're countin' on him comin' through with the cash. He's our last chance."

"On Halloween, I'll have plenty of money of my own," she said. "Suppose I promised to give you that if you'd let me go?"

"I wouldn't believe you," he said and his voice was cold. He got up and went back into the cabin.

She stood there looking after him. When he'd put his hand over hers, she'd had the strangest feeling that he might be about to kiss her, and then she'd had said something that upset him. "Are you crazy, Rosemary?" she scolded herself. "You would have let an outlaw kiss you?"

She wasn't sure. At the moment, a kiss sounded more tempting than a chocolate eclaire. She closed her eyes and wondered how that kiss would feel. Would it be gentle and tender or savage and rough? If only she was slender and pretty, he might have kissed her, might have fallen in love with her, even. She had never disliked being Rosemary Burke as much as she did at this moment.

She saw his big silhouette appear in the cabin door. "Missy," Waco called, "you better come in here now. You needn't be thinkin' about gettin' away."

Funny, she hadn't been thinking about getting away or even food. She'd been wondering what it would be like to be kissed into submission by a virile, handsome outlaw. "Don't be stupid, you ninny," she scolded herself. "You can't even buy a man to love you."

"Missy, do I have to come out there?" Waco called.

"And do what?" she challenged, feeling more daring than she ever had in her life.

He came outside, walking toward her in long strides. "Don't give me any trouble, now."

"I'm tired of being ordered around."

"Well now, I can't leave you outside, you might get away." He stood looking down at her.

"Not hardly, with my horse hobbled and you watching me like a hawk."

"You got leaves in your hair," he said and picked them out gently, looking down at her.

She put her hands on his wide chest, feeling the hard muscles there, and heard his quick intake of breath.

"Missy," he warned, "don't play with me or I'll—"

"You'll what?" She looked up at him, a little shaky and excited, not sure what she was doing or what he might do. He was breathing hard and there were only inches between their faces. She tilted hers up.

"Stop it!" he growled. "You could get yourself in more trouble than you can handle."

"I don't know what you mean." She kept looking up at him, feeling his warm breath on her face.

"No, I don't suppose you do. Little rich gal like you, you've been used to dealin' with boys. You don't know anything about men."

He was standing so close to her, she could feel the tension in his big body, feel the bulge of his aroused manhood against her. She had the sudden feeling he was about to pull her to him, kiss her savagely, and she almost stood on tiptoe, waiting breathlessly.

"Missy," he growled, "you don't know what a

temptation it is not to throw you down on the grass and kiss those pouty lips, make love to you like I've wanted to do since the first moment I laid eyes on you back at the bank."

He had broken the spell by making fun of her. She whirled away from him. "You're a damned liar," she snapped, starting for the house. "I know I'm plain and no man would really—"

He reached out and caught her hand, whirled her around and jerked her up against him. "Nobody calls me a liar," he breathed in a raspy voice. "If you were a man, I'd kill you for it, but missy—" He broke off and turned away. She thought he might be trembling, which took her by surprise.

"What?" she asked.

"Never mind." He turned her loose and shrugged. "I just don't take lightly to bein' called a liar. No more than I like a woman who teases."

She didn't know what he was talking about for certain, except it must have something to do with that electrically charged moment when he had held her, looking down at her with his eyes so intense and his breath coming hard.

"I'm sorry," she murmured, but she was not certain what she was apologizing for. He was still looking at her intently. Waco breathed hard and she saw by the look on his face that he wanted her as a man wants a woman, and it almost scared her. In the love stories she read, this was always where the words said, "And here, dear reader, we draw the curtain of privacy around the loving couple . . . "

Tom came to the door and broke the intent moment by yelling. "Hey, you two, come on in."

She broke away from the big man and ran for the cabin in her ragged scarecrow clothes.

"Missy, when you play with fire," he called after her, "don't be surprised if you get burnt!"

"You unspeakable cad, you!" she flung over her shoulder as she ran into the cabin. She felt more than a little foolish. He hadn't really done anything and she wasn't certain if he was playing with her or trying to convince her he really cared about her. What did it matter? Pretty soon now, they'd figure out Godfrey wasn't going to send the money, and then what would happen?

The next morning, she took a good look at her reflection in the river. She was a tiny bit slimmer, but that wasn't what caught her attention. "Oh, look at my hair."

Waco leaned against a tree and grinned. "You look like you've been dragged under the porch by a pack of hound dogs, but I don't care. Maybe you could wash it some."

She gestured helplessly. "Wash my own hair? I've always had a maid to take care of my hair."

"Too bad. It's about time you got more independent."

She looked down at her scarecrow clothes. "These are filthy and so am I. Eww!"

"Tell you what," Waco offered. "Tom's gone into town to see if there's a message from your daddy, and Zeb and Zeke are in the cabin. If you want to wash your clothes and take a bath in the river, I promise not to peek."

She couldn't imagine any man would want to

watch a plump girl take a bath, but she wouldn't take the chance. "Get me some soap and a towel."

When Waco returned, he was more than a little disappointed. Rosemary had only pulled off her outer layer and knelt by the river in her corset cover and lace drawers. She was attempting to untangle her hair. "I've got a curry comb," he offered.

"Just leave the towel and soap and go away," she ordered. "My mother would be turning over in her grave at a man seeing me in my underwear."

"I can't really see anything." Waco smiled. "Your modesty is purty safe."

"Go away." She took the soap and began to wash the faded plaid shirt and rub it against a big rock.

Waco didn't go very far. He retreated partway up the hill and sat down under a tree. From here, he could see the outline of full breasts and a pleasing round rear as she scrubbed her clothes and hung them over a branch to dry. Then she waded out into the river and wet her hair. "Watch out," he called, "there's some holes out there. Can you swim?"

"Of course not. If I could swim, I'd escape down the river."

"Uh-huh." He watched her. She was getting a little too deep for comfort. "Missy, that water has a current ahead of you. Stop right there. It's deep enough to wash in."

"Stop telling me what to do!" And about that time, she stepped into a hole.

"Oh, hell!" Waco threw away his smoke and ran for the river. He pulled off his boots and dove in as she came up again, gasping and coughing. He grabbed her and she hung on to him, terror on her round face. "I told you it was deep, don't you listen to anything?"

She came up choking as he dragged her toward the edge. "This is all your fault!"

"My fault?" He laid her on the ground and pounded her back. "I warned you about the holes."

"Stop beating me!" She half turned and slapped at his big hands.

"I'm not beatin' you! I'm tryin' to get half that river out of you."

She coughed again. "I wouldn't even be in this river if you hadn't kidnapped me. I'd be home with a maid doing my hair and bathing in a fancy copper tub with French soap."

He drew back and surveyed her. The wet underclothes were almost transparent, but he wasn't about to tell her that. He was enjoying the view too much. "Here." He grabbed the ragged towel, hauled her into a sitting position, and wrapped it around her. "Are you cold?"

"No, I'm just mad." Her lips were trembling and turning blue.

"So hush, Rosie." He began to rub her bare legs.

"My mother—" she began.

"I know. She'd be turnin' over in her grave at a man puttin' his hands on her daughter's legs."

"Limbs," she corrected. "Men are so vulgar."

"You could at least thank me for savin' you."

"If it hadn't been for the ransom money, you'd have let me drown—"

"Rosie, don't tempt me," he warned.

The color was coming back to her face. She had pretty, pouty lips. Or maybe he'd just been without a woman too long.

"If you'll get your hands off my person, I'll go back to washing my hair."

"Okay, just don't venture out too far."

He retreated up the hill where he could watch her wash her hair and rinse it. Then she scrubbed herself with her underwear on. Damn. He'd hoped she'd pull it off. He'd like to see her naked.

Rosemary was aware that he watched her, but she didn't think she could do anything about it. Besides, she didn't want to admit it even to herself, but she rather enjoyed the look in his eyes. He was watching her the way a small child stands in front of a candy counter when he has no money. Who was she fooling? Herself? No man could want a fat girl. There, she'd said it. In spite of all her daydreams, she was just a plain, fat girl whom no man could want except for her money. Tears came to her eyes at the thought. She finished washing and wrapped herself in the threadbare towel. She felt her clothes, but they were still damp. A breeze had picked up and she figured they would be dry in another hour.

About that time, Tom rode in and she watched Waco stride over to meet him. She couldn't hear what they were saying.

Waco grabbed Tom's bridle. "Well?"

Tom shook his head. "No signal."

Waco chewed his lip. "I just can't believe he isn't fallin' all over himself to save her, everyone says he adores her so."

"Maybe he really can't raise that much money,"

Tom said as Zeb and Zeke came out of the cabin and joined them.

"Oh, Lord," Zeb said, "does that mean we're stuck with her?"

"And don't forget her worthless dog," Zeke complained. Then he seemed to notice Waco's clothes. "How'd you get wet?"

Waco looked sheepish. "I warned that hardheaded little thing there was holes in the bottom, but she wouldn't listen to me until she stepped in one and I had to go after her."

Zeb frowned. "You should have let her drown."

"Then we'd never get the money," Zeke complained.

"Aw, a Texan can't stand by and let a lady drown," Waco said.

"I think I could make an exception in her case," Zeb said. "That's the contrariest, hardheaded gal I ever met."

"Ain't that the truth?" Waco said and was surprised that he admired her for it. "She's purty nigh as stubborn as a Texas gal."

"She's spoiled rotten," Tom said.

"Well, she is that," Waco admitted, "but it's just 'cause she's had everything handed to her on a silver platter."

Zeke turned and looked toward the water. "Most gals would have been crying and whining if they got kidnapped."

"Speaking of which," Tom took off his Stetson and scratched his head, "what are we gonna do now? The banker still ain't tryin' to deal. You reckon he don't care if he gets her back or not?"

Waco turned and looked at the girl wrapped in the old towel. "Can't be. No daddy would do that.

He might have the law searchin' for her. If not, I reckon we'll lower the ransom until we hit a sum he can afford to pay."

"We're already below what we got to have," Zeb reminded him. "You know what Colonel—"

"I know," Waco snapped. "As well as I know that I got you three into this."

"No, you didn't," protested the others in unison. "We wouldn't have done that, no matter how much Captain Bennett commanded—"

"Well, it don't matter," Waco said. "We'll lower the ransom to fifteen thousand and wait to see if he comes up with it. Tom, did you see any troops or law searchin' the countryside?"

Tom shook his head. "I reckon he is keepin' his mouth shut, afraid we'll hurt her."

"Well, then that just goes to show he really does want his darlin' daughter back," Waco said. "Otherwise, he'd have the army and the law searching everywhere. Maybe the bank's poorer than we thought. I'll write the note, and Tom, you take it to town."

"What are you men talking about?" the girl called.

"Nuthin, missy," Waco yelled. "Boys," he lowered his voice, "let's keep this quiet. We don't want to scare the lady none."

"Ha! I don't think a charge of cavalry could scare that one," Zeb grumbled.

"I don't know." Tom smiled, watching her. "I'm beginnin' to think she's right pretty."

Zeke shook his head. "Young 'un, you been without a woman too long."

Waco said, "You men watch your mouths. I don't cotton to disrespectful talk about a real lady."

Tom watched her. "I don't reckon she might be interested in pleasin' us a little?"

"Don't even think about it!" Waco growled.

Tom raised his eyebrows. "You gettin' serious about her?"

"Of course not, but you think her daddy will pay to get her back if she's used goods?"

"Reckon not." Tom sighed. "Okay, Waco, you write the message and I'll take it to town."

Zeke said, "We're runnin' low on supplies, although the gal ain't gobblin' food like she used to."

Tom said, "I saw a nice farm the other direction. Must belong to a rich Yankee, because I saw a big chicken house."

"Mmm." Waco rubbed his chin. "Fried chicken and fresh eggs sound good. We got enough corn, bacon, and melons left for tonight. Maybe tomorrow night, we'll trying liftin' a few eggs."

"What will we do with the gal while we do that?" Tom asked.

"Well," Waco said, "we can't leave her alone at the cabin, so we'll have to take her with us. She did okay when we stole the melons."

"Let's lock up her dumb dog," Zeke grumbled. "It almost got us caught last time. Worthless mutt."

Waco pulled out his watch and checked the time. "It's too late, Tom, the bank will be closed. You can take the new note in tomorrow morning. Then tomorrow night, we'll rob the henhouse!"

Chapter Eleven

Rosemary's clothes were finally dry about dusk and she put them on before she came up to the house. "I don't suppose any of you varmints has a comb?" She tried to run her fingers through her tangled hair.

Waco grinned. "I got a curry comb."

She started to complain, then decided it wouldn't do any good. At home, there would be a maid who would wash and dry her hair, put it up in curls with the curling iron. "Go get it. I'm sure the horse won't mind. By the way, when are we going to eat? I'm hungry."

"You're *always* hungry," Zeke said.

She felt sudden shame. Her mother always complained that she ate too much. Girls were supposed to have dainty appetites. "Well, I haven't been eating as much as I used to."

"Now, that's a fact," Waco said kindly.

Her mind had been too preoccupied with her predicament to think about food. No, not her predicament. She was preoccupied by a certain big outlaw.

Waco sent Tom out after the curry comb, then when he returned he said, "We'll finish off the stuff we took the other night. Tomorrow night, we're goin' out and get something."

She paused in dragging the curry comb through her hair. "Don't tell me we'll be stealing melons again?"

"Oh, no," Waco said.

"Good, because I felt stupid, a woman of my position out there with a dog tearing the back out of my pants."

"That is a ragged outfit." Waco shook his head. "You look worse than a scarecrow."

"Thanks a lot!" The way he was looking at her made her uneasy. His eyes were intense, and she felt a surge of strange power between them and wished she had let him kiss her out there by the river.

After they went to bed, she made another mark on the beam and then lay on her cot staring up at the rafters. If she had just smiled at him or given him some signal, he might have come up the ladder tonight. Like the slender heroine of one of her stories, she might have found out what love was all about. Did she really want to know, especially with a wanted outlaw as a teacher? She finally dropped off into a restless sleep.

Morning came and Tom rode out. The day dragged by with Waco seeming to avoid her.

In late afternoon, Tom rode in, tied up his horse, came into the cabin, shook his head. "Nuthin'."

"Nuthin'?" Waco asked almost as if he couldn't believe it.

"What?" Rosemary came down the ladder. "What are you all talking about?"

"Nuthin' that you ought to worry about," Waco said. He smiled, but he looked concerned.

She didn't speak as she tied up her hair with a scrap of rag. So Godfrey wasn't coming through with the ransom. Why should he when if these outlaws killed her, that would solve his problem? What did worry her was what these four Texans would do with her when they finally accepted the fact that Godfrey wouldn't pay one thin dime to get her back. Could she convince them to help her instead? They might not believe her, and besides, they seemed to be running out of time.

Tom walked over to the water bucket and got himself a drink. "We goin' out for food?"

"Late tonight." Waco nodded.

She looked from one to the other. "I hope not to that place with the big white dog?"

"Naw, another one," Zeke said. "But we ain't takin' your dog. He nearly got us caught last time."

"Who, Prince? He's a good dog."

Prince woke up, yawned, and wagged his tail at the sound of his name.

She thought fast. "Why don't you all just leave me here? You men do it."

"So you can escape while we're gone?" Waco asked. "I don't think so. Besides, you can help carry chickens."

"Chickens? Live chickens?"

"They will be till we eat them," Tom said.

"I don't think I like this." Rosemary snorted.

"You want to eat, don't you?" Waco asked.

"I'm the richest girl in the county," Rosemary complained. "I shouldn't be out stealing food."

"Well, in that case, we'll tell the farmer that as we're takin' it." Waco smirked. "I'm sure he'll be glad to bill your rich daddy."

"I hope they hang you all!" she snapped.

"Now, that ain't nice," Waco said, "especially after I kept you from drownin' yesterday."

She gritted her teeth and decided she wouldn't point out that she wouldn't have been in that river if it wasn't for him.

They waited until very late to leave the cabin to make the raid on the farmer's chicken coop.

Rosemary said, "Are we at least going to take the horses?"

Waco shook his head. "It's hard to hide horses. Besides, if you got a head start on us, you might outrun us."

That was what she'd been hoping for.

"I'm hungry," Tom complained. "Can't we get movin'?"

"Lock the dog inside," Waco ordered. "He caused too much trouble last time."

Tom put Prince inside and closed the door. As they left, they could hear the dog barking and scratching to get out. The five of them started through a field to the south.

Once Rosemary stepped in a prairie dog hole and fell. "I think I broke my ankle or something."

"Reckon we'll have to shoot you," Tom said.

"Yeah, you're a mite heavy to carry," Zeb snapped.

"That was not a gentlemanly thing to say," she complained as she struggled to get to her feet.

"Naw, she's not that heavy." Waco picked her up easily and stood her on her feet. "How's that ankle?"

She took a tentative step. "All right, I think."

"Women!" Zeke snorted. "That's why I never married, too much trouble."

She drew herself up proudly. "You might consider that I'm an unwilling participant in this endeavor."

Zeb paused in the moonlight and looked at her. "Is that English?"

"Hush up and keep walkin'," Waco said. "She's naggin' us about draggin' her along."

"Oh."

They walked until Rosemary could feel the sweat on her face and back. Other girls glowed. She just sweated. "You must have picked out a farm ten miles away."

"Not quite," Tom said, "but he's got thousands of chickens. He probably won't miss a couple."

Rosemary could not see over the dried corn stalks they were pushing through, and she'd never learned anything about directions and following the stars. She didn't have the least idea where they were. A plan began to form in her mind. When they made the raid on the chicken coop, the noise of the cackling would surely bring the farmer out to investigate. When she saw him coming, she would run toward him, shouting who she was, and he'd surely save her. Godfrey wouldn't have posted a reward, but in a few more days, she'd be in control of the bank and she could reward the farmer herself.

They came to the edge of the cornfield and everyone crouched low, looking through a rambling wood fence. In the moonlight, she could see a distant farmhouse and a barn. Closer to them was a long, low white chicken coop with a fence around it.

"There it is." Tom motioned. "There's several hundred chickens and some nests inside the buildin'."

"Won't the chickens squawk and wake everyone up?" she asked.

"Not if we do it right," Waco said. "The chickens are asleep, too. You grab them by the legs. The ones we grab will squawk, but maybe they won't make enough noise to wake the farmer."

She stared at him, eyes wide. "You surely don't expect me to go in there and grab live chickens?"

"That's why we brought you along." Waco shrugged.

"I'm scared of the dark." She gulped. "I can't even imagine stumbling around there grabbing chickens."

Zeke spat to one side. "Can you imagine eatin' them, miss?"

"This is outrageous! I've never done anything like this in my whole life."

"See?" Waco grinned. "You're gettin' a whole lot of new experiences you never had before."

"I can't see how learning to steal melons and chickens will be of much help in my social life." She was huffy.

"Well, Rosie, you never know when you might lose all your money, and learning to live off the land will come in mighty handy."

About that time, she felt a cold wet nose on her skin and Prince whined. "The dog got out."

"Oh, hell, damned dog," Zeke grumbled. "He'll start barkin' and alert the farmer. He ain't worth nuthin'."

She patted the dog. "Oh, shut up. He's a good dog, aren't you, Prince?"

The dog whined and licked her face.

"Good for nuthin'," Zeke said.

"You know." Zeb rubbed his whiskery chin. "I could cotton to some fresh eggs, too."

"Well, missy here has big pockets in that old shirt," Waco said. "Rosie, why don't you grab as many eggs as you can carry and slip them into your pockets?"

"Now you've got me stealing eggs?"

"You want to keep eatin' just biscuits for breakfast?"

"You know," Tom pointed out, "we could crouch out here and jabber all night, but that won't feed us none."

"You got that right," Waco drawled. "Okay, we'll open the fence gate and sneak into the henhouse. Missy, you grab as many eggs as you can carry in your pockets, then take a couple of chickens. If we get two each, that's ten chickens. That'll feed us awhile."

Everyone murmured agreement.

Rosemary was thinking fast. She'd pretend to be delayed getting the eggs and then when she fell behind, she'd run toward the farmhouse, shouting. When the sleepy farmer came out, she'd explain while the four startled outlaws hightailed it through the cornfield.

"Come on, Rosie." Waco gestured and she crept

along behind the four as they slipped through the shadows of the trees, the dog trailing along behind.

They must have done this before, she thought, because they moved as silently as spirits.

Waco opened the gate to the pen and it creaked. Everyone froze in place for a moment, but nothing happened. Then he gestured toward the henhouse door. There was a full moon tonight that lit up the landscape bright as day. Tom opened the henhouse door and she held back, thinking she might make a run for the farmhouse, but Waco took her arm and led her inside.

It was warm in the henhouse and it smelled bad. She wrinkled her nose and gasped. What would the girls back at Miss Pickett's Female Academy think if they could see her now? Her heartbeat increased as her eyes grew accustomed to the shadows, and she could make out hundreds of white chickens asleep and roosting on poles across the building. Over to one side were boxes. Prince stood so close to her she could feel the heat of his shaggy body, and he trembled and whined with excitement.

Waco whispered, "The eggs will be over there in those boxes, missy. Get as many as you can."

"Stick my hand in those?" Her voice rose to a terrified note. "No telling what's there; maybe spiders."

"Can you shut that gal up?" Zeke complained. "She's enough to wake the dead."

Waco gave her a slight push and she stumbled over to the boxes while the men moved up and down the rows of chickens.

Gingerly, she stuck her hand in a box and came

up with an egg. She put it inside the big pocket of her shirt.

"Hurry up, everyone!" Waco commanded. "We need to be out of here in a couple of minutes."

She grabbed an egg, then another, hurrying between the boxes. Behind her, she heard the startled racket of a chicken being rudely awakened by a hand grabbing its legs. First one chicken, then another squawked, waking up others.

Her pockets were sagging with fresh eggs as she whirled around.

"Rosie, you got chickens?"

She shook her head as the chickens hanging from the men's hands squawked and fluttered their wings.

It seemed it was all too much for Prince. He began to bark, running up and down the henhouse, waking sleeping chickens. Feathers flew everywhere.

"Damn dog!" Zeke shouted.

The squawking and the barking were enough to wake the dead. Between the confused chickens flying about in the henhouse, the feathers drifting and the dog chasing them, it was bedlam.

She looked toward Waco and he gestured wildly. "Rosie, grab a couple and let's get out of here! If that farmer ain't deaf, he'll be out here with a shotgun!"

The men were already running ahead of her. All the hundreds of chickens seemed to be awake and making an ungodly racket. She grabbed one by the legs and it pecked her hand. She drew back, terrified.

Waco paused in the doorway. "Come on, Rosie! I just saw a light come on in the house!"

This would be her saving. She grabbed a couple of chickens as slowly as she could and walked out into the chicken yard. In the moonlight, she saw Zeke, Zeb, and Tom already almost to the cornfield, but Waco had hung back, and Prince stood next to him, a white chicken in his mouth. It clucked and squawked, trying to get away. Now there were more lights on at the farmhouse.

"Gawd Almighty! Come on, Rosie! You want to get shot?"

That hadn't even occurred to her. A man in a long white nightshirt came out on the back steps of the house, waving a shotgun. "Who's out there? What's going on?"

She turned and ran toward the farmer. "It's me! I've been kidnapped! Help me! Help me!"

Behind her, she heard Waco cursing.

"Help! I'm Rosemary Burke! I've been kidnapped!"

The two chickens dangling from her hands squawked and flapped their wings. Feathers flew and the load of eggs in her pockets made her stagger. She was shouting for help, but the startled hens made more noise than she did and the farmer couldn't seem to hear her because he raised his gun and fired. "Damned chicken thieves!"

The shot seemed to echo and re-echo, too close for comfort. She paused, the chickens still flapping from her hands. "No, don't you understand? I've been kidnapped!"

Boom! The farmer fired again, then stopped to reload. Prince had had all he wanted. The dog dropped his chicken and took off toward the far fence. The chicken ran about, squawking and complaining, white feathers flying everywhere.

Behind her, Waco yelled, "Come on, Rosie, he can't hear you!"

The farmer ran toward her, firing again. The shotgun sent a splatter of buckshot near her, tearing up the dirt. Obviously he hadn't heard her and he was aiming at her. She dropped the squawking chickens and turned to run toward Waco. He had paused to wait for her; the other three had already disappeared into the cornfield.

"You little idiot!" Waco shouted. "You're gonna get us all killed!"

The farmer fired again and now she was really terrified. She ran past Waco, heading for the fence. She failed to notice Prince, who had paused to wait for her. She tripped over the dog and fell flat on her belly. Prince ran over and licked her face.

"Damn dog!" Zeke yelled.

Behind her, Waco said, "Hurry up, Rosie, he's comin' hard!"

That spurred her into crawling on her belly through the rambling fence. She'd forgotten about the eggs. She felt the shells crush and the sudden smell of fresh eggs. *Oh hell.*

Now Prince crawled under the fence and licked her face as she struggled to get into the cornfield.

"Big brave guard dog you are!" she snapped, pushing him away.

Ahead of her, the trio gestured her to come on, which was difficult since they all had a white chicken in each hand. She stumbled to her feet, feeling the raw eggs running down her chest. They felt wet and slick. She whirled to see Waco now running for the fence with the farmer in his nightclothes pausing to reload his shotgun.

She hadn't meant to get anyone hurt. "Come on, Waco!"

He was almost to the fence when the farmer paused and aimed and fired. Waco yelped suddenly like a scalded hound and paused, then continued running for the fence, but he let go of the two chickens he held and they fluttered up so that the farmer's next shot hit one of them and it fell like a rock with white feathers fluttering in the moonlight.

"Damn, I'm hit, fellas!" Waco stumbled toward the fence and Tom turned loose his chickens and ran back to pull him under the fence.

"Waco, is it bad?" He half dragged, half carried him into the cornfield.

Rosemary watched as behind them, the farmer tripped on the edge of his nightshirt and went down, the shotgun blasting toward the dark sky.

"I can make it, let's get out of here!" Waco ordered. He leaned on Tom's shoulder, and the three of them joined the two old men. Behind them, the chase had evidently ended. They could hear the farmer cursing as he returned to the house.

All four of the men paused, breathing hard and glaring at Rosemary and Prince, who was too dumb to know anyone was mad at him. He ran from one to the other, licking hands.

"Damn you and your stupid dog!" Zeke swore. "Lady, you almost got us all killed. Where you hit, Waco?"

"Caught that buckshot right in the butt," he sighed.

She felt guilty. "Does it—Does it hurt?"

"Well, it don't feel good, missy," he snapped.

"Let's get back to the cabin," Tom said. "At least we got four chickens and some fresh eggs."

The eggs. They all seemed in too bad a humor to tell them she'd fallen on the eggs that she could feel wet and sticky running down inside her shirt. Obviously her plan hadn't been too good after all, and now they would be mad at her.

"Next time," Waco groaned as he limped through the dead corn stalks, "we'll tie up Miss Rosemary and her dog and leave them behind."

"I didn't mean to get you shot," she apologized. "I was just tryin to get rescued."

Zeb said. "It do look like her daddy ain't gonna send any money. Do you reckon we could pay him to take her back?"

"That's the best idea I've heard all week," Waco complained as he limped along.

"This is humiliating!" Rosemary said as she stumbled through the cornfield, "I never heard of a ransom where the kidnapper paid to get the family to take the victim back."

"It's beginnin' to sound like a good idea," Waco said, "except we ain't got no money."

"Don't have any," she corrected without thinking.

Zeke groaned. "Lord save us from educated women! I knew this was a bad idea, knew it from the start. I'd rather have took my chances against all them soldiers and just tried to rob that bank."

"It would have been suicide," his brother said.

"Maybe, but puttin' up with this gal is like being nibbled to death by a duck: slow torture."

"And how do you think it is for me?" she challenged.

Waco laughed without mirth. "Rosie, you have to admit it's an adventure."

"Oh sure. I've been attacked by a big white dog, shot at, and almost drowned in a cold river."

"Poor little rich girl," Tom snapped. "Waco, why don't you just tie a rock to her and throw her in the river? We could keep askin' for the ransom. Her daddy wouldn't know she was dead."

"You wouldn't dare!" *Or would they?* She felt a chill run up her back.

"Oh, missy," Waco groaned as he limped along, "don't tempt me. Right now, I'd give him my gold watch to take you back."

She stuck her nose in the air as she walked. "I've never been so insulted!"

"Rosie, do you never shut up?" Waco groaned. "Because of you, I got a butt full of buckshot, but I'll feel better once I get some fried eggs and chicken."

The eggs. They were now puddling around her rope belt.

"Uh, Waco, Will, there's something I need to tell you."

"What is it this time?" He didn't sound like he was in a very good mood.

"Never mind."

They finally made it back to the cabin just before dawn. Tom laid Waco on a quilt on his belly. "Somebody bring a lamp. Let's see how bad it is." He began tugging at Waco's pants.

Waco protested. "You ain't gonna pull them off in front of a woman, are you?"

"She can go outside with Zeb and Zeke."

She went out and watched the two old men stake their chickens out to graze in the yard. The four white hens seemed perfectly content to peck around in the circle of their leashes.

Tom came to the door of the cabin. "You fellas better come in. My eyesight ain't all that good."

Zeb and Zeke looked at each other. "Tom, you know both of us got shaky hands. We'd hurt him worse than you would."

Tom glared at her. "So now what do we do?"

This was all her fault.

"I—I can give it a try," she offered.

"He ain't gonna like it." Zeb spat tobacco juice on the ground.

Tom sighed and pushed his hat back. "He ain't got a lot of choice. Lady, you be gentle, you hear?"

She nodded, and feeling guilty, she followed the three back into the cabin. Waco lay on his belly, his pants down. She'd never seen a man's rear before except when she'd peeked out the window when they were swimming. Waco had a lean and muscular rear, but there were small, bloody specks there.

Prince bounded into the cabin and put his cold, wet nose on Waco's behind, which caused him to jump and curse. "Somebody do something about that dad-blamed dog!"

"Damned dog." Zeke caught the pup and put him outside, then closed the door.

Tom handed her a pocket knife. "Here, miss."

Waco turned his head. "That female in here? I don't want her lookin' at my naked butt."

"Oh, shut up," Tom said. "We got to get that buckshot out, and none of us hombres are too steady."

"You want me to dig pellets out of his behind? I don't think so." Rosemary backed away.

"I don't want her to neither," Waco howled. "She'll probably try to kill me."

"Oh, shut up," she said. "If I was going to kill you, I wouldn't take a knife to your rear, I'd take it to your throat."

"See? See?" he demanded, thrashing around on the quilt. She's just lookin' for a chance to do me in. Besides, she's left-handed and you saw what she did when she tried to peel a potato."

Zeke's hands shook noticably. "Waco, we figure maybe she'll do a better job than any of us. Women's got a lighter touch."

"Not that one. She'll stab me in the butt."

"It's a tempting idea," she said.

"See? I told you she'd like to kill me."

She took a deep breath. She could refuse and he might get an infection or die of blood poisoning. Even though he was holding her captive, she didn't want that to happen to him. "Oh, shut up. You're whining like a baby." She knelt next to the quilt and took a look. He had half a dozen small puncture wounds in his muscular rear. She was past feeling embarrassment. "Okay, I think I can do this."

"*Think*?" he howled. "Think?"

"Now hold still or I may stick this knife in up to the hilt," she warned him.

"I told you fellas she'd try to kill me."

She really wasn't certain what to do. "Have we got any whiskey?"

"Good idea," Waco groaned. "I could use a drink."

"I meant to sterilize the knife," she snapped.

Tom brought out a half bottle. She poured it over the blade, then her courage wavered. "Maybe we'd all better have a drink," she said.

She took a slug right from the bottle and passed it around. The cheap whiskey burned all the way down, but her courage was renewed. She was Clara Barton, battlefield nurse, and it was up to her to save the life of this handsome cavalry lieutenant. Then he would marry her and she would discover he was a rich heir from Boston and on the social register besides.

"You must have a real gentle touch," Waco murmured. "I don't feel nothin'."

"I haven't started yet, Lieutenant."

"I'm not a lieutenant, I'm a sergeant," he muttered.

"What?"

"Never mind."

Brave, willowy, and beautiful Clara Barton leaned over the Boston lieutenant with her pocket knife and used the tip to probe for the buckshot.

"Ow! She has the touch of a butcher!" Waco yelled and tried to get up off the quilt. "She must have stuck it in up to the hilt."

Tom and the others grabbed him and held him down. Rosemary dug in again with the knife and the buckshot came out and bounced across the floor. She felt sick at the sight of blood. Clara Barton would never faint at the sight of a bleeding wound. She took a deep breath and dug out another.

Waco howled again.

"Oh, shut up, you big baby." She dug out a third and a fourth. "I think I'm getting the hang of it."

"Yeah, practicin' on me, you lady butcher."

She dug out the rest of them. Her hands were shaking. "Zeb, hand me that whiskey."

"Thanks," Waco moaned, "I need a drink."

"It isn't for your mouth, you idiot, I'm using it to clean the wound." She tilted the bottle and poured a little on the wounds.

"God damn! That smarts! She's tryin' to kill me, I tell you!"

Tom said, "Seems like a waste of good whiskey."

"Well, you can lick it off if you want it." Zeb laughed.

"You men are all so vulgar," she said.

"Oh, she's so damned proper." Waco moaned. "It was a rotten day when we first thought to kidnap this infernal female."

"You hungry?" Tom leaned over him.

Waco sighed. "Yeah, the thought of scrambled eggs sounds good. How many have we got?"

She might as well confess. "Uh, they're scrambled all right." She stood up and looked down at the rivulets of yellow yolk all over her faded shirt.

"Oh, hell," Tom said.

"What's the matter?" Waco twisted to look.

"Never mind," said Zeke. "There just ain't gonna be any eggs tonight. Maybe one of the chickens will lay one in the mornin'."

Waco managed to turn enough to look at her. His face was ghastly pale. "You," he said in a defeated tone, "you are a curse. No wonder your daddy ain't eager to pay to get you back."

"We should toss her in the river," Tom said.

"We can't do that to a lady," Waco said. "Hell, I don't know what to do with her."

"I did get the buckshot out," she reminded him.

"I wouldn't have got shot if'n I wasn't tryin' to save you," he snapped back.

"I think," yawned Zeke, "that we'd better all get some rest. Things will look different in daylight."

"Then we'll drown her," Tom said.

"I think I'll go wash the egg off my clothes," Rosemary said.

Waco said, "Then, Zeb, you or your brother need to go along. She'll try to get away."

"What if I promise I wouldn't?"

"Ha! I'd trust a riverboat gambler before I'd trust you, missy," Waco said. "Everyone keep an eye on her. She might escape."

Zeke brought out his mouth organ. "I'm beginnin' to wish she would so's we could go back to Texas."

The other three looked at him.

Zeke said, "I know, I know. Okay, Miss Rosemary, let's go down to the river and you can wash up. Then for breakfast, we'll have fried chicken and biscuits. Can you fry chicken?"

"Now, you know I can't."

He sighed. "Why did I even ask?"

Lying on his old quilt, Waco felt like his butt was on fire. "Waste of perfectly good whiskey," he muttered.

Prince ran over and licked his face, then scampered away after Rosemary and Zeke.

Waco thought maybe Zeb was right, maybe it was a good idea to give her back, ransom or not. Miss Rosemary was just too spunky and spirited to deal with. He grinned. He had to admire that in a woman.

Chapter Twelve

Godfrey leaned back in his office chair and stared first out the window at Main Street, then to the note in his hand. As each day passed, the ransom had gotten smaller. So now she only wanted $10,000. *Does Rosemary think I am a complete fool?*

He lit a fine cigar, then crumpled the note and used the cigar to catch it afire, watching it burn in his ashtray. Sooner or later, she would give up this charade and come home. So what if she didn't? He grinned. No, he couldn't be that lucky. Was there a chance she really had been kidnapped? Godfrey shrugged. If so, the kidnappers had his pity. Rosemary was such a handful, no wonder they kept lowering the ransom, trying to get rid of her. Things were looking really good for him now. Certainly he'd had a real change of luck since he'd been Elmo Croppett, an uneducated nobody from Cincinnati. All he'd had going for him then were his good looks and his ability to charm women. Even though the police were looking for him in three states, his future seemed secure here in Prairie View.

Mollie was an increasing problem now that the new maid had arrived. Mollie might be stupid, but she could see that handwriting on the wall. He hoped he didn't have to kill her, that would be messy and so inconvenient. Besides, two murders were enough. He didn't want to push his luck.

Still smoking his cigar, he went out into the busy lobby, greeting customers, charming old widows who eagerly put their life savings in the Prairie View Bank. The bank would remain sound unless he decided someone suspected him; then he would clean out the vault and move on.

"Ah, good day, Mr. St. John." Reverend Post paused to shake hands.

"And a good day to you, sir." Godfrey feigned warmth and interest. "And how is the effort to raise money for an orphanage going?"

"Not too well." The frail old man shook his head. "So many children left alone from the War, you know, but maybe someday, we'll have enough to buy a big house for them."

Godfrey managed to stifle a yawn. He didn't give a damn about orphaned kids. He'd been one himself and he'd made it, hadn't he? The little buggers should get out and steal fruit and snitch pennies from old ladies like he had. "Too bad." He feigned a concerned look. "I'll make a hundred dollar donation, no, make that five hundred."

The preacher wrung his hand warmly. "Oh, Mr. St. John, you have no idea how your generosity will help. Maybe it will inspire others to give more."

"Let us hope so."

"By the way, I haven't seen Rosemary at service last Sunday or around town. Is she ill?"

"No, no," Godfrey hastened to assure him. "She's gone to visit friends over in Thackerville."

"Oh? I thought everyone in town came this past week when I went over to conduct a big wedding. I didn't see Rosemary."

Oh, damn. He sure didn't want anyone to get suspicious. "Maybe I was wrong, maybe it wasn't Thackerville. She'll be back directly."

"Oh." The pastor looked confused. "Not like a girl to go off visiting for weeks right when she gets home after she's been gone so long."

"Well, uh, I think—I think maybe this was an old friend she hadn't seen in a while. Rosemary's been writing me and I've been begging her to come home. She's such a dear girl and I miss her." Godfrey glanced up at the clear blue sky outside. He wasn't at all religious, but for a lie like that, anyone might expect lightning to strike him dead.

"Humm. Well, all right." The old man waggled his finger. "Do tell her next time you write that we miss her at Sunday services."

"I surely will." Godfrey patted the preacher's shoulder and escorted him to the bank's door. "I hope things pick up with your orphanage fund."

"Thank you. With your generous gift, I'm sure others will be motivated. Now if we just had a big building to house the children, we could do wonders." He turned and walked away.

Godfrey watched him go. Damn it, it was getting harder to explain why Rosemary wasn't making any appearances around town. Surely she would give up and come home when Godfrey didn't pay the money. If not, maybe he could concoct a good story about her meeting a young man in Thackerville and eloping to some faraway spot, never to return.

Unfortunately, he got the same question when he returned to the mansion that night from Mollie.

"Aye, all the help is beginnin' to wonder about Miss Rosemary," she said as he entered the library where she was dusting.

"I got a note from her today at the bank." Godfrey sauntered over to the desk and poured himself a brandy. "She's having a lovely time visiting her friend."

"It does seem strange that she didn't ask me to pack anything, just went off without tellin' anyone."

He frowned and sipped his drink. "Rosemary was always difficult. She had a purse with her, I'm sure. Probably bought a whole new wardrobe in Thackerville."

"But—"

"I don't want to hear any more about it!" He whirled, almost thundering at the maid. "You're as bad as the preacher, wanting to know where she is. She hasn't been gone but a week."

Now the pretty freckled face turned pouty. "You didn't used to shout at me that way. It's that new girl, Francine, isn't it?"

He tried not to smile, remembering Francine's big breasts and passionate nature. "No, of course not." He took Mollie's hand, looked down into her eyes, trying not to look at her crooked teeth. "I'm sorry, my love," he whispered. "I'm just tired and out of sorts, worrying about business, you know, and what nice gift I'm going to buy for you next. Perhaps a new coat for Christmas?"

Her blue eyes lit up. "Ah, and you're too generous, you are. Would you like to go to me room?"

"With all the servants around?"

"Aye, this is their day off, remember?" she reminded him, looking up into his eyes, her mouth moist and open. "They won't be back till almost dark."

"Even Francine?"

"Now why would you ask about her after I skipped takin' a day off now, hopin' to see you? Yes, they're all gone."

He had never been a man to pass up opportunity. If Francine wasn't around, Mollie would do. He'd get in Francine's bed later when Mollie was gone on an errand. "Then, my little Irish love, let's go to your room and let me show you how much I cherish you."

She started to giggle and he sighed. That infernal giggle and her bad teeth. He was past weary of Mollie, but she might start nosing around and thus be a danger to him. There was no other way out but to murder her. He couldn't do it the way he'd done the last one, it might raise some questions. Maybe he could help her trip and fall down the stairs like he'd done the old lady in Cincinnati?

She took his hand, giggling. "A penny for your thoughts."

If she only knew. "Not worth a penny, I'm afraid." He smiled at her. "Now let's go to your room."

It was evening as Waco settled himself gingerly on a pillowed chair and watched Rosemary attempting to cook. She turned and looked at him. "Are you still sore?"

"I'd rather not talk about it," he sighed and tried to settle himself.

"Well, it's been more than three days."

"If you hadn't been so ham-handed digging out the buckshot, I might be sitting a little easier."

She looked at him. "So now it's my fault?"

"I did hang back to rescue you, you know."

He had, sort of gallant. But on the other hand, she wouldn't have been out there being shot at if she hadn't been with the chicken thieves. She turned back to the cabinet. "I haven't the least idea what to do with this raw chicken." She shuddered at the sight.

"Well, don't ruin it. It's the last one we got. I'll call Zeb in to fry it. Honest to God, I never saw a woman so helpless. If you weren't rich, you couldn't survive on your own."

"I'm smart enough to learn, I just don't want to."

"And stubborn to boot."

"Any news from the bank?" she inquired.

"Now if there was, don't you think we'd be talkin' about it?"

"He isn't going to send the money," she said.

"Now what makes you so sure, missy? You don't think your adorin' daddy—"

"He's not my real father, you know. He's my stepfather."

"What?" He sat up straight, which made him wince because of his buckshot wounds. "Why didn't you tell us that before?"

"I figured when you found out, you might panic and kill me."

"Believe me, it's been temptin'. But everyone seemed so convinced he adored you."

"Uh-huh. Well, now that you know differently, you might as well turn me loose and let me go home."

"Aha! Not so fast. And here I was about to believe you."

"I'm telling you the truth, which is more than you've done with me."

"I don't know what you're talkin' about." He didn't look her in the eye.

"Sure you do. I'm not sure what's going on, but I don't think you four are ordinary outlaws just trying to get some money." She walked over and stood looking down at him.

"Sure we are."

"Would you swear on the Lone Star State that's true?"

"That's blasphemy." He snapped and stood up. "We don't ever swear on Texas or the Alamo."

"Somehow I figure this has something to do with the War."

He shook his head.

"You're a poor liar, Waco. Besides, I've heard your men call you 'sir.'"

"They all worked as my cowhands on my ranch before the War pretty much destroyed everything, so of course they might call me sir."

"I don't believe you. I remember you admitting to being a sergeant. Anyway, I don't think you're going to get the money from the Bank of Prairie View, so you might as well head back to Texas."

"We haven't given up hope yet." He reached into his pocket for cigarette makin's.

"Then you must be desperate, and there has to be a reason behind it."

She had struck too close to the truth, and it made Waco nervous. He rolled his cigarette, then limped outside into the growing darkness. "Zeb, do you think you and your brother could get some supper goin'?"

"That gal ain't offerin' to cook still?"

"After you've had a couple of her meals, do you want to risk her burnin' that good chicken?"

"Reckon not."

"Where's the other two?"

Zeb gestured. "Out feedin' the horses."

Waco paused, lighting his smoke. They were desperate, all right, but he didn't want the girl to know how desperate. The four were caught between a rock and a hard place. They only had until mid-November to come up with a pile of money or they all faced a firing squad. And if they got caught up in Yankee country out of uniform, they faced a firing squad as spies. If the banker didn't come up with the ransom money, there was no backup plan.

That thought made Waco shudder. He pulled out his gold watch and checked the time. The banker might be home by now. Maybe he was the one they needed to kidnap. Waco ambled out and sat down very gently under a tree, watching the swift current of the river run past. The starry sky turned cloudy and a wind came up, cool and smelling of rain. Back home, the pastures would still be green and the cattle fat. His house was probably suffering from neglect with him away at war. No one missed home like a Texan.

"Mind if I join you?" He looked up suddenly to see Rosemary standing near by.

"Can't stop you." He shrugged.

"What I said in the kitchen—"

"Don't try that again. I'm not gonna believe that your adorin' daddy won't ransom you, so I should let you go."

She sat down next to him in her ragged, faded clothes. "So why do you think he hasn't sent it, even though you keep lowering the amount?"

He shook his head. "Maybe he didn't have that much in the vault. Maybe the bank isn't as rich as we were told it was."

She watched his silhouette as he smoked. This was a man's man and yet, the kind that could turn a woman's heart. Several times she had caught him looking at her in a way that was charmed, but troubled. Could he possibly be interested in her? She had lost some weight because she'd spent more time thinking of him than of food. Of course, she would never be as slender as the girls in her romance stories, but maybe a man might love her anyway. Could she seduce him into letting her escape?

Be reasonable, Rosemary, she told herself, *you don't know the first thing about seducing a man.* She'd probably make such a clumsy mess of it, he'd laugh at her. She'd had enough ridicule in her life, from her mother nagging her about her weight to always being the last girl at the ball to be asked to dance, and even then, asked only because fortune hunters knew she was rich.

She reached out and put her hand on his arm,

and he didn't shake it off. "Will, I've got a secret that nobody in town knows."

"What kind of a secret?" He didn't believe her.

"One only me, my stepfather, and a lawyer in Thackerville know."

"Then why would you tell me?"

"I—I don't know, really. I guess over the last couple of weeks, I've grown fond of you and the boys."

"Oh, sure you have," he scoffed, patting Prince, who ambled over to lie down next to him.

"No." She shook her head "I mean it. What if I were to give you the money myself? I inherit it all on Halloween."

He threw away his smoke and laughed. "In the first place, I don't believe you'd give me the money, and why should I believe it'll all be yours then?"

"Because I turn twenty-one October the thirty-first, and I intend to take the bank over and run it myself."

"Now why would your daddy turn it over to you?"

"Because the will says he must . . . unless I die, then he gets everything."

"That's the wildest story I ever heard. And what happens if you both die?"

"The mansion gets deeded to Reverend Post to turn into an orphan home, and old Bill Wilkerson takes over the bank. He's quite capable."

"So we should take you at your word, wait a few more days, and you'll hand over the money, just like that?"

"That's right." She leaned closer.

"Rosie, my mama didn't raise no fools. The longer

we hang around Kansas, the better our chances are of runnin' across lawmen or Union troops."

"Well, it doesn't seem to be working your way," she reminded him.

From the cabin came the smell of frying chicken, and the breeze blew colder.

She shivered. "Looks like it will rain tonight."

"Maybe. You cold? Here, take my jacket." He put it around her shoulders. "I got to hand it to you, Rosie, you've been a good sport about this whole thing."

"It's not as if I had a lot of choice," she laughed.

"No, I mean it. The way you helped steal the melons and the chickens. Other gals would have been cryin' out of sheer fright."

"Ha! When that white dog grabbed my pants, I wasn't thinking good thoughts about you and your buddies." In the darkness, she could see the sinews of his strong neck. "I'm still cold." She nestled her head against his shoulder.

"You shouldn't do that, Rosie." His voice was gruff, but he put his arm around her. "You ain't gonna soft-soap me into lettin' you go."

"That's okay. I just wanted to thank you. You've been pretty good to me."

Now it was his turn to laugh. "We've dragged you around the country, put you in a shack, gave you raggedy clothes to wear. I'm sorry, Rosie, but I don't trust you. I don't trust any woman, not after one promised to love me forever and then while I was in Kentucky, she run off with a Yankee block-ade runner."

"All women aren't like that."

"Can't prove it by me. If I don't trust one, I don't chance gettin' my heart broken again."

She sighed. "This time with you has certainly been an adventure. All I ever did in my other life was hide food in my room to eat, attend teas and do embroidery, and read little etiquette books."

"You do good embroidery?"

"No. I'm left-handed, remember? I don't have any skills, really, except horseback riding. Mama always said I was lucky I was rich or I'd never get a husband because I was so plain and dumpy."

"I don't think you're plain, and you're just sturdy, that's all. You'd fit right in on a Texas ranch."

Their faces were only inches apart.

"Tell me about Texas," she whispered.

He sighed wistfully. "Heaven on earth. Miles and miles of prairie with lots of cattle and horses. A man can make a place for himself down there, lots of room. All he needs is hard work and a good woman workin' beside him."

She didn't know how to do it, but she leaned over and kissed him gently on the lips.

For a moment, he froze, his mouth warm on hers, and then he pulled her to him and kissed her deeply, thoroughly. She was overwhelmed by the power and the passion of this man. The kiss sent her mind into dizzy reeling. It was better than any of the dainty love scenes in the novels she read.

She didn't care what happened next, she was so caught up in the moment and the emotion of being in this man's arms.

About that time, behind them, Zeb called, "Supper's ready! Come and get it!"

Waco pulled away from her, breathing hard.

"Oh, no, you don't, missy. You ain't gonna talk me into lettin' you go by kissin' up to me. I may have been a long time without a woman, but I know a highfalutin' gal like you couldn't be interested in some dirt-poor Texas rancher."

"You—you might let me decide that," she gasped, breathing hard. She wanted him to take her in his strong arms again and kiss her breathless.

"You ain't gonna bribe me with your kisses." He stood up, looking angry. "For a minute there, I almost forgot what you was up to. Now let's go in and eat." He held out his hand.

So much for seducing the Texan. Frankly, she had forgotten her own intentions, and if Zeb hadn't called out to them and Waco had wanted to take her to the ground and pull all her clothes off, she wasn't sure she would have stopped him. Now who was seducing whom? He wouldn't believe her anyway.

Lightning flashed across the sky as she took Waco's hand and they started for the cabin, Prince bounding ahead of them.

"It's going to rain," he noted.

She wondered then what it would have been like to stay under that tree, making love with warm rain dripping on their naked, writhing bodies. The thought both thrilled and horrified her. Now she had to escape before things got any more complicated.

As they went inside, Waco said, "Tom, you better put the horses in the shed, it's gonna rain."

Tom nodded and went out as Zeb dished up fried chicken and fried potatoes.

Zeb said, "If'n we're gonna stay here much longer, we'll have to get some more supplies."

She took a tin plate and sat down at the rickety table, bit into the hot, crispy chicken. She had never had anything so good before. She shared bites with Prince, who licked his chops and watched eagerly for the next crumb.

Rosemary looked at Waco and saw the pleasure on his face as he helped himself to a biscuit. Suddenly, she wanted to be able to cook well enough to bring that look to his face. She wanted to kiss him again and see that expression of need in his pale blue eyes. Something was changing, and it scared her. Yes, she had to get away.

"Well," Waco said, "now I don't know whether to lower our offer to her daddy again or not."

"We lower it much more," Zeke griped, wiping his beard on his faded shirt, "we'll be payin' him to take her back."

"Except we don't have no money and we're runnin' out of time," Zeb reminded him. "I say we call it a bad deal and head for the Kansas border. We'll think of some other way to get the money."

Waco paused. "She'll slow us down if we take her with us."

"I wasn't plannin' on takin' her," Zeb said and stuffed a biscuit in his mouth.

"Stop it!" Waco commanded. "You'll scare her."

She pretended she didn't hear the conversation. Outside, it had begun to rain.

Tonight, she thought, *tonight is the night I'm going to have to escape.*

Chapter Thirteen

Rosemary lay on her cot in the loft, listening to the light rain outside and the four men and the dog snoring down below. She got up and checked the many marks on the beam; less than a week until her birthday. Now she tiptoed to the ladder and looked down. Waco lay in a spot near the window where an occasional flash of lightning lit up his features. He was naked to the waist, masculine and virile. She remembered his kiss and sighed. No man had ever kissed her before. She touched her lips and smiled, remembering.

She was slender and willowy Juliet with Romeo beneath her window. *Romeo, Romeo, wherefore art thou Romeo?*

What was she thinking? Rosemary snorted in disgust. She'd let herself be kissed by an outlaw, a bandit. No, she had kissed him. If she'd been Lady Wendamere, with a handsome highwayman stopping her carriage, that would have been totally different.

Yes, fair lady, for the price of one precious kiss, I'll let you go your way without stealing the rubies and emeralds around your slender, swanlike neck. One kiss from your lovely lips is more precious than a fortune in gems.

This was the perfect night to make her escape. Certainly they wouldn't be expecting it with all this rain. She tiptoed to her loft window and looked out. The rain came down in blinding sheets. She'd be wetter than a drowned cat by the time she found her way to some farmhouse and a ride back to Prairie View, but it would be worth it to see Godfrey's shocked face. She'd started out thinking this was a joke, but now she knew better. Evidently, he didn't intend to ransom her at all and was hoping she'd just disappear.

Very slowly, she raised the window, and cold rain blew in. Her ragged scarecrow outfit wasn't going to be much warmth against the chill autumn weather. Rosemary stuck her head out and looked around. There was a vine that crawled up the side of the house past her window. It might hold her weight if she could get out the window and slide down it. Or maybe not. From here, it looked like a long way to fall.

Slender and lovely Guinevere, held captive by the evil duke's henchmen, had only to slide down the ivy on the castle wall, avoid the sleeping dragons below, and make her way home to her rightful throne and her handsome prince.

Rosemary reached out and caught the vine, hesitated, then clambered out the window. The vine seemed to groan under her weight and she held her breath. *Suppose it gives way?* Her mother had been right about eating all those cookies, but sometimes sweets had been the only comfort in her lonely life. If only she weighed twenty pounds less—*Oh, for gracious sakes, be honest, Rosemary.* Okay, thirty pounds less. Her life might depend on her weight tonight.

With one foot, she felt for a toehold on the vine while the cold rain lashed her body. There, that felt pretty secure. She started to move down with the other foot. At this point, she realized her ragged shirt had caught on the vine above her head. Oh hell, why did she have to be so clumsy? Delicate Lady Guinevere would have slid all the way down. So there Rosemary hung, trying to decide what to do next. She didn't intend to stay there all night so that the outlaws found her hanging outside like a wet rat the next morning. There was nothing else to do but yank hard on the faded shirt. It ripped, making a loud noise, but it freed her. Then she swayed on the vine, which creaked like it might give way and drop her.

From inside, she heard Prince pawing the door to get out. She'd like to get the dog, but if she opened the door, it would wake the men up. She thought she heard Waco murmur something in his sleep and turn over several times. She held her breath, wondering what he was dreaming about.

What difference does it make? She took another hesitant step down the vine, and its sharp thorns scratched her skin. A flash of lightning lit up the sky and she looked down. The vine seemed to be shaking and it looked ten miles to the hard ground below. What if lightning struck her? In her mind, she imagined Waco finding her in the morning, all fried to a crisp and still clinging to the vine. Would he shed a tear or bemoan the fact that his chance at money was gone?

Damn Godfrey, too. When she got back to town, he was going to be surprised when she took over the bank and kicked him out. If she could only find her way back to town.

She was nearly to the ground when she felt the vine giving way under her weight. She tried to grab on to the cabin planking, but there was no hand-hold there. The vine began to tear loose from the house. She must not scream because if the fall didn't kill her, she might still get away.

In a panic, she looked below. There was a big mud puddle right below her. Did she want to miss it or hit it? Would she have any choice? *Good-bye, cruel world.*

Then the vine jerked away from the side of the house and she hung on. For a split second, she felt herself falling and then with a big splash, she landed on her bottom in the mud.

For a moment, she just sat there, the vine tangled in her wet hair. Was she still alive? She wiggled her toes. She felt the wet mud soaking through her ragged pants. How undignified. Well, at least only her generous bottom was muddy.

Clambering to her feet, she took a step, tangled in the vine, and crashed down full length on her face. Gracious. No, hell, hell, hell. Rosemary stumbled to her feet, covered with mud, and limped toward the shed. The horses neighed as she approached, and she did her best to shush them. "Shh! Lady Be Good, be quiet, horses."

She turned and looked toward the shack. Had the outlaws heard anything? She might not have time to put on a saddle, even if she could find it here in the dark. The shed smelled of hay and warm horses, a pleasant scent. A flash of lightning lit up the wall and she saw bridles hanging there. She felt her way across the shed and got a bridle, then felt her way to Lady, whispering to her all the time. "Whoa, Lady. Good Lady. Be still now."

The horses were nervous, stamping and blowing because of the storm, but she managed to get the bridle on her horse. She had to stand on the stall gate to mount up. Then she opened the gate so the other horses could escape the shed. It might take hours for the outlaws to catch their mounts, hours they couldn't be chasing her. Then she rode Lady out of the shed and galloped away into the rainy darkness. She rode in a panic for a few minutes, reined in and looked around. Nothing looked familiar. She had to admit she was lost and she had no clue how to return to Prairie View.

The thunder made Waco stir uneasily in his sleep. It had been rainy that summer night in the Ohio Valley area, too, and now he rode that trail again as he had that night in late August.

"Sergeant." Tom had ridden up beside him and saluted. "The men want to know where we're goin'."

Waco felt the cold rain dripping off his gray cap and into the neck of his uniform. "Captain Bennett has the orders, we're crossin' into Kentucky."

"Beg pardon, sir, but we got enough Yankees to fight hereabouts, without ridin' deep into their country."

"I don't make the orders, I only follow them,

Corporal. This patrol was chosen because we're mostly Texans who ride like bats out of hell."

"But Captain Bennett—"

"You're dismissed, Corporal. Get back to your men."

"Yes sir." Tom saluted again, wheeled, and rode along the line of wet, miserable Confederate cavalry.

Waco watched him go, then stared at the muddy path ahead. He had no confidence in Captain Jake Bennett, but he was following orders. He'd long ago lost any enthusiasm for the war. It was a lost cause, everyone knew that now.

At dawn, they camped in a grove and tried to dry out their soaked clothes. Waco made sure the camp fire was small. They didn't want Yankee troops spotting the smoke or smelling the fire. They were dangerously deep into enemy territory now and everyone knew it.

Captain Bennett, burly and bearded, sauntered over to the fire, slapping his leather gloves against his leg. "Well, men, I know you must be wondering what we're doing on this raid."

Sergeant Waco McClain saluted. "Yes, sir, the men have been askin'."

Bennett marched up and down like a toy soldier. It was whispered he was more of a guerilla sometimes, working both sides of the war. "You all know the South is desperate for gold and silver to buy guns and boots and food."

The men nodded. Everyone had been asked to contribute gold watches, lockets, even women's wedding rings to try to bolster the Confederacy's dwindling treasury.

"Nobody wants to give the South credit anymore," Bennett complained. "England, France, yes, even our own blockade runners are demanding hard cash, not Confederate paper dollars."

A murmur of agreement went through the tired patrol. Everyone knew the Confederacy had tried to invade the West, hoping to lay hands on California gold mines and Nevada silver mines, but they had been defeated and turned back at the battle of Glorieta Pass, New Mexico Territory.

"You know," said Captain Bennett, running his fingers through his beard, "there was even some talk of invading Colorado to get that gold and silver, but that was too long a chance. Our supply lines couldn't reach that far, and Colorado Territory is pretty much for the Union."

In the firelight, Waco saw the men exchanging glances. Some of them were almost barefooted, and food rations were slim. They were running out of money to carry on this war; everyone knew that.

Waco took a deep breath. "Sir, just what is this mission?"

"I'm getting to that, Sergeant. You know some of our troops tried to invade from Canada and rob a bank in Vermont. They only got a few thousand dollars, not enough to do any good."

"Sir," Waco said, "Confederates are men of honor, not bandits."

Bennett frowned at him. "This is war, Sergeant McClain, and this is our mission: we hear there's a fat bank in the little town of Owensboro, Kentucky. We're to rob that bank and also do any damage to the enemy we can."

"Won't there be lots of Yankee troops in the area?" Waco asked. "We got less than twenty men."

"Sergeant, I resent your attitude," Bennett

snapped. "There well might be, but this patrol has a reputation of being excellent horsemen. Our mission is to hit that town and some of the others in the area, find banks, rob them, do whatever damage we can, and then hightail it back to our own lines."

A sigh went through the men. So now they were reduced to being common thieves. The glances exchanged told Waco the men didn't like it much. On the other hand—he looked at Zeb and Zeke; they had holes in their boots and no jackets, and in three months, winter would be here. Waco felt guilt run though him. His ranch hands had joined up because he had, all for the glory of Texas and the South, even though none of them owned slaves or knew anyone who did.

"Any questions?" Bennett snapped.

The patrol looked toward Waco. None of them really trusted Bennett; he was prone to wild raids without a lot of thought. He might get them all killed.

Waco sighed. "No, sir." He snapped a salute. "You lead us to the town, we'll get that gold if there is any."

They rode into the town of Owensboro in the late August morning, but someone had seen them and hurried to spread the word. Most of the people had fled the town, including those in the bank.

"Sergeant, see if you can get into the vault," Captain Bennett ordered.

"We don't have any blastin' powder or tools for this," Waco pointed out.

"Damn it, just do it!"

Waco and his men tried. They kicked open the

bank doors, but the vault was steel and iron and it would have taken a cannon to get into the vault. They tried using their handguns and rifles against the door, but they needed powder kegs. After an hour of trying, Waco had to report back that it was no use. "I'm sorry, sir." He saluted. "It just can't be done."

Captain Bennett went into a fury. "Dammit, are you telling me we rode deep into enemy territory and we're getting nothing for it?"

"Seems that way, sir."

"Then tell the men to start robbing anyone you see!" The captain shouted orders: "Take jewelry, wallets, anything of value. Break the store windows and grab anything we can use."

Waco hesitated. "Beg your pardon, sir, but my men aren't common thieves. They won't cotton to the idea of robbin' civilians."

"They're enemy!" the senior officer roared. "Do it!"

The men fanned out, kicking in doors of houses, breaking shop windows and grabbing food, boots, anything they could use and a lot of things they couldn't.

"Damn," Tom muttered to Waco, "we ain't common thieves."

"That's what I told him," Waco said. He and his three partners sat their horses in the middle of Main Street. Here and there, enthusiastic Confederate soldiers had started fires to burn the town. Somewhere, a woman screamed and an old lady followed a soldier out of her house, whacking him with her broom. "Dang ye! What are we supposed to eat this winter if ye take all our food?"

"Soldier, put it back!" Waco yelled. "Give that old lady that ham and sack of flour you're carryin'—"

"But Captain Bennett said—"

"You heard me!"

The town was in flames now, and Waco and his trio watched helplessly as the fires spread.

Captain Bennett rode into their midst with a sack of stolen loot. A handgun and some jewelry peeked out of the top of the sack. "Damn it, Sergeant, aren't you obeying my orders?"

"Most of the men are, sir, but me and my partners here don't cotton to robbin' old men and scarin' ladies and children."

"You're deliberately disobeying my orders!" Bennett shouted, a crazed look in his eyes.

"Reckon we are, sir."

"I can have you shot for this!"

Waco didn't answer. In the smoke and screams, he turned to look at Zeb, Zeke, and Tom. All of them shook their heads at him. *No, we won't do it.*

About that time, Bennett shouted to the bugler. "Sound recall, soldier. Let's get out of here before the smoke draws some Union troops!"

The sharp notes of the bugle rang out over the screams and crackle of burning wood. The patrol came from everywhere, falling into formation.

Captain Bennett turned in his saddle to glare at Waco. "Sergeant, I'll deal with you when we get back to camp."

"Yes, sir." Waco saluted and shouted orders to fall into formation. Reassembled, the patrol rode out of town and along the river.

That's when they ran across a Union barge drawn up to the river bank. They drew fire from the barge.

"God damn!" Captain Bennett snarled. "We got Yankees now! Sergeant, spread out and deal with it."

"Yes, sir." Waco motioned his men off their horses and behind logs and bushes. He soon realized the barge was defended by not more than half a dozen black troopers.

Captain Bennett crept over to him. "We got the firepower to wipe them out."

"Yes, sir, but we might be here half a day, and that smoke behind us is gonna draw more enemy troops. My suggestion is to clear out of here quick."

The firing from the barge came less and less frequently.

Waco said, "I think they're about out of ammunition, sir. Why don't we just ride on and leave them be?"

Captain Bennett roared at him. "Are you blind, Sergeant? Them's black soldiers firing at us, and that barge could be used against our troops. Let's capture and burn it."

"Yes, sir." From his post behind a shrub, Waco could see blue uniforms and faces of various shades of brown. "Hold up, men!" he shouted to his troops. "Give them a change to surrender!"

The firing gradually died out. Cautiously, Waco raised up from behind the bush and shouted, "You Yanks aboard the barge, surrender. We got plenty of ammunition and we'll wipe you out if you don't!"

Behind him, Captain Bennett muttered curses about blacks having the sheer gall to join the Yankee army.

First one black soldier threw down his rifle and

put up his hands, then another. In all, there were not more than six or seven.

"Okay, men!" Waco shouted. "Take control!"

His men ran on to the barge, kicking away the rifles, shoving the black troopers into a line.

Captain Bennett looked furious, his face red as he stalked over to the barge. "Burn the damn thing!" he commanded.

Someone lit a dry bit of brush and threw it onto the deck. The deck caught the flame and began to burn, acrid gray smoke snaking up to the sky.

"Sir," Waco said, "what about the soldiers? We can't take them as prisoners, they don't have horses and we're moving fast. The Yanks will catch up with us. Shall I just turn them loose?"

Captain Bennett scowled at Waco, then at the black Yankees. "We ain't taking them with us and we ain't leaving them to fight again. You black bastards have your nerve, fighting against white men."

"We fightin' for freedom," one black said proudly.

"Kill them!" Bennett snapped. "Don't leave one alive!"

"What?" Waco wasn't sure he'd heard correctly. "Captain, I don't think—"

"You heard me, shoot the bastards!"

The black troopers looked at each other uncertainly as the Rebels moved toward them.

"No!" Waco shouted. "I can't massacre unarmed men. No, I won't do it!"

"You're disobeying an order! I'll have you court-martialed and shot for this!" There were flecks of foam on Bennett's mouth and his glazed eyes had the look of a madman. "Shoot the bastards! Do you men hear me? Shoot the black sons-a-bitches!"

He began firing at the panicked black troopers and one fell. Reluctantly, others of the Confederate patrol began firing—all except Waco and his partners.

"No!" Waco swore. "Damn it, no! We can't kill unarmed prisoners!"

But the other members of his patrol were firing now. Maybe a black or two managed to get away, but the others were falling across the deck of the burning barge.

Waco could only stare, frozen with horror. He looked into Tom's eyes, then the two old brothers. None of the trio fired, but the echo of heavy gunfire was deafening and the smell of the burning barge and gunpowder choked them as the black troopers fell and lay still.

"All right." Captain Bennett swung up on his lathered gray horse. "Let's get out of here! We're headed to Lewisport and then on to Hartford. If you see anything of value, take it!"

Captain Bennett turned on Waco. "Sergeant, you and your friends are prisoners. Lieutenant, take their weapons!"

Now that the slaughter was over, the other men of the patrol looked guilty and ashamed, but they followed orders and took the four men's weapons.

Captain Bennett glared at Waco with glittering, mad eyes. "You four will stand for court martial when we get back. I expect you will be shot."

However, at the court martial, the panel of officers hearing the case noted the past heroism of the four and decided to be lenient. The colonel in charge ran his finger over his white mustache. "Sergeant McClain, you do realize we can't have disobedience in our ranks?"

Waco snapped to attention. "Yes, sir, but we Texans are not used to terrorizin' and robbin' women, shootin' down unarmed enemy."

"They were niggers," Captain Bennett said in the background.

The colonel frowned at Bennett. Evidently there was no love lost there. "They were unarmed troops."

"Nevertheless," Captain Bennett remind him, "our mission was a failure. We went after Yankee gold to help the Confederate treasury and came up empty, thanks to Sergeant McClain and his friends."

Waco started to point out the fact that they had tried valiantly and failed to rob the bank. Captain Bennett had led the patrol into danger without checking his information. Waco decided his comment wouldn't make any difference in the proceedings.

The colonel frowned at Waco. "Sergeant, you do realize how serious the charges are against you and your men, disobeying direct orders from a superior officer while under fire?"

"Yes, sir, but I won't rob ladies and kill unarmed men on nobody's command."

"You're very stubborn," a balding major on the panel snapped.

"I'm a Texan, sir, and Scotch-Irish besides."

"Umm," muttered the colonel, "Scots-Irish have a reputation of being stubborn beyond belief. And Scots-Irish Texans—"

"We Texans have our own rules we live by."

Waco drew himself up to his full height. "I don't apologize for that."

"I think we need to retire and discuss our decision." The colonel pulled at his mustache thoughtfully and surveyed the other officers of the panel sitting under the faded tent. "Although we need good men, and it seems a waste to shoot four of them, especially Texans. They always seem to be our best fighters. Guards, take the prisoners away for a few minutes while we discuss this."

That gave Waco and his men a little hope. They sat under a tree, chained together with a guard nearby, and talked.

"Waco, I mean, sir," Tom said, rolling a cigarette, "you think they're gonna shoot us?"

Waco shrugged. "Even if they do, we were true to ourselves as men and as Texans."

"That's right." Zeb spat to one side. "I wouldn't change anything if I had to do it over again."

Zeke began to play "The Yellow Rose of Texas" on his mouth organ.

It seemed like an eternity before the court martial proceedings were called to order again.

"Attention, prisoners!" a captain barked.

Waco and his men rose and squared their shoulders, resigned to being shot by a firing squad.

The mustached colonel cleared his throat. "This is a clear-cut case of insubordination."

Captain Bennett smirked.

"However, this is a highly unusual case." The colonel focused his attention on Waco. "I have heard that Sergeant McClain and his Texans would charge hell with a dipper of water, they're that brave, and we've a shortage of good soldiers."

Captain Bennett looked as baffled as Waco felt.

The colonel looked up and down at his panel of officers gathered around the scarred table under the faded tent. "The mission was to bring back gold, which the Confederacy needs in the worst way. Our spies have brought us word of a fat little bank in Kansas."

Everyone looked puzzled.

Captain Bennett jumped up from his chair and said, "Excuse me, sir, but I think they deserve the firing squad for disobedience. In fact, I demand it."

The colonel frowned. "Sit down, Captain. Sergeant McClain, what this panel has decided is highly unusual, but I think you are a brave and honorable man, as are your soldiers."

"We are, sir. Texans pride themselves on it."

"Good." He nodded and stared directly at Waco. "Then I'm offering you what may be a suicide mission. It's this or the firing squad."

"Sir, that doesn't seem to give me much choice," Waco said.

"Then will you take your trio of Texans, rob that Kansas bank, and bring back whatever you can get? Fifty thousand dollars would be great, but of course, we don't expect that much."

A murmur ran through the assembled crowd.

Waco blinked. "I beg your pardon, sir?"

Captain Bennett shouted, "They'll run off to Mexico, that's what they'll do!"

"Sergeant at arms, remove that man!" The colonel gestured and Bennett was dragged, kicking and cursing, away from the tent.

"I'm asking you, on your honor, Sergeant," the colonel said, "if you four will ride up to Kansas, rob that bank, and bring us whatever money you find? You know we're low on food, our soldiers are barefooted and without tents. The money in the Prairie View bank might make the difference."

"And what if I say no or our mission is unsuccessful?" Waco asked. "What if your information is faulty?"

The colonel shrugged. "Then when you report back, we'll put you before a firing squad." He smiled. "You will report back, won't you, Sergeant?"

"Yes, sir." Waco saluted. "We give you our word. We'll do our best to bring in that money, sir."

"Good. We'll send you back to Texas and you can get to Kansas through Indian Territory. Probably take a couple of weeks of September to ride to Kansas. We'll expect to hear from you by mid-November. Agreed?"

This was late August, Waco thought. There were all sorts of complications ahead of the four. And suppose something went wrong? The alternative was facing a firing squad. "Yes, sir." He saluted again. "Me and my men will hit that bank and bring the money to Confederate headquarters."

"Objection!" The balding major slapped his hand on the table. "What if they rob the bank and hightail it to Mexico with all that money?"

"We're Texans, sir," Waco said softly, "and we've given our word. His word is sacred to a Texan."

"I believe you," said the colonel with a nod. "Sergeant, we'll see you and your men in mid-November and we'll expect you to have that money. Otherwise—"

"We'll bring it, sir," Waco said with more confidence than he felt. "We'll get that money or die tryin'."

Thunder cracked and Waco woke suddenly and sat up on his quilt in the shack, looking around in the darkness at his snoring partners. Here it was nearing the end of October and they hadn't come up with a penny yet. That sleeping girl up in the loft held the key to the quartet's fate. Right now, it looked like their future was a Confederate firing squad. Heading for Mexico was tempting, but of course, he had given his word as a Texan to return.

Waco lay sleepless for a long while, listening to the rain pour down and trying not to think how close November was. Then he remembered kissing Rosemary and smiled. If only times and events were different. He wondered for a moment what would happen if he went up the ladder now to the sleeping girl. Would she open her arms to him and want him to spend the rest of the night making love to her?

Then he scolded himself. *Don't be a fool. She's a rich girl, she wouldn't spit on the likes of you. Besides, you know you can't trust women.* It was a long time before he drifted back to sleep.

Rosemary rode through the wet night without the least idea where she was headed. She and her horse were both soaked to the skin and shivering in the October chill. If she could stop awhile and get warm, she could wait until daylight to ride on.

Maybe by then, she'd see a familiar landmark and could find her way back to Prairie View.

Up ahead in the cold rain, she made out the shadow of a small hill and some piles of boulders. She headed in that direction. It was almost as if she could smell a campfire. Then she shook her head. She was hallucinating because she was so cold. She wouldn't be able to start a fire, of course, because she had no matches, but maybe she and Lady could find an outcrop of rock to keep the rain off them. She imagined hot coffee and dry blankets and maybe some food.

It seemed as if she could smell bacon frying and yes, coffee brewing. She must be going mad from the chill. And then she rode up near the rocks and saw the shadows and glow of a small campfire. She was saved.

She urged her horse into a lope, riding near the circle of the campfire. "Hello, the camp! I'm lost! May I get down?"

A man stood up suddenly and grabbed her bridle, and he wasn't smiling. Now she saw other men sprawled around the fire. "Who the hell are you and who's with you?"

Too late she realized the ragtag bunch were wearing mixed pieces of blue and gray uniforms. *Guerillas*, she thought, *outlaw guerillas, raiding both sides and loyal to neither, like the infamous Quantrill. Folks say they'd kill you for a nickel, and I've stumbled into a nest of them.*

Panicked, she tried to wheel her mare and ride away, but the dirty outlaw hung on to her bridle even as her horse whinnied and reared. He grinned without mirth through broken teeth. "Hey, girlie, what's your hurry? Get down and visit a spell."

The other men laughed as she slapped at the thug with her bridle reins, fighting to free her horse from the man, but he hung on to the bridle and now another stepped forward to pull her from her horse. She fought him, biting and scratching as he hung on to her. *Talk about out of the frying pan and into the fire.* She was now in twice as much trouble as before.

Chapter Fourteen

"Let go of me!" Rosemary fought the dirty man as he dragged her from her horse, but he and his crowd of guerillas only laughed and gibed at her.

"Hey, honey, you got here just in time! We was lookin' for a little fun after our long ride."

A tall, bearded man appeared suddenly on the outskirts of the fire, blinking sleepily. He looked like a big, hairy bear. "What the hell's all the fuss about? I told you not to wake me up."

The men quieted suddenly and Rosemary realized he must be the leader. She turned to him, pleading, "Please, sir, I rode into your camp by mistake, meaning no harm."

The leader looked past her to her horse. "Fine horse for a ragged, muddy slut to be ridin'. Where'd you steal it, honey? The law after you?"

The crowd of men guffawed.

Money, she thought, *they'll be interested in money.* She jerked away from her captor and straighted her wet, torn clothes with as much dignity as she could. "No, she's my horse. I didn't steal her."

The men laughed again. Evidently, they didn't believe her.

The leader grinned. "Now that ain't too likely, a fine horse like that and a ragged gal like you."

"I am not a poor girl." She drew herself up proudly. "I am Rosemary Burke of Prairie View, and I've been kidnapped. No doubt you've heard about the kidnapping."

The men looked at each other, then back at her.

"No doubt we ain't." The leader rubbed his hairy chin. "And if you're so rich, why are you dressed like a tramp?"

They weren't going to believe her. "No, you see, I've been kidnapped and my clothes stolen. I've had to take clothes off a scarecrow. Now if any of you would ride to Prairie View and alert the law, I'm sure there's a nice reward—"

The men interrupted her with hoots and catcalls. "Hey, Bill, she's a rich 'un, don't you see by her clothes?"

The leader said, "Burt, you was in Prairie View to get supplies a couple of days ago. You heard anything about a rich girl missin'?"

"Nope, Bill." One-eyed Burt shrugged. "Town sleepy and quiet."

So Godfrey was keeping this quiet, she thought. Well, what had she expected?

"I tell you," Rosemary insisted, "I am rich and I've been kidnapped. All you have to do is take me to the bank there and next week, I'll see you are rewarded."

The men roared with laughter again.

"You must believe me!"

"Girlie," the leader said with great patience, "you

think a bunch of guerilla fighters under Bloody Bill Anderson are gonna ride in that close to the big new fort to claim a reward that don't exist for a gal that ain't missin'? You tryin' to get us all killed?"

"But it's a Union fort. Aren't you Union—"

"We ain't anything," the leader snarled. "Like my friend Quantrill, we're fightin' both sides and profitin' from it. Both sides would like to hang us high. We ain't about to all ride into Prairie View."

"Well, if you'd just head me that direction or ride into town with me, there's money—"

"It's a trap," several of the men muttered. "She's trying to get us ambushed."

"I'm not. I tell you, I'm rich and I'll reward you—"

"You gonna reward us, all right." Bloody Bill laughed. "I'm gonna take that fancy horse you stole and you can reward all of us personally before we leave camp and ride back to Missouri."

She felt her blood freeze. "What—what do you mean?"

"Oh, don't be innocent with us, honey." The leader winked. "You're a mite raggedy and dirty, but we ain't seen any women in a while, and so you'll do."

She must not faint. She whirled and tried to run to her horse, but her captor grabbed her, ripping her faded shirt. "No, you don't, honey. Now ain't you gonna be sociable and pay us back for the food and coffee we're gonna give you?"

God, she wished Waco was here. All of a sudden, he and his Texans seemed like protective friends. Maybe they had already discovered she was missing and were even now searching for her. All she had to do was stall for time. "Okay." She tried to smile in a flirtatious manner. "Feed me and let me rest awhile and I'll entertain you all."

The men roared with approval. She could see the lust reflected by the firelight in their eyes.

"Joe," the leader ordered, running his hand through his shaggy black beard, "bring the lady over by the fire and we'll give her some grub and a chance to get warm. Then we'll see how good she is at pleasin' a man."

She tried to step with dignity as she was led to the fire. Even though she was facing a terrible ordeal, the smell of the roasting meat and hot coffee had her salivating. At least she was buying herself some time, she thought as one of the men dished up a tin plate of steaming stew and a cup of strong coffee. She would eat slowly and waste as much time as possible. She dipped her spoon in the stew and gobbled it even though she intended to delay, she was that starved. The coffee seemed to warm her all the way down her throat.

"For a rich gal," the leader said, "you seem awful hungry."

"I've been kidnapped," she insisted. "I can give you a big reward if you'll just—"

"Don't start that again," her captor snapped.

"Who gets her first?" one of the men yelled.

"I do, of course," the leader said. "Then the rest of you can draw straws and line up."

She looked around and did a quick count. There must be ten or fifteen of the guerillas. The thought made her choke. She had to stall. She just had to, and hope Waco came to her rescue. That was a forlorn possibility, she thought as she ate as slowly as possible. Probably he didn't know she was missing yet, and he might be glad to be rid of her. Right now, it appeared she was going to be raped by all of these thugs.

"Can't you eat any faster?" one of the outlaws complained.

"No. I'm really hungry. May I have some more, please?" She glanced around at the men. The dirty thugs had gathered around her like a pack of wolves.

"You tryin' to eat us out of house and home?" The leader sneered. "Quit stallin', gal, we're ready to have a little fun with you."

Oh God, Waco, where are you when I need you? At least the Texans had behaved like gentlemen. What could she do to stall some more? "Would— would you like to see me dance?"

"You dance, girlie?" The leader eyed her suspiciously. "Oh, I'll enthrall you." She stood up.

"What's enthrall?" one of the others muttered.

"Please and thrill you," she answered with a weak smile. Now could she remember any of the ballet training her mother had made her take to make her a little less clumsy?

Waco woke up suddenly, listening. As a leader of troops, he was always on the alert for noise, or lack of it that might mean trouble. He listened a moment, straining to hear. It was silent. The rain had stopped. He breathed a sigh of relief and relaxed, listening to his men snoring. He stared up at the ceiling, thinking about Rosemary. He had begun to admire the stubborn girl. No, maybe it was a little more than admire. He remembered the inexperienced kiss and sighed. Others might think her difficult, but he thought he could see through that protective armor, and she really felt scared and unloved in a hostile world that only judged her on her money and her looks.

Yet he was running out of time to get that money for the Confederacy, but if he came back without it, he and his men would be shot. Now it appeared her rich father wasn't going to pay the ransom, no matter how low Waco made it. He was really between a rock and a hard place.

Prince scratched at the door and whined to get out.

That was what had awakened him, the dog's scratching. "What's the matter, boy?"

The dog renewed his scratching. Waco got up quietly and went outside, sat on the damp step, and rolled a smoke. Prince ran up and down the yard, panting frantically. "Be quiet, dog, you'll wake everyone up."

In answer, the dog ran to the stable, then back to Waco.

"Must be a rat in the barn," he muttered absently, patting the dog's head.

Scudding clouds drifted over the moon and he had no idea what time it really was. He pulled out his gold pocket watch, held it up to the faint light from a few stars and squinted at it. 3:00 A.M.

He looked up at the upper window and wondered if she might be awake and they could talk. He realized then that the thought was only an excuse and he really wanted to have a chance, maybe to hold her and kiss her again.

Now what is that vine doing torn away from the side of

the house? Maybe it had been struck by lightning. Throwing away the cigarette, he slipped back inside and went up the ladder to the loft. In the shadows, he could see her form under the blankets. He didn't want to startle or scare her.

A damp breeze blew against his face suddenly and he blinked, wondering. Then he realized the window was open. *Surely the little filly couldn't have—*

He strode to the window and looked down. The vines that climbed the wall were mostly lying on the ground. *What the hell?* Waco took two steps to her pallet and yanked back the cover. The sassy female had piled her blankets to look like she was there, but she was gone. "Well, damn, I knew I couldn't trust her! All women are the same."

Now what? He struggled between anger and admiration as he took the steps down the ladder two at a time. "Hey, boys, get up! She's gone! The gal has escaped!"

"What?" All three of them came up off the floor grabbing for pistols. "Yankees? What's happenin'?"

"Grab your boots," Waco ordered. "Our captive has slipped away like a coyote out of a trap. Reckon that's what Prince was tryin' to tell me last night."

All three began to search through the semidarkness for their clothes.

"Damn it to hell," Zeb muttered. "I say good riddance and let's head for the border."

"We can't do that," his brother griped, struggling to put on his boots. "They're waitin' with a firin' squad in Texas."

"You know," Tom said as he pulled on his pants, "we could just head for Arizona or some place where they won't catch us."

"We swore on our honor as Texans," Waco reminded him. "Besides, I feel responsible for Rosie. Suppose she runs into trouble?"

"Then you'd better save your sympathy for the trouble." Zeb scratched his beard and yawned. "She's a handful."

"Oh, shut up," Waco snapped. "We're responsible for her since we kidnapped her. Grab your gear."

"Did it occur to you," Tom ran his hand through his red hair, "that even now, she may be back in town gatherin' up soldiers and a posse who might be on their way out here to hang us?"

Waco paused. "It did cross my mind," he admitted, reaching for his Stetson, "but if not—"

"Okay, okay," the two old men muttered and they stumbled toward the door. "Gonna get as wet as fish out there."

"Aw, you ain't made of sugar, you won't melt." Waco led them toward the barn, Prince bounding ahead of him in the rain and mud. Waco came to the fence and frowned. "Oh, hell, she's left the gate open. We'll have to catch our horses."

"That's one fiesty, ornery gal," Tom said.

"Ain't she, though?" Waco grinned in spite of himself. He didn't want to admire her spunk, but he did. "Now let's spread out and catch them horses. It'll be daylight in a few hours."

It took thirty minutes to catch the horses, and Tom tripped and fell in the mud catching his. Then the dog, wet and dirty, gave a good shake that threw mud and water all over everyone.

"I oughta shoot that mutt," Zeke grumbled, wiping the muck off his beard.

"Just shut up and saddle the horses," Waco ordered.

It began to rain again, and all four were as angry as rattlesnakes in a bed of cactus when they finally rode out in the rain, the wet dog bouncing along through the mud with them.

Waco said, "Well, her tracks is washed out. I ain't got the least idea which way to go."

Prince paused ahead of him, sniffing the air.

Waco reined in. "You don't think that dog's smart enough to track her?"

"That dog's dumb as a stump," Zeke grumbled, pulled his hat down over his eyes, and hunched his shoulders against the cold wind. "He might be able to track a plate of food, but nuthin' else."

Waco dismounted and searched the ground. He had always been an expert tracker, but in the darkness and hard rain, he couldn't find so much as a broken twig. "The only thing I know to do is wait for daylight. No tellin' which way she went."

Prince turned east, sniffing the wind and barking.

"Stupid dog." Tom rode up next to Waco as he remounted. "I hope she rides clear to hell." He wiped rain from his face.

"You got to admire her grit," Waco said and smiled in spite of himself.

"That gal has been more trouble than sand in scrambled eggs," Zeb complained. "I say we head for Texas and take our chances on the firin' squad. Anything beats dealin' with that fiery gal one more day."

"We're goin' after her," Waco said. "I wouldn't

feel right if something happened to her. We ain't got nuthin' else to go on. I say we follow the dog; he might be able to track her. Go on, boy," he encouraged Prince, "find Rosie."

The mutt wagged his tail and started east, stopping now and then to sniff the ground.

"So now," Zeke grumbled, leaning on his saddle horn, "we're followin' a dog that can hardly find its way to a plate of scraps?"

"You got a better idea?" Waco asked and turned his slicker up against the cold rain.

Silence.

"You do realize," Tom said, "that if we head east, we're liable to run into some of them Missouri bushwhackers?"

"What?" Zeke asked.

"You know, guerillas that have no allegiance to either side, just robbin' and killin' anyone that crosses their paths, like Bloody Bill Anderson or Quantrill."

"If we do, we'll deal with them," Waco said.

Out at the guerilla camp, Rosemary danced around the fire as gracefully as she could. Of course she couldn't get up on her toes, but even if she'd had ballet shoes, she couldn't anyway because she was a sturdy girl and she wasn't too good at dancing on her toes. The men seemed enthralled but were getting restless, and she was running out of breath.

"Enough!" the leader finally said and slammed his fist down on his knee. "Gal, it's time for another kind of entertainment."

The men cheered and waved theirs fists in the air.

"Uh, I can sing, too," she gasped.

"What can you sing?" One of them asked.

"What about some Stephen Foster or 'Lorena'?" She could only hope to stall for time.

"Do you know 'After the Battle, Mother'?" Bloody Bill asked.

"Naw, not that one," another said, "that always makes me cry for my own dear mama."

"Your old lady is in jail," someone pointed out.

"I'll sing 'Jeannie with the Light Brown Hair'," she said and began to sing. She knew she wasn't very good and she was breathless and a little off-key, but the men seemed to like it. More than one wiped his eyes.

She sang two more songs before the leader became restless again. "Enough, chubby gal. You're what I want now."

The others cheered and nodded.

"Wouldn't you all like a drink first?" She paused and licked her lips, so terrified she was shaking.

"Yeah, that sounds good, too." One of the men, the one with the eye patch, nodded. "Let's have a drink while we wait for our turn at the slut."

The men cheered again.

Rosemary looked around the circle and then past the men at the prairie beyond the rocks. If she took off running, they would surely catch her, but it would delay things for a little while. "Look." She tried to keep her lips from trembling. "Look, you've just got to believe me. I am a rich girl with lots of money in the Prairie View Bank. Now if you'll just take me there, I'll give—"

"You think we're stupid?" the leader growled. "We'd be ridin' into a nest of soldiers."

"We wouldn't tell the soldiers," she babbled, knowing she couldn't get the money until Halloween, but maybe soldiers would come to her rescue. There were plenty of them at the new fort. "We'll just ride in at dawn and I'll get the money and you can ride out."

"We've wasted enough time, gal." The leader stood up and leered at her. "None of us believe you're a rich gal, not the way you're dressed. Now you just lie down on this here blanket and pleasure us and we'll let you go. There ain't but fifteen of us. That won't take much of your time." He tried to grab her arm but she stepped away from him.

They might all rape her, but she wasn't some timid, whimpering wretch. She would not surrender without a fight. She didn't have a chance of outrunning the men, but she had to try. She took off suddenly, rushing past the startled man and into the night. The ground was muddy and sucked at her boots as she ran.

Behind her, she heard the exclamations of surprise and cursing as the men stumbled to their feet. Most of them were probably drunk, but they could still chase her. If she could just swing in a circle and find her horse, she might have a chance. The men could surely hear her breathe as she swung to the left and came around toward where all the horses were staked. Behind her, she heard running feet and cursing. She saw the horses silhouetted in the dim light that comes before dawn. *Oh, Lady Be Good, you've got to run tonight!*

She was almost to the horses now and hope

began to build in her heart that she might have a chance, but she was breathless and slowing. She heard the men gaining on her.

She made it to the staked horses. She jerked Lady's rope off the picket line and tried to swing up on her back. She was going to make it.

And then the bearded leader stepped out of the shadows and grabbed her. "Gotcha, you sassy little bitch!"

Oh God, no. She struggled with him as he dragged her away from her horse. She bit and scratched and fought him. "No, I won't give in! I won't let you! I'm a rich girl, you hear? I'll pay—"

Then he slapped a dirty hand over her mouth. "Shut up, you bitch, nobody believes that story!" He wrapped his other arm around her waist, dragging her back toward the blanket by the fire. "Come on, boys! I've got her now!"

An angry howl went up from the panting men. "Damn her, we'll make her pay for all this trouble!"

She managed to bite the leader's hand and he slapped her hard, stunning her as he put his hand familiarly on her breasts. "You little bitch, you're gonna pay for this. Wait till my men get through with you, you'll submit and be glad to do it."

She must not cry, although she was shaking in terror as he dragged her toward the fire and threw her down on the blanket. When she tried to get up, he slapped her and reached down to rip open the front of her faded shirt. "Now get a look, boys, you ever see a pair of tits as big and purty as those?"

She tried to cover herself with her arms, but now two men grabbed her arms and pinned them on each side of her head as she struggled.

"Umm!" The leader's beady eyes darkened with lust. "I can hardy wait to get a mouthful of them."

"Rip her pants off!" someone yelled. "I wanta see what we're gettin'"

One of the others guffawed. "Now, Joe, you ain't had a woman in two months, you'd take on a heifer or a sheep if you could get it."

"Now that's the truth."

All the men laughed as she struggled to get away.

"Ain't you gonna cry and beg for mercy?" asked one of the men who were holding her down.

In answer, she spat in his face and he slapped her. "Just wait till it's my turn, girlie, I'm gonna flip you on your belly and see how you like takin' it from the back end."

The men howled with laughter.

The leader said, "Now I get her first and you all can watch how a master does it."

He pulled at her pants and she tried to jerk away, but the men were all gathered around like a circle of hungry wolves.

It didn't seem right that she was going to lose her virginity to this filthy pack of cutthroats and thieves, but there was no help for her now. She'd be lucky if they didn't kill her when they finished!

Chapter Fifteen

Waco was wet and cold as he and his men rode through the darkness, trailing the dog while his compadres followed, grumbling under their breath. He was probably a knothead for trusting the dog, hoping it could track Rosie, but with the rain pouring down and the sky black as the inside of a cow, he didn't have any better ideas.

Once Prince paused, running in circles and sniffing the ground.

Behind him, Zeke said, "That dog don't know nuthin'. He's probably leadin' us to some farmer's chicken coop."

"Yeah," Tom said, "reckon she's made it back to Prairie View and a big troop of cavalry is ridin' out right now to catch us?"

"Well," Waco wiped rain from his rugged features, "the Yankees will shoot us for spies since we ain't in uniform, and if we ride back to Texas without the money, our own side will shoot us. You think a Yankee bullet hurts any less than a Confederate one? Our only hope is catchin' up with Rosie."

The dog barked and took off running east again.

"Come on, boys," Waco said and nudged his horse, following Prince. He glanced at the eastern sky, thinking it wouldn't be long until daylight. What if the boys were right and Rosemary had found her way back to Prairie View, and even now, an army troop or at least a posse was mounting up?

Behind him, Zeb grumbled, "I think we should light a shuck for the border. If that gal's got people lookin' for us, we might make it into Indian Territory before they pick up our track."

"Yep," said his brother, "I'll take my chances in Texas. At least if I die, they'll bury me in Lone Star dirt. Kidnappin' that dad-blasted female was a *loco* idea."

"Have you got a better one?" Tom challenged.

"Oh, shut your yammerin'," Waco threw back over his shoulder. "Now that we stole her, we're responsible if something happens to her."

"No such luck," Zeb complained. "I pity the poor devils who get her."

Waco was wet and bone tired. He ground his teeth and kept riding. "Any man who wants to can head for the border."

"Without you?" Tom asked.

"Yep. As a Texan, I feel obliged to return her safely to her dear papa." Actually, although he didn't want to admit it, he'd gotten attached to the sturdy girl the same way he might to an ornery mule that can't be broken.

"Hell, we ain't gonna desert you," Zeke said and the others murmured agreement. "If you're *loco* enough to keep lookin', I reckon we're as crazy as you are."

"*Gracias*, I think," Waco grinned back at the wet trio. Rain dripped off the brim of his Stetson and down his neck. If it weren't for that dad-blamed gal, he'd be back in that cabin under a warm blanket. The boys were right. He'd known from the first that it wasn't right to kidnap a lady, and God was getting even with him.

The dog paused a hundred yards ahead of them, whining faintly.

Waco reined in, looking ahead at the faintest glow of a campfire. "Whoa, fellas," he whispered. "There's a camp up ahead, no tellin' whose. Let's sneak up there and see. Leave the horses here. If they smell other horses, they'll nicker and alarm the camp."

They dismounted and tied their horses to nearby shrubs. The mud squashed under Waco's worn boots as he grabbed his Winchester off the saddle and crept forward. Prince had paused at a boulder, whining softly. "Shh! Be quiet, Prince!"

He heard his men stepping through the mud behind him. Waco crept up the boulder and peered over the top at the campfire below. Then his heart almost stopped. "Oh, no."

"What?" the other three whispered and crept up beside him.

Below them, a ragtag band of ruffians sat around a fire. They wore bits and pieces of several uniforms. *Guerillas, probably Quantrill or Bloody Bill*, Waco thought in dismay. Worse than that, the outlaws had Rosemary. She was dancing about the circle to the hoots and hollers of the drunken bunch. He couldn't hear what was being said, but she looked scared.

He turned back to his men. "I know we're out-numbered, but I'm duty-bound to rescue the lady."

"I say the guerillas deserve her. They'll be ready to let her go in a day or two and glad to do it," Zeb said.

"You hombres don't have to help me, but I got to do this," Waco said.

Prince growled again and Waco said, "Quiet, pooch, you'll give us away."

"Now, Waco, you know we ain't gonna let you ride into a fight by yourself," Zeke whispered.

"Okay, then let's sneak back to our horses. If we ride in at a gallop, yelling and shooting, they may think the whole army is after them and they'll panic and ride out before they stop to count us."

"Well, we've followed you into barroom brawls and fights with rustlers," Tom said, "I reckon we can do this."

"I don't know that she's worth it," Zeb grumbled. "She don't even dance too good."

"Oh, how would you know?" snapped his brother.

"You two stop it!" Waco ordered. "Let's get back to the horses. Remember, we'll ride in at a gallop, shoutin' and shootin'."

"Reckon what will happen if they count us quick and see there's only four of us?" Tom asked.

"I reckon they'll stop amusin' themselves with Rosie and have a good time lynchin' us."

"I wish you hadn't of said that," Zeb said.

"Gawd Almighty!" Waco swore. "She just took off runnin' away from the fire. That only makes it worse! Get mounted! Good luck, men." Waco

doubled-checked to make sure his weapons
were loaded.

Rosemary continued to fight her captor vigor-
ously. Abruptly there was noise and shouts and galloping horses coming down the hill toward her.
She and her captor froze in confusion for a split
second. *Oh, God, there are more of the guerillas.*

Behind her, she heard men shouting in alarm
and fear as they tried to get away from the fire,
running for their horses. "Soldiers! Let's get the
hell out!"

Her captor turned her loose and she fell in the
mud, confused at the gunfire, rearing horses, and
shouting men. Abruptly, a muddy, wet Prince was
all over her, whining and licking her face. "What?"

"Gawd Almighty, Rosemary! Get out of the way,
for God's sake!"

And then she recognized the big bay stallion
galloping toward her and saw the rider's strained
face. She stumbled over to one side as the horses
galloped past. The sound of gunfire echoed all
around her, making her ears ring, and she choked
on the acrid smell of gunpowder.

Prince barked and barked, adding to the noise
and general confusion. In the early dawn light,
the guerillas ran about, colliding with each other,
many too drunk to mount a defense. Now most of
them were running for their horses.

"It's a posse!" Rosemary screamed. "There must
be a hundred of them! Hang them, Sheriff, hang
them all!"

The guerillas were not stopping to see if they

were being attacked by soldiers or lawmen; they were mounting up and riding out, leaving their camp behind in confusion. It was a complete rout, the four riders chasing the guerillas out into the coming dawn to gallop away in panic.

For a long moment, Rosemary stood in the middle of the destroyed camp, watching the backs of Waco and his men disappear over the rise, still shouting and shooting. She took a deep breath and realized she was all right except for her torn shirt, which left her partially naked. She fell to her knees and hugged the wet, smelly dog. "Good boy! Good boy!"

That was not her biggest problem, she thought as she blinked back her tears. *Stop it, Rosemary*, she scolded herself, *you're not the heroine of a romantic novel who can now collapse and weep until the hero returns to sweep you up in his arms. You'd better get out of here before your kidnappers return.*

Easier said than done, she decided as she ran to the picket line, the dog romping along with her as if it were a game. The surprise attack had scattered all the horses. The only thing still tied there was a pack mule, and he laid his ears back at her as if he had no intention of letting her mount. She had neither saddle nor bridle, but the mule did wear a halter. She untied him from the picket line. "Whoa, mule, let's get out of here."

She tried to mount up bareback, but the mule wasn't interested. It moved around in a circle as she tried to mount. "Stop that, I'm not that heavy. I'll bet you've carried packs bigger than me." She managed to get aboard, feeling the mule's backbone under her well-padded rear. "Okay, now let's go."

The mule moved reluctantly, his ears laid back. She dug her heels into his sides and urged him forward. A jolting trot was the best he would do. Prince bounded alongside, barking frantically. Behind her, she thought she heard horses returning. *Is it Waco or the guerillas?* One thing was certain, she didn't intend to wait around and find out. She urged the mule forward again and he balked, giving a loud and protesting "hee haw, hee haw," and then he bucked her off.

She felt herself flying through the air and she came down in the mud with a splat. The mule looked back at her inquiringly, wiggling his ears, then he turned and galloped away. "Damn you, now you start to run."

Tears ran down her face and she struggled to wipe them away with a muddy hand. She'd tried hard and nothing worked out. Why, Lady Wendemere would land in a bed of flowers and only look slightly mused and romantic as Lord Thistlebritches rushed to her on his fine steed, gathered her up, and took her back to his castle for the wedding.

Well, Rosemary wasn't licked. She could still run, and it wasn't quite light yet. Maybe she could lose herself among the rocks.

Rosemary stood up with great effort and a big sucking sound as the sticky mud pulled at her. She took two steps, the mud sucking at her fine boots, lost her balance, and fell again, but this time forward. "Oh, hell and damnation!" she muttered as she tried to stand and fell again.

"Ladies ain't supposed to cuss." Waco rode up and reined in, grinning.

She could just kill him. "Look at me! Just look at me!" she shrieked. "I've been kidnapped, helped you rob chicken houses, and almost been ravished by a bunch of outlaws—"

"I'm lookin'." He grinned again as he relaxed and leaned on his saddle horn.

Rosemary looked down. Her generous breasts were bared by the torn shirt. "You are a rotten blackguard, sir," she snarled and crossed her arms over her breasts.

"That ain't a nice thing to say to the man who just saved you." He dismounted.

"Saved me? Saved me? Why, you—" She managed to stand up again and took a swing at him, but he sidestepped and she fell again. She'd had all she could take. Rosemary buried her face in her hands and began to sob. The dog ran up and licked her face.

"I'm sorry," Waco said in his soft drawl, "I didn't mean to cause you to cry."

"Go away. I'm just a fat, clumsy mess."

"No, you ain't. You're a beauty in distress. Here, let me help you up." He paused, took off his shirt, and draped it around her shoulders. On her cold body, the rain-wet shirt, was still warm from his muscular chest and smelled faintly of tobacco and wood smoke.

She pulled it around her and looked up at him. "You got me into all this," she sobbed. "If I had a gun, I'd kill you."

"Ladies don't shoot people." He gave her a warm, engaging grin as he held out his hand.

Hesitantly, she took it although he seemed to grimace at the mud. For a split second, she had the

urge to yank him off balance down into the mud
with her, then decided against it. Waco McClain
was not a man to mess with. His hand was big and
warm and calloused, enclosing hers. "I'm really
sorry, Rosie," he whispered. "I never could have
forgave myself if something happened to you."

She tried to take a step, lost her balance, and fell
forward into his arms. He held her close for a long
minute.

"I just got you all dirty," she said.

He wiped at his muddy chest with distaste. "That's
all right, Rosie. I been muddy before."

His horse stood behind him, all saddled and
bridled in the early morning light. It would serve
him right if she managed to steal it and left him
afoot until his friends returned.

"Waco, I—I think I lost one of my boots out
there in the mud. Would you find it for me?"

"Sure thing." He turned her hands loose and
stepped past her, searching the dark shadows.

At that point, she made a run for the horse, got
her foot in the stirrup, and tried to mount. The
dog barked and jumped about with excitement.

"Why, you little—!" Waco whirled and came
after her.

She almost had her leg over the saddle. All she
needed was a split second and she would gallop
away, leaving him here in the mud. However, now
he grabbed her leg, pulling her toward him. For a
long minute they struggled while the horse whinnied and stamped restlessly, then Waco pulled her
from the horse, lost his balance, and they both
tumbled into the mud.

"Well, I'll be God-damned!" he swore. "If you ain't the sneakiest little coyote."

She tried to kick him and pull away, but now they both struggled and went down, rolling over and over in the mud until he ended up on top. He lay with his bare chest against her bare breasts and she felt the heat and the power of the man. So this was what it felt like when a couple began to make love. The thought made her flush furiously.

"Hey, Waco, where are you?" called Tom. "We run the guerillas off, but they might come back."

"Here," he called, grinning down at Rosemary in the coming dawn.

"Let me up, you rascal," she snarled through clenched teeth.

"Now, you got yourself in this fix, ma'am." He smiled, but he got up, pulled her to her feet, and jerked her shirt closed. "I'm over here, boys, rescuin' the ungrateful lady."

She snorted in disgust.

Waco turned to face the trio riding up. "Anyone find the lady's horse?"

"We got her, but she's limpin' a little."

"Lady!" Rosemary forgot about herself and ran to examine her beloved mare.

"She'll be all right," Zeb said, "just needs not to be ridden for a while." Then he suddenly seemed to notice the pair's appearance. "What happened? Fall in the mud?"

"Not exactly." Waco winked at her and she wanted to brain him. "Tom, you lead the lady's horse and we'll double up on mine."

"I will not ride with you!" She whirled on him.

"Excuse me, ma'am," Zeke said respectfully, touching the brim of his hat, "but none of us three would cotton to takin' on a rider as muddy as you."

"Now that's a fact," nodded his brother.

"See?" Waco said and held out his hand. "Come on, Rosie, I'm as muddy as you are, so I don't mind."

"I do mind." She crossed her arms and glared at him.

"Well, I reckon you can walk back to camp," Waco said agreeably. "Come on, boys."

He mounted up.

"You—you're going to let me walk? Sir, you are no gentleman."

"I offered. You expect me to give you my horse and me walk?"

"No, I'd like to drag you behind it!" she snapped.

"Look, it's gettin' daylight," Waco said patiently as if speaking to a small child. "Them guerillas might come back, so we need to get out of here. Make up your mind."

There was a long moment of silence. She certainly didn't want to walk. "All right. I will share a horse with you."

"Damned nice of you," Waco grinned, "since it's my horse."

She glared at all four of the men, then put her nose in the air and sloshed through the mud with as much dignity as she could manage to Waco's horse. He held out his hand and she took it. He lifted her lightly up on the saddle before him. She could feel his warm, naked chest through the shirt and into her back. For a split second, she remembered the feel of his chest against her breasts, flesh against flesh. She didn't like the emotions those images brought to her mind, so she sat up very straight and tried not to let her body touch his. This was impossible, of course, because he had to reach around her to handle the reins. The other three turned and rode out and Waco urged his horse to follow.

She could feel his warm breath against her neck as he pulled her closer. "Relax, Miss Rosemary, it's a long ride back to the cabin." His arm went around her waist and she liked the power and the heat of it against her bare flesh. She looked down, realized the shirt was not buttoned, and jerked it closed.

"I've already seen them," he whispered against her hair. "Nice ones, too."

"Sir," she muttered, "I hope the sheriff catches you and hangs you from the nearest tree."

"Aw, you don't mean that."

"I do. In fact, I'd volunteer to kick the box out from under you and stay to watch your feet jerk."

"I don't reckon it matters. I'm bound to hang, might as well be here as there."

"What do you mean?" She turned her head slightly to look at him in the growing light. He didn't look as if he were joking.

"Never mind, Miss Rosemary, it ain't your problem."

"I'd say you've made it my problem by kidnapping me."

"Well, we were desperate for cash and thought your anxious father would send the money right away."

"Not likely."

"Maybe he don't have that much," Waco suggested against her hair. "Maybe we need to give him more time."

"Don't bet on it," she snapped.

"What?"

"Never mind." She had said too much. She was certain Godfrey wouldn't send the money, and if these men knew it, they'd—they'd—she wasn't certain what they'd do. She didn't want to speculate on that now.

She had meant to watch the landscape and see if she recognized anything as they rode back through the wet dawn to the cabin, but she was wet and cold and Waco's arms were so warm and strong. She had never felt so protected as she did in his embrace. In spite of herself, she dozed off as they traveled.

Rosemary awoke with a start as Waco reined in.

"Whoa, hoss," he said quietly. "Oh, I didn't mean to wake you."

"I'm okay." She struggled to sit up and looked around. They were back at the cabin now. She'd missed whatever chance she might have had to figure out where she was so she could escape back to Prairie View later.

"Here, Tom," Waco said, "take my horse and I'll get her inside."

Tom took his reins and Waco dismounted, held up his arms for her. She slid off into his arms without thinking and looked up at him. The dog ran around their legs.

"Are you cold?" Waco asked.

"The sun's coming out," she snapped, "and I'm warming up."

"We're both a muddy mess. I'll see what we've

got to put on and we'll go down to the river and wash up."

"Not with you." She protested and struggled until he stood her on her feet.

He smiled. "You got mud on your face, *señorita.*"

"I wouldn't have if it weren't for you. I'd be home hosting a morning tea for the young ladies of the town."

"Sounds dull," he answered and wiped at her face.

"Don't touch me." She stepped backward.

"You could be a little sweet," he complained and pushed his Stetson to the back of his head. "I just saved you from a fate worse than death."

"And whose fault is it I was in that spot?" She flounced off down to the river.

"You could be some grateful," he called after her. She didn't answer.

"I'll be down in a minute," he yelled, "soon as I find something for us to wear."

She whirled, annoyed with him. "Why? Is there another scarecrow to steal clothes from?"

"That smarts." He winked at her and disappeared into the cabin.

Rosemary sat down on the river bank and ran her fingers through her hair. It was a muddy mess. She must look a sight. She leaned over and looked at her reflection in the water. It was worse than she had thought. If her mother could see Rosemary, she'd roll over in her grave. At least she didn't have to wear that terrible corset anymore.

Waco ambled down to the water, carrying faded clothes over his arm. "The boys is lookin' after the horses. I found a blanket to wrap you in after you wash up and another old shirt and pants."

"The ladies of Kansas City and St. Louis would be so envious of my fashionable wardrobe," she snarled.

"What?" He sat down next to her, looking puzzled.

"Never mind." He obviously didn't understand sarcasm. "I just wish I had a decent dress, that's all." She took the blanket and the faded shirt and pants.

"I'm sorry." He shook his head. "I got to go after supplies later. Maybe I can find something for you."

"What? Going to steal more clothes off some poor farmer's clothesline?" She glared at him.

"I know you're upset, Rosie, and I don't blame you—"

"Upset? Upset?" Her voice rose. "Now why would you think I'd be upset? And don't call me Rosie."

"All right." He smiled at her, thinking she was pretty even with her hair caked with mud and her face all smudged. He thought he understood her as no one ever had. Maybe no one had ever really loved and appreciated this girl. "Let's wash off a little and then maybe the boys will have some grub ready."

She backed away. "If you think you get to watch me wash—"

"No, you go off down behind those bushes," Waco motioned.

"You planning to watch?"

"Texans would never stoop to that."

"Only if they got a chance!" she said and rose and walked toward the bushes with a huff.

Frankly, he wished he could watch her undress

and bathe. He thought every inch of her was desirable, from her generous breasts to her dimpled knees. He leaned back on one elbow to pull off his boots and discovered that that position gave him a small view of her disrobing. He knew Texans shouldn't spy on a naked lady, but he just couldn't help himself. As she peeled the muddy clothes off, he got an eyeful of creamy white flesh and voluptuous curves. She was a lotta woman, more than enough for any man. Waco sighed wistfully. Well, this wasn't doing any good. He might as well clean up himself and get ready to eat. He pulled his boots and his muddy clothes off, dove into the river, and came up dog-paddling. The water felt cold and good. He could hear Rosemary splashing in the shallows.

"You need any help?" he called.

"Don't you wish!" She snorted and continued to splash behind the bushes.

"Don't say I didn't offer," he yelled and dived deep, enjoying the current pulling at him. He swam and dived, then took his bar of soap in the shallows and washed himself, standing in knee-deep water. Then he submerged himself and came up, shaking his head like a dog. "I'm about finished, Rosie. What about you?"

"I'm not coming out until you head back to the cabin," she called.

"Okay, I can take the hint." He grinned as he leaned over, picked up his denim pants, and put them on. "I think the boys might have some food ready. I'm going up to the cabin."

She stuck her head out of the bush and watched him sauntering away, bare-chested and carrying his boots. He had a few scars, she noted, but he was deep-chested and powerful without his shirt. She remembered what it had felt like to be held against that bare chest as they rode, and a little shiver went up her back. She must not be attracted to her kidnapper, that would be absolutely stupid. Rosemary pulled on the oversized and faded pants and shirt and tried to wring the water out of her long hair. She must look a sight. What would Major Mathis say? Rosemary gathered up her muddy clothes and walked back into the cabin.

"Oh, there you are." Tom looked up suddenly and all conversation ceased. She had a definite feeling that she had interrupted conversation about herself. Were they thinking of letting her go? Killing her? Somehow, she didn't think so. In fact, she smiled to herself, she thought they weren't quite sure what to do with her if Godfrey wouldn't pay the ransom.

Zeb and Zeke had opened some beans and made some coffee.

She looked the food over. "Is this all we have?"

Zeb snapped, "Well, we ain't exactly like a French chef, missy."

"Stop it, you two," Waco sighed. "I'll go into town later and see what I can find."

"Prairie View?" she asked.

"None of your business," Waco answered. "Anyone got any money?"

Zeke and Zeb between them came up with eight pennies.

"We're all about out," Tom said. "I think I got a couple of dimes."

"We got anything we can trade?" Zeb asked.

"I got my silver spurs," Waco said.

"Naw, Waco, don't trade them off," young Tom protested, "them's the finest spurs in Texas."

Waco shrugged. "We need supplies more than I need a pair of silver spurs."

Rosemary snorted. "I guess I can forget about some decent clothes."

Waco looked embarrassed. "I'll see what I can do," he told her. He pulled out his watch and checked the time. "I'll be back directly. Now boys, you keep a good eye on her, you can't trust her. She's slippery as calf slobber."

"Thanks a lot," she snapped.

"We'll keep her from runnin' off," Zeke said.

"Good." Waco went out to saddle up his horse. "I'll be back after while."

Rosemary watched him swing up in the saddle and ride out. With only a handful of change and a pair of spurs to trade, she figured they'd be eating beans again tonight.

The men must have felt the same.

Tom sighed. "I think I'll set some snares," he said to no one in particular. "Maybe I can get us a fat rabbit."

Rosemary didn't say anything. Perhaps while Waco was gone, she'd get another chance to escape.

Chapter Sixteen

Waco had gathered up the little money they had, and taking a circular route as he rode out, headed into Prairie View. The town was quiet for a late October afternoon, leaves turning red and gold, a spotted hound dog asleep in the street. People came and went from the bank, and the other stores seemed to be doing a good business.

Waco watched for soldiers or lawmen, but no one seemed to pay him any attention as he reined up in front of the general store and dismounted. He thought there ought to be some reward posters up around town about the missing heiress, but he saw nothing but a farm auction sign and several announcing a big Halloween celebration on Main Street. Was the month that close to ending? He'd lost track of the days. Waco tied up his horse and almost collided with a small, freckled-face boy pushing a hoop on the wooden sidewalk. Through the big window across the street, Waco could see the elegant banker working behind his desk.

"Hey, son," he said to the boy, "how'd you like to make five cents?"

The boy eyed him critically. "Make it a dime."

"Gawd Almighty, you Yanks drive a hard bargain. Okay, a dime it is." He pulled a scrap of paper from his pocket and a stub of pencil. "I want you should take a note to the banker."

"Gimme the dime first." The freckled-face urchin held out a grubby hand.

Waco finished scribbling and gave him the note and the dime. "I'll wait here for an answer."

"That old grouch probably won't give you one. He ain't give anyone an answer so far."

"Just take him the note," Waco ordered.

Godfrey St. John looked up to see that same dirty urchin in his office. "What do you want this time?"

"Another note."

"This is getting ridiculous," Godfrey complained and held out his hand.

"Gimme a dime first."

"Highway robbery," Godfrey grumbled and handed over the dime, then grabbed the note. "What are you waiting for, kid?"

"He said bring back a reply."

Godfrey read the note: *We still have ur dotter. We will take $5,000 for her or we might kil her. Giv the boy ur ansir. Signed Desperiate Men.*

Godfrey almost threw his head back and laughed. If Rosemary wasn't at the bottom of all this, the kidnappers deserved to be stuck with her. Evidently, she was wearing thin on them or they wouldn't keep lowering the amount.

"What about an answer?" the boy asked.

Godfrey didn't even care enough to stand up

and walk to the window to see if he could figure out who sent the note. "Tell the man he should give *me* five thousand dollars to relieve him of his problem."

"That don't make no sense," the boy said.

"Tell him that anyway," Godfrey snapped. He was getting weary of this charade.

The boy shrugged and went out of his office.

Waco stood at the hitching post across the street patting his horse when the boy ran up. "Okay, what did he say?"

"Gimme a dime first."

"Dammit it, I ain't got another dime, you little bandit."

"Well, it don't make no sense, but he said you should give him five thousand dollars for him to take your problem off your hands."

Waco blinked. "Are you sure that's what he said?"

"Yep." The boy nodded. "And he was grinning, too."

"Okay, thanks. That explains a lot." Waco shook his head and ambled up the steps toward the general store. Actually, it made no sense at all. The banker didn't want his darling daughter back? In fact, he wanted Waco to pay him to take her? Waco had to admit she was difficult, but this turn he couldn't understand. He walked into the store.

A plump old man with bushy eyebrows and a dirty white apron greeted him from behind the counter. "Howdy, stranger, you new to these parts?"

"Uh, just passin' through," Waco drawled. "I need a side of bacon, some coffee and corn meal, yes, and some tobacco. That is, if you'll take a trade. I'm a little down on my luck." He laid the silver spurs and what change he had on the counter.

"Hmm." The old man rubbed his hands together and picked up the spurs. "These look like real silver."

"They are. I've had better days, but now I'm lean as a starvin' fox. I can live without silver spurs, but not food."

The old man nodded sympathetically and began pulling boxes from the shelves.

Waco leaned against the counter and said casually, "Nice little town. Anything much happenin' around here?"

"Naw." The old man paused in digging through the shelves. "New fort has brought some soldiers in, and there's a spellin' bee at the school tonight. Of course, there's the big Halloween celebration coming up. Half the county and all the soldiers will be in town for that, I guess."

Strange, Waco thought. *Everyone should still be talking about the kidnapped heiress.* "Looks like a busy bank across the street."

"It is." The storekeeper nodded as he tied the purchases up with a string. "Banker's daughter came back to town couple of weeks ago. She's been in Europe."

"You don't say? I ain't never been as far as Kansas City myself." Waco grinned.

"Me neither, but then, that family's rich."

"She pretty, too?"

The storekeeper paused. "Well, she's a mite plump for my taste, and a handful, if gossip is to be believed. 'Course, she's not in town right now."

Waco's ears perked up. "Oh?"

"Nope. The banker says she's gone to Thackerville to visit a girlfriend. He hinted the other day that she'd met a fella and might elope with him."

"Is that a fact?" Had Waco grabbed the wrong girl?

"Is there two daughters?"

"Nope, just the one, Rosemary." The old man wiped his hands on his apron. "Anything else for you, young fella?"

Waco shook his head. He barely had enough to pay for what he'd bought. He'd like some canned peaches or tomatoes, but there was no money for that. He picked up his package and started to leave, then noticed a dress hanging on a rack. It was a blue-flowered print with lace around the collar and cuffs. He thought of Rosemary in his ragged faded shirt. "That's mighty purty."

"Ain't it, though?" the other man agreed. "Little big for most of the young ladies around here."

"I got a gal back home who might could wear that." Waco hesitated. He didn't have any more money, but that dress would look so pretty on Rosemary. He imagined the smile on her face when she saw it. "I reckon she'd need the lace drawers, stockings, and whatever else a gal would want, maybe a blue hair ribbon to go with it."

"Shoes?"

Waco shook his head. "Reckon just those things might add up. She's got nice ridin' boots."

"It do add up," agreed the old man.

Waco considered. He was ashamed that his kidnapped lady looked so poor and raggedy. "I don't have any more money. Would you consider another trade?"

The old man looked interested. "What you got to offer?"

It was a big sacrifice, but Waco wanted her to

have that dress, wanted to see the light in her eyes when he gave it to her. He reached into his pocket

Back at the cabin, Rosemary wandered down to the river and sat under a tree with Prince. She looked toward the corral, but Zeke was working in the barn and was keeping a close eye on the horses. She remembered the way it had felt to be in Waco's arms when he rescued her. *Are you crazy?* she scolded herself. *You wouldn't have been in that mess if it hadn't been for him and his friends.* He didn't seem like an outlaw, but then she'd never met a real outlaw, so how would she know? It had been as if Lancelot had come riding through the boulders to rescue her, and she'd felt so warm and safe in his embrace.

She patted the dog as she heard a step behind her and turned. "Oh, hello, Tom."

He stood first on one foot and then the other, Stetson in hand. "Am I botherin' you, Miss Rosemary?"

"Not at all." *What does he want?*

"May I set a spell?"

She motioned to him to do so.

"I want to apologize personally for us kidnappin' you," he said and his freckled face turned red as his hair.

"That's okay." She nodded. "I don't suppose it was really your idea."

"We started out to rob the bank, but when we seen that there was a lot of soldiers in town, we decided we'd never get away with it. Waco said it wasn't gentlemanly to kidnap a lady, but we had to have the money."

She gave him a warm smile. "Tom, why do you all need so much money?"

"I—I can't tell you that." He shook his head.

"Fifty thousand dollars is a lot to divide among four men. You could live nicely on a lot less."

"Oh, it ain't for us," Tom blurted, "but our lives depend on gettin' it."

That baffled her. "Why?"

"I can't talk about that, ma'am." Again his face turned cherry red. "Do you think your daddy will send any money so we can go back to Texas?"

She didn't think Godfrey would send a penny, but she couldn't admit that. "What happens if he doesn't?"

"We ain't thought that far ahead. Oh, Waco might have. We're in big trouble."

She reached out and put her hand on Tom's hand. "Want to talk about it?"

He shook his head and scooted a little farther from her. "I can't, ma'am. I just wanted to tell you I'm sorry and wondered if things were different, would you have let Waco call on you?"

Every young man who had ever expressed an interest in calling on her had been after the bank's money. "You're so nice, Tom, but you see, things aren't different. It's hard to think about such things when I'm being held prisoner."

"Is there some sweetheart?" He fumbled with his hat.

"Oh, no, I'm afraid all the young men I know are looking for a prettier girl."

"You are pretty," he declared loyally. "Why, Waco

says you got the purtiest eyes he ever saw and he likes a sturdy gal."

"Does he now? I figured Waco had lots of women who'd marry him."

"Oh, they chase after him all right, but Waco don't trust women. Not after that one broke his heart. She run off with another man while Waco was in Kentucky—"

"What was he doing in Kentucky?"

"We was all there, but I can't talk about that neither." He shook his head.

She worked that puzzle over in her mind. What were these four all doing off in Kentucky? Maybe they'd been over there buying blooded horses. *In the middle of a war?* No, it had to have something to do with the war.

Tom looked up. "Oh, here comes Waco." He stood and pointed.

She turned her head and saw Waco riding to the cabin. Tom and the dog went to meet him. Prince wagged his tail and licked Waco's hand. "Traitor," she whispered.

She decided to stay where she was as he dismounted and went into the cabin. After a few minutes, he strolled down to the river, carrying a small parcel. "Rosie, I got something for you."

"My name is Rosemary," she replied in an icy tone. "Besides, I thought there was just barely enough money for bacon and flour?"

"There was." He sat down next to her and tossed the package in her lap. "But I saw this and knew it would look pretty on you."

Puzzled, she began to open the package. "What is it? Did you steal something?"

"I beg your pardon." He was noticeably offended. "I'm not a thief."

"You were planning on robbing a bank," she pointed out as she ripped open the package and saw what it held. "Oh, why, it's lovely." She held the dress up, deeply touched by his thoughtfulness.

"You don't have to be polite if'n you don't like it," he murmured, red-faced.

"No, it's beautiful, and there's everything to go with it. Where'd you get the money?"

"Never you mind," he said gruffly. "Now, I'll keep the fellas away from the water and you clean up some for supper. There's a hair ribbon, too."

Tears came to her eyes. She wasn't certain how he had managed this, but it was evident he wasn't used to buying things for women. He was too shy and embarrassed. "Thank you, Waco."

"My given name is Will," he said.

"Well, thank you, Will."

"I like the way you say my name," he said then got up and walked swiftly back to the cabin.

She got some soap and a towel and spread the new clothes out on the grass. She washed herself and her hair in the river, then toweled off and put on the new clothes. Her riding boots would have to do. She brushed the mud from them. Dusk was settling in as she walked up to the cabin.

The men were all sitting around the table drinking coffee when she walked in and they stared, then stumbled to their feet.

Tom gulped. "Why, ma'am, you look purtier than a speckled pup in a red wagon."

"Purtier than an ace-high straight," Zeb said.

"Thank you, boys." She smiled at Waco, who was

staring at her with his mouth open. "Will, what do you think?"

"Beautiful," he whispered and his eyes widened. "I'm glad I done it now."

She felt small and dainty as she whirled around the enthused men. "I do feel pretty." She smiled at all of them.

"You *are* pretty," Waco said with conviction. "Lucky the man who marries you."

"I don't know where you got the money, but thank you anyway." She sat down at the table and saw the men exchange glances, but no one said anything. Maybe he had stolen the dress off someone's clothesline? No, this dress was new, there was no doubt about it.

"I reckoned I owed you something for snatchin' you," Waco said.

Zeke stood up. "I almost got dinner done. We got stew made from some vegetables we took out of that farmer's garden and a rabbit Zeb shot this morning."

Zeb jumped up. "I'll help you, brother."

Tom said, "I got time to look after the horses before we eat?"

"If you hurry," Zeke said.

Waco nodded. "Put my horse away, would you, Tom?"

"Yes, sir." Tom went outside, Prince tagging along behind.

"It seems my dog likes you and all your friends," Rosemary said.

"Wish you did," Waco said and looked away.

That made for an awkward silence that left Waco and Rosemary sitting at the table looking at each other. It was fast getting dark. Zeb went over and began tinkering with the oil lamp. She reached across the table and took Waco's hand. "It was thoughtful of you."

"Glad to do it, Miss Rosie." He ducked his head shyly and hesitated, then squeezed her fingers. "It goes with your eyes, and I like your hair done up with ribbons that way."

He really was a big, virile man. If only he weren't an outlaw. In her mind, they were riding away from a bank together, the posse shooting at them.

She was Sadie, the Outlaw Queen, riding along with this handsome outlaw. *Even if they string us up,* the Outlaw Queen sighed as they galloped away, *it was worth it for the moments I spent in your arms.*

I love you, I love you, my beauty, he yelled to her as they galloped through the cactus, the posse gaining on them, *and I'd do it all again for your love. I hope they allow me one last, precious kiss before I die.*

"Would you like some cornbread, miss?" Zeke nudged her shoulder and she started, came out of her daydream. Waco held her hand and she realized she had puckered up and he was staring at her.

"Uh, yes, of course." She pulled her hand away and felt as embarrassed as Waco looked. In minutes, everyone gathered around the table as they ate.

"Cornbread makes me think of the night my mother died," she said.

"Oh?" Waco said. "Why would you remember that?"

She shrugged as she dipped into the hot, savory stew. "Because we never had it. I was away at school, but I was told Doc Graham came to dinner and he liked beans and cornbread so Mother was humoring him, even eating some herself. She thought it was so country and not at all something upper-class people should eat."

"What happened to your ma?" Tom asked.

Tears came to her eyes. "Doc said later that night, she went into spasms of pain. He thought it must be acute appendicitis. She lingered on for several days before she died. I didn't even get home for the funeral. Of course, Doc's not a very good doctor, but he's the only one in town."

"Maybe bad food?" Zeke said.

"No, they all ate the same thing, and no one else got sick," Rosemary said. "In fact, Doc said Mother liked the pinto beans so well, Godfrey went into the kitchen and got her another helping."

"I'm sorry about your mother," Waco said.

"We didn't get along too well." She sighed and returned to her food. "I think she was disappointed in me."

Waco looked at her. "I don't know why anyone would be disappointed in havin' a daughter like you," Waco said, and he looked sincere.

They finished eating in silence and Tom started to pick up the plates, gather the scraps for the dog.

"No, wait, let me clean up the dishes," Rosemary protested and got up.

"I'll help you," Waco said. "You got fine hands, they shouldn't get all rough."

Actually, she found she liked helping out. She wondered if she could learn to cook. Was she out of her mind? Cook for a bunch of outlaws?

Zeke got out his harmonica. "With a pretty lady like this one, I think we need a dance." He began to play a Stephen Foster tune, "Jeannie with the Light Brown Hair."

"Play something a little more lively," Tom said and bowed before Rosemary. "Miss Rosemary, may I have this dance?"

She smiled and nodded, and Tom took her in his arms awkwardly. "I won't break," she said.

Tom didn't dance too well, but he tried. Then she danced with Zeb. Waco sat at the table and watched them. She paused in front of him as Zeb ceased playing. "Aren't you going to ask me to dance?"

"I reckon," he said and stood up, grinning shyly.

She went into his arms as Zeke played a slow country waltz. Waco was a big, powerful man, she thought as his arms went around her and she put her hand in his strong one. He made her feel so tiny and pretty. She could feel his warm breath against her hair and his heart beating against her breast. He danced her around the room slowly and she relaxed and rested her face against his shoulder. After a while, Zeke stopped playing, but they kept on dancing. She could stay in this man's arms forever, she thought, but of course that was only if things were different. No man could really love her, she was heavy and plain. Hadn't her mother said so? She couldn't trust any man to really love her; they were all after her money.

Dimly, she heard Tom say, "What time is it, anyway?"

Waco paused and felt in his pocket, then frowned. "What difference does it make?"

She waited for Waco to pull out his gold watch, but he didn't. Instead, he shrugged.

"Waco, what happened to your watch?" she asked.

"Uh, I lost it." He took her hand and led her out of the cabin into the darkness.

"Lost it? Gracious, then we need to go look for it. That watch was real gold."

"It was; belonged to my grandfather." They paused under a tree and he put his arm around her shoulders as they looked toward the river.

"Then we need to look—"

"Rosie," he murmured and shook his head. "I—I didn't have enough money for the bacon and stuff."

"You traded it?"

"Well, I told the storekeeper I might redeem it sometime, along with my silver spurs."

Sudden realization came to her and she felt both guilt and horror. "You traded it for that dress for me, didn't you?"

"It don't matter none." He shrugged.

She was deeply touched. "But it was your grandfather's watch."

"Forget it. You needed a dress more'n I needed to know the time."

"Now I feel terrible about it."

"Maybe after the war, I'll ride into Prairie View and buy it back."

That wasn't too likely. He had let go of the thing he valued most to get a dress for her. "I wouldn't have let you do it if I had known."

He tilted her chin up to look deep into her eyes. "It was my watch. I didn't need to get permission."

"I never expected you would do that."

"I know, but you were so ragged and the dress looks purty on you, so I'm happy." There was a long silence and then he said, "Rosie, if things were different—"

"Yes?" She waited.

"Oh, I don't reckon it makes no never mind. You'll be goin' home if your pa decides to pay the ransom. Funny thing, though, I was in town and it was as if no one knew you were gone. Why would your pa be tellin' everyone that you were over at Thackerville visitin' a friend?"

A chill went up her back. "I—I have something I ought to tell you, Waco. Maybe he's creating an alibi."

Waco blinked, looking down at her. "What are you gettin' at?"

She might as well tell him the whole truth. "I don't think he has any intention of paying the ransom; he's surely thrilled to think I might be murdered. If I die, he inherits the bank. If I don't come back, he'll tell everyone I went back to school or ran off with some boy and got married."

"So that explains what happened today." Waco sounded annoyed as he sat down under a tree.

"I—I was afraid you'd do me in."

"Well, I couldn't hurt a woman," he admitted. "But now I don't know what to do with you."

"You could just let me go."

"That doesn't solve our money problem." He ran his hand through his hair. "And what about you? Send you back to a man who cares so little, he'd rather we murder you than pay a ransom?"

"I think I could deal with Godfrey." But she wasn't so sure.

Waco sighed. "Now what? I reckon we could

just ride for the border and let you go when we got there."

"What about the money?" she asked.

He shrugged. "So we don't get it. I don't know what we'll do."

She put her hand on his arm. "Waco, tell me what kind of trouble you all are in."

He shook his head. "It's not your problem."

"You don't trust me with the truth?"

He looked at her and finally admitted, "I don't trust women, Rosie, and you couldn't do anything about it anyhow."

"Waco, I'm not like that girl who ran off with another man."

His head jerked up, his pale blue eyes wide. "How can I know for sure?"

"Never mind. I'm just tellin' you you can trust me."

He laughed without mirth. "Don't make me laugh. Turn my back and you're stealin' a horse, tryin' to escape, but I can't really blame you none for that."

"Well, looks like we either trust one another or forget it."

He twisted his hands together. "So I reckon the laugh's on us and we got to ride back to Texas without the money."

"Who needs that money, Waco?" she asked, her voice soft.

"I might as well tell you. We've all been sentenced to a firin' squad for disobeyin' orders."

"As Rebels?"

He nodded. "Confederates, not rebels. That's a Yankee term. And we're out of uniform, so if the

Union troops get us, we'll be shot as spies. Don't reckon it matters which side shoots us."

Quickly, he told her the story. "So you see, we disobeyed orders on shootin' the black troops. The South is desperate for food and supplies, even for boots. If we don't come back with the money, they'll put us before a firin' squad."

"Is this true?" It was a wild, unbelievable story.

"Sorry to say it is. And there's a deadline; mid-November."

"I wish I could help you," she murmured.

He shrugged. "I'm sorry we dragged you into this by kidnappin' you, but the bank was too surrounded by Yankee troops to rob it."

She put her hand on his shoulder. "So now what will you do?"

He turned and looked at her. "Head for the south Kansas border tomorrow, I reckon. When we get there, we'll free you and you can go home."

"Why don't you just leave me when you ride out?"

"And have you go back to town and have a posse hot on our trail by tomorrow night?"

"I—I don't think I'd do that," she whispered.

He shook his head. "Can't take the chance. Anyway, I wouldn't blame you none."

"You could just head for California or some place."

He shook his head. "Rosie, I gave the colonel my word we'd return. If a man's word is no good, he ain't much of a man."

"But they're going to shoot you," she reminded him.

"Well, they ain't shot us yet. Maybe something lucky will happen." He put his arm around her shoulders. "If things had been different . . ." he began.

"Yes?"

"Oh, never mind. I don't have the money or the social position for a girl like you."

Was he stringing her along? Hadn't her mother always told her it was lucky Rosemary was rich or she'd never get a husband? She had no idea if he wanted her or not, but she'd heard men were not too choosy when they needed a woman. If she could seduce him, would he free her?

She turned in his arms and looked up into his face. "What if things were different? What if I could get you the money you need?"

"There's no use talkin' about that again. I don't believe you."

He didn't trust women and he wouldn't believe her. On the other hand, suppose she gave him the money and he took it and deserted her? She wanted to, but she didn't quite trust him either.

She felt like the weepy heroine in one of her romantic novels. She didn't want to see this man or any of his friends shot, but she needed to escape. Perhaps she could seduce him into letting her go. "We seem to be caught in a tumultuous time. Perhaps we need to grab all the pleasure we can, for who knows what will happen tomorrow?" She ran her hand gently over his rough-hewn, tanned face. "There's a poem I read—'Had we but world enough and time . . .'"

"But we don't." Both his big hands came up to cup her face. "You're a lady, Rosie, and someday you'll marry a highborn man who deserves a beauty like you."

"You really think I'm beautiful?" She felt the tears overflowing her eyes.

"Yes, I do. And if I had money and didn't have a death sentence hangin' over my head, I'd ask you to marry me and go back to Texas with me."

She hadn't meant to kiss him, but she did. She would seduce this man and he would let her go. Then he and his friends would escape and ride away into the sunset. The kiss deepened as he pulled her to him and she opened her lips and let him kiss her deeply, his tongue exploring her mouth as she put her hands on the back of his strong, corded neck. "I—I think I'm fallin' in love with you, Will."

"Don't say that," he murmured against her lips. "This is a big enough mess already." He kissed her eyes and her cheeks and came back to her mouth. She let him press her back against the soft grass as the kiss deepened again. "I can't promise you, anything, Rosie, even if I trusted you. I'm a sergeant in the Confederate army under a death sentence and in enemy territory, and you're a rich Yankee girl."

"I'm not interested in the war. I don't care which side wins." And she kissed him again. "I wouldn't turn you in."

He wished he could trust her, he wanted so badly to trust her, but he knew she would say anything to escape. He wanted to make love to her, desperately needed to make love to this voluptuous, vibrant woman. He kissed along the hollow of her throat. "We—we need to go back inside," he murmured but he didn't move, waiting for her to agree and get up off the grass, but instead, she pulled him down to her.

She wasn't sure what to do next, but he was older and more experienced; surely he would know. She reached to unbutton the top button of his shirt, stroked there with featherlike strokes. He caught his breath and seemed to shudder.

"Do you like that, Will?"

"You little scamp, you know I do. We ought to go in, Rosie."

She reached up and put her hands on the back of his neck. "Just a few more minutes. The cabin is so crowded."

He sighed deeply and kissed her again, his mouth trailing down the side of her neck. She could feel the warm dew of his lips against the beating vein in her throat. She began to unbutton the tiny pearl buttons at the neck of her blue-flowered dress.

"You shouldn't do that," he warned, but his lips followed her hands down as she unbuttoned the pearl buttons and paused in the hollow of her throat.

Her heart seemed to be beating so wildly, she was certain he could feel it as his mouth touched the rise of her breasts. "I know you've been wanting to kiss these for ages," she whispered and pulled her lace petticoat down.

"Oh, Rosie," he moaned, and then his two big hands cupped her breasts and he kissed her nipples over and over again.

In the moonlight, she could see his rugged face, his eyes closed as he kissed and caressed her breasts. She hadn't realized it would feel so good, so exhilarating. "More," she demanded, "more!"

His mouth went to her nipple and he ran his

tongue over the tip until her nerves seemed to be screaming for more touch, more caress, more kisses. She breathed hard as she felt his hand go to her thigh, pushing her skirt up. She ought to object. She knew it, but her mouth couldn't seem to form the words. No lady would be making love under a tree to some outlaw who might or might not have told her the truth about being a enemy officer, but she didn't feel like a lady. Tonight, she was Sadie, the Outlaw Queen, making love to her paramour.

"Rosie, I want you more than you know, Rosie . . ." His hand was hot as he pushed up her skirt and pulled at her lace drawers. His hand stroked and pulled at them and then his fingers were inside, touching her, stroking her in a way no man had ever touched her before. She was trembling so hard, she was sure he could feel it as he caressed between her thighs, and she wanted him as much as he wanted her.

"Will," she whispered, "if I let you, will you let me go?"

It was the wrong thing to say, she knew immediately. He jerked up, his blue eyes bright with hot anger in the moonlight. "So this is it, then? You don't care about me? You're wantin' to trade your favors to escape?"

"Well, I—"

"I thought you were a lady, not a slut. I thought you really might care about me. No sale, sister." He stood up, rearranging his clothes. "And to think I was ready to believe anything you told me."

"But, Will—"

"Let's go back to the cabin." He reached out,

jerked her to her feet, and started walking back, almost dragging her with his long strides.

"I didn't lie to you," she protested, trying to keep up with his long legs. "I did want you to make love to me."

"At least a whore would be honest," he thundered as they headed up the hill. "I don't like to be laughed at."

She sighed as they went inside. She'd tried to seduce him and made a mess of it. Now things were worse than before.

Chapter Seventeen

Rosemary and Waco interrupted the three men's conversation as the two entered the cabin.

"What—?" Tom began, but then she saw Zeb nudge him into silence.

"I—I think I'll bed down," she stammered and climbed up the ladder to the loft and watched what happened below.

"What happened out there?" she heard Zeke ask.

"None of your damn business," Waco growled. "She tried to—oh, never mind."

"Waco, you better remember she's a lady," Zeb warned.

"She ain't actin' like one," Waco said. "Willin' to trade her favors for—"

"Whoee! If'n she made me an offer like that," Tom whooped, "I'd give her anything she wanted."

"Oh, shut your pie hole," Waco snapped, "or I'll shut it for you. We got to keep our mind on what we came for."

"You're the one who needs that sermon, not us," Zeke said.

"If I believe her, and I'm not sure I do, her pa ain't gonna give us any money to get her back, no matter what. In fact, we might have to pay him to take her off our hands." Waco paced up and down below her, the yellow dog following his every step.

"What? Then we're wastin' time here," Tom said. "We need to figure out something else. We're runnin' out of time."

"You think I don't know that?" Waco snarled, turning on him. "I just can't believe her pa would let us murder her to keep from payin' any ransom. It's a rich bank."

Up in the loft, Rosemary shuddered at the words. She had never really thought they intended to hurt her. She shook her head. No, she was certain that Waco was deep inside a caring, tender man. She remembered the way he had kissed her and sighed. If only she had kept silent, he would be making love to her right now.

My word, are you out of your mind? Do you think you're the daffy heroine in one of your novels? That thought soothed her and she lay down on the cot and stared out the broken window at the big harvest moon. She had wanted to be made love to as Lancelot would have made love to Queen Guinevere or Sadie, the Outlaw Queen, both much more slender and desirable than she was. Waco was wanting to make love to her, all right, but it was just because there was no one else around, no gorgeous, thin saloon girl. Funny, Rosemary had felt so beautiful and beloved in his arms.

Money. The ransom. Did she trust him enough to give him the money? How long until Halloween? Quickly she got up and checked the scratches on the timber in the moonlight. By her calculations, day after tomorrow was the thirty-first. There was only one thing to do. Tomorrow, she would tell Waco about the money again and make him believe her. Even if he didn't love her, she could save him from the firing squad.

That decided, she closed her eyes and became the heroine of one of her novels, making passionate love to the handsome hero who looked a lot like Waco. In her restless sleep, he took off her clothes and kissed her naked body all over. She awoke several times, wishing she slept in Waco's arms.

Godfrey awoke early, humming to himself as he dressed and went down to breakfast. Tomorrow was his stepdaughter's birthday and she had neither turned up nor had he been sent any more ransom notes after he'd sent that final message by that urchin. If she had been kidnapped, certainly the hapless strangers had killed her by now, or if she was sending the notes herself, she had decided she wasn't going to be able to squeeze any money out of Godfrey and was trying to decide what to do next. He hoped she was dead; that would save him the trouble of killing her.

As he finished breakfast and made ready to leave the house, Mollie caught him in the hallway. "All right, be honest with me, what have you done with Miss Rosemary?"

"Me?" He touched his silk tie in mock horror. "I haven't done anything, I tell you, she's away at Thackerville, visiting a friend."

"Aye, and I don't think I believe that." Mollie got

right up in his face. "I didn't pack her no clothes and I ain't seen nuthin' of any letters."

"I—I burned them after I read them. Besides, she says there's a young man that she's interested in and she might elope with him."

"A prominent society girl don't elope," Mollie said suspiciously.

"Now, dear," he reached out and patted her face, "you know how much I care about you. Maybe if she does elope, we can get married."

"I don't trust you no more. You think I don't hear that floorboard squeak when you sneak down the hall to that French maid's room?"

He made a mental note to get that squeaky board fixed. "Now, you're imagining that, my dear."

"If you've done something to Miss Rosemary, I ain't gonna be part of it," the little maid threatened. "I don't hold with murder."

"Me? Perish the thought. I'm late for the bank, dear. We'll talk more later." As he went out to his buggy, he decided that Mollie had become too much of a problem. He wondered who he could hire to kill her and get her out of his life before she talked. Life had become just too complicated.

That afternoon, Rosemary checked her marks on the post again. Yes, there was no mistaking it; today was the thirtieth. Tomorrow was her birthday. She came down the ladder and looked around. Tom was cleaning up the lunch dishes. "Where is everyone?"

"Zeb's in the barn and Zeke's off down the river fishing, which is what I intend to do as soon as I finish here. Fried catfish and hush puppies would be tasty."

"I guess it would," she said. "Where's Waco?"

He nodded toward the door. "Out by the river."

She went through the door and down the pasture to the river. Waco sat with his back to her, staring at the water. Bright red and gold leaves swirled from the trees and the wind had turned chilly. "We need to talk."

"Okay." He looked troubled.

"What are your plans?" She sat down beside him.

He looked at her in the blue-flowered dress and smiled. "I'm glad I bought you that. You look like a Texas girl now. I'll always remember the way you look at this moment, you know that? You're so pretty."

She looked into his pale blue eyes and realized he was sincere. "Thank you," she said. "You sound like you're ready to pull out."

He sighed. "I don't know what else to do, Rosie. I reckon the banker's called our bluff. We never intended to hurt you—no true Texan would harm a lady. I reckon before the weather turns any colder, we'd better head back down south."

"And face a firing squad?" She put her hand on his arm.

"I reckon, unless we stumbled into buried treasure on the way home. At least we'll die honorably. I hope you don't hold no grudge against us for keepin' you hostage all these days."

"Actually, it was sort of an adventure; most exciting thing that ever happened in my life. So you're going to turn me loose?"

He smiled and nodded. "You can come along

almost to the border, then we'll give you a map to get home so you can get on with your life."

She thought about her future and sighed. It seemed colorless and dull. She saw it stretching endlessly before her: running the bank, overseeing the big elegant house that she had never really liked. Suitors would call on her and she would suspect they were all after her money. These weeks had been the most exciting time she'd ever known. "Tell me about Texas."

He smiled, his thoughts obviously far away. "God's country; just ask any Texan. It's warm there most of the time, and I've got lots of pasture and thousands of cows, nice ranch house. After the war, it could make a family a nice livin' if I had a little money to fix the roof, build a bigger barn."

"And a wife?"

Waco frowned. "Well, the girl I thought was gonna look after a garden and sit beside the fire with me run off with another man. I never figured I'd find another gal I liked even better until I met you. I could see you on that ranch." He laughed without mirth. "Who am I foolin'? I couldn't expect a rich, spoiled gal like you to live on a ranch. It'd be a hard life."

"Not if you loved the girl and she loved you." Now that he would be leaving, she realized how much she would miss him and his friends.

"Anyway," he shrugged, "what difference does it make? I'm a condemned man now that our mission has failed."

"Waco, I've got something to tell you." She leaned close, thinking of that snug ranch house. Besides a garden, she'd also like a few chickens and a cow. "Tomorrow is my birthday."

"Sorry we ain't got a cake for you. You'd probably have a fancy party at home."

"That doesn't matter. What does matter is that on my twenty-first birthday, I inherit the bank and the big house and a bunch of cash."

"This is the same story you already told me. So what?" He looked guarded.

"Don't you understand? We'll ride into town, I'll claim my inheritance and give you the money."

"Oh, sure you will."

"I will," she insisted.

"Why are you just now makin' this offer?"

"Because I knew you wouldn't trust me or believe me."

"My mama didn't raise no fools, Rosie. I'm not stupid enough to ride into town and right into a bunch of soldiers who'll hang me from the nearest lamp post as a spy."

"I wouldn't turn you in," she insisted.

"After what we've put you through?" he snorted. "You'd just walk me right into the bank, hand over the money, and let me walk away without sending a posse after us?"

"I don't want to see you get hanged back in Texas."

He shook his head. "You don't think I believe that, do you?"

"I'm sorry you don't trust me, Will. I'd trust you."

"I've given you no reason to do so."

She laid her head against his shoulder. "I've grown to care about you, Will, and I'd do anything to help you and the boys."

"I wish I could believe that, Rosie." He pulled away from her and stood up. "I don't trust women, and all I see here is I'd be walkin' into a trap."

She felt tears welling up. "What can I do to make you trust me? Don't you care about me at all?"

He shifted his weight from one foot to the other. "It don't make no never-mind how I feel about you. I can't let my heart get in the way of my good sense."

"We've got to trust each other. Believe me when I say I'd like you to take me back to Texas with you." She looked up at him, tears trickling down her face.

"Don't start cryin' now. I can't bear to see you cry. I—I do care about you, Rosie, but maybe you shouldn't trust me, either. Supposin' I just said I'd marry you and after I got my hands on that money, I ran off and left you here in Kansas?"

"Love means trust, Will. We'd just have to trust that each of us is telling the truth and wants only the best for the other. Besides I don't think you'd do that." A small doubt surfaced in her mind. Yes, she'd be taking a chance, too. Would he take her money and then desert her, he and his friends laughing all the way back to Texas? Love means trust, and she realized she loved Will McClain.

"I don't want to talk about this anymore, it's *loco.*" Abruptly he turned and strode back to the cabin.

Rosemary watched him go and then she put her face in her hands and cried like one of the heroines in the novels she loved. *Lady Roxanna hears that her knight, having pledged his love, is riding away to the Crusades. He could have at least asked her to wait for him to return.*

Who was she fooling? She was plump and plain,

and Waco didn't really care about her. Maybe she could make him care. She took a deep breath and wiped her eyes. Tonight, she wanted him to make love to her, even if he was riding away tomorrow, never to see her again. She at least wanted to have one precious night of memories for all those dreary long years ahead of her as she ran the bank as a powerful and wealthy spinster. And every night, she would sit in her fine mansion and eat and eat to fill her loneliness.

That night, she and her dog stood out in the yard watching the sun sink slowly in the west. Waco came out to stand beside her. Without thinking, he put his arm around her shoulders. He cared for this girl, really cared, but he couldn't ask her to share the hard life he lived. And anyway, it appeared his days were numbered. He and the boys had failed to bring back the bank money to help the Confederacy. Because he had given his sacred word as a Texan, Waco had to return to face the colonel.

She looked up at him and he thought how soft her eyes were and how warm she felt standing next to him. "Will, what are you thinking?"

He leaned over impulsively and kissed the tip of her nose. "Nuthin' much." How could he tell her he was wondering how it would feel to have a firing squad's bullets piercing his heart? Would he have a brief second of pain or would he even feel it? "If things were different, Rosie, I would ask you to marry me and go back to Texas. We could have made a nice life on my ranch."

"Waco, I meant it about the money. Please trust me." She laid her face against his chest and he reached to stroke her brown hair.

"I said I was gonna turn you loose when we leave. You didn't have to offer me money."

"I'm not trying to buy my freedom," she insisted. "I'm trying to help you and the boys out of this mess."

He laughed softly. "Gawd Almighty, you really think you can just waltz into the bank after bein' gone for weeks and get a few thousand out, then leave without any explanation?"

"They'll want one, but I don't have to give it."

"Rosie, there's a big Halloween celebration and dance tomorrow night. The town will be full of people, especially soldiers."

"Are you afraid?" She looked up at him.

He held her close and watched the sun sink below the horizon as the sky became pink and purple. "No, I'm not afraid. I've battled Indians, Yankees, rattlesnakes, and grass fires. Nuthin' scares me much anymore."

"I think love does," she murmured. "Love scares you."

"Maybe it does," he admitted sheepishly. "I thought I had it once. In fact, I was so sure, I would have bet my ranch on it." They began to walk down the path.

"Are you not willing to bet your life on me?" she asked softly. "You think I would betray you?"

"I—I hope you wouldn't, Rosie, but how am I to know? If it was just me, I wouldn't think twice about takin' the chance, but I hate to get the boys ambushed. At least if the Rebs shoot us, we face death honorably like men, not shot down in the street like robbers."

The far sky was turning dark purple now, fading to black as twilight deepened into dark. They sat down under a tree.

She looked up at him, loving him, wanting him. "Waco," she sighed, "I think I trust you not to deceive me. If you can bring yourself to trust me, we can have a great future together."

"Rosie, you don't understand. I need fifty thousand dollars. That's a mountain of money."

"I think I've got that much," she insisted.

"What about the bank and your fancy life?"

"I don't care about any of that, although I'd like to fire Godfrey and turn the bank over to Mr. Wilkerson to run. He's honest and reliable."

"But you've got that fancy mansion—"

"I'd trade it for a little ranch house. Besides, if I fire him and leave town, I can legally turn the big mansion into an orphans' home."

He shook his head. "Let's not talk any more about this, okay? I haven't even mentioned it to the boys."

"Mention it to them," she whispered. "I think they all trust you to make the right choice." She turned her face up to him. "You don't have to decide tonight, but I do wish you would make love to me."

He seemed startled. "Rosie, ladies ain't supposed to be that bold."

"Then kiss me and I'll hush," she ordered and reached to put her arms around his neck.

He kissed her then, kissed her at first hesitantly as if afraid she might pull back, then tightened his grip and kissed her deeper, and deeper still, his tongue slipping between her lips to tantalize and explore her mouth. His big hands fumbled with the tiny pearl buttons of her blue dress and she reached to undo them herself.

She had already made her decision; she wanted this man to make love to her in a way she had only fanaticized about in her daydreams as she sighed over her books, wanted him to possess her and make her feel as she had never felt before and would never feel again once he rode out tomorrow.

His big hands pulled away the top of her dress, trailing along the edge of her lace underwear at the swell of her breasts. She reached to undo the laces. "I want you to kiss and touch my breasts as no man has ever done," she whispered.

"Rosie, are you sure you want this?"

"Very, very sure," she said and then gasped as he bent his head to lave her nipples with his tongue, caressing her breasts with his fingers until every nerve of hers seemed to be on fire. "Ohh, Will, Will . . ."

"Rosie, my love," he murmured, his breath hot against her bare flesh, "I've dreamed of doing this since the first time I saw you." His hands stroked and caressed, making her gasp with surprise and pleasure. She arched her back, wanting more and more as he kissed her mouth, her eyes, her cheeks, and then returned to her breasts again. "You are so pretty and I want you so much."

She didn't really believe that he thought her beautiful, but she wanted to believe it. In her mind, she was Lady Windemere, all slender and blond.

And then his big, rough hands stroked her thighs, pushing her skirts up. He was pulling at her drawers and she stood up to shed them, but before she could come back to the grass, he pulled her to him, her skirt still pushed up, and he caressed her upper thighs and femininity with his lips.

She gasped and embraced his head, holding his hot mouth against her as her excitement built, not even dreaming a man would want to kiss her in her most secret place. She slid slowly down to the grass again and his hands were hot and expert under her skirt, stroking and teasing while she shuddered and began to beg for more. "Please, Will, I—I don't know how much longer I can wait."

"You'll wait," he gasped, "because I'm not through pleasurin' you yet, darlin', I want you to really want me before we end this." He took her hand and put it on his manhood, which throbbed hard under his jeans.

She reached to unbutton his pants, freeing the throbbing maleness of him. She knew this one was all man, big as a stallion and virile with seed to fill her womb.

He touched and stroked between her thighs and she grasped his manhood and begged for more.

"Are you sure, Rosie? Sure you want this?"

"Yes, yes, yes! I want you, Will, I'll always want you!"

Swiftly, he laid her on her back, pushing up her skirts so that he could look at her naked body in the moonlight. "You are the most beautiful girl I ever saw," he breathed, and she was almost sure that he meant it, his eyes said he meant it. "You are all woman, Rosie, and no other girl can hold a candle to you."

"Do you mean that, Will?"

"I never wanted a girl like I want you now," he gasped as he poised himself above her. Then he came into her very slowly.

For a long moment, she did not think she could take him, he was so big and so rigid, yet her body ached for him and she reached up, grasped his hard hips, and pulled him down into her.

"You're wet," he gasped, "so hot and wet." Then he began to ride her in a slow, grinding motion that drove her senses wild with feeling.

"More!" she ordered. "More! I can't ever get enough of you, Texan, I want more and more and more!"

Her words seemed to excite him and he quickened his pace, riding her harder and deeper as she locked her legs around his muscular body. They were both bathed in a sheen of perspiration, even though the night was cool and she had never experienced anything like this in her whole life. She forgot that she was plain and plump and that no man could ever really love her. She was the slender, beautiful heroine of one of her novels and the man in her arms loved her with all the passion any human could offer.

The feelings and the motion intensified and she dug her nails into Waco's back, wanting more and deeper as her excitement mounted. Then she was reaching a crescendo like racing to the top of a mountain, and for a long moment, she stood atop that peak, too breathless and thrilled to do anything but cry out as she began to tumble into blackness. She was vaguely aware that he kissed her, and then for a long moment, she knew nothing at all but sensual pleasure, and nothing so wonderful had ever happened to her in her lonely, lonely life.

Chapter Eighteen

"I—I never knew it could be like this," Rosemary whispered as she lay on her side in his arms.

"Neither did I." He sounded surprised. "At least, it was never this good before with anyone else."

"Do you mean that? You're not just trying to flatter me?"

"I wouldn't mind sleepin' in your arms the rest of my life, lady, but of course, I know that can't be."

"Sure it can be, Will." She reached up and brushed his sun-streaked hair off his forehead. In the moonlight, he now looked serious and sad.

"Let's not fool ourselves, Rosemary. You're a rich girl and you'll be goin' back to that life. I got to go back to Texas and my fate. I only wish . . ." His voice trailed off and he sighed.

"Don't decide tonight, Will," she whispered and kissed his lips gently, tenderly. "We can make this work, in spite of everything. Trust me."

"I trust you tonight. That's real and that'll have to be enough," he said and kissed the side of her face, his lips moving along her temple.

"Then if tonight is all there is," she said, "do we have to go to the cabin?"

"No." He gathered her into his strong arms and kissed her again as if he could never get enough of her. "We can stay here till dawn if you want."

"I want you to make love to me again." She smiled. "And then I want to sleep in your arms, just to feel what it would be like to be married to you."

He frowned, raising up on one elbow. "Don't, Rosie, don't talk like that, you only make it worse."

"Then just make love to me this one last time and I'll not ask for more. I won't think about the ranch and the war ending, and children—"

"You're hurtin' me, Rosie, and makin' me want to turn my back on everything after I gave my word. A Texan's word is sacred."

"All right," she sighed. "I won't be selfish, then. Just make love to me." She felt such sadness that her throat ached, to have almost had something so special and to realize that she was only going to be allowed this one taste of what life and love could be like, and at daybreak, it was going to be taken away. The memories of this night would have to last her a lifetime.

He must have felt the same, because he made love to her so gently, as if prolonging their pleasure could make the dawn not come. Then they slept in each other's embrace under the shadow of the trees. Prince curled up next to them as if he knew tomorrow they would all part ways.

* * *

When she awakened, Waco lay with his head propped on his elbow, looking down at her with an expression that was both loving and sad.

"It's almost mornin'," he said.

"Already?" She looked up at him, then closed her eyes again, wishing that the sun would not rise.

"Happy birthday," he whispered. "You're now twenty-one, a woman of property."

"Let me trade it all for a life in Texas." She reached up and touched his dear face.

"We've been through this before, Rosie. We'll be ridin' out for the border this mornin' and then we'll turn you loose."

"I give you my word I would never turn you in. Trust me."

"I think I almost would, but I can't ask the others to do that. Not with their lives at stake."

She sat up and brushed the leaves from her hair in the pink glow of the coming dawn. The cool wind picked up and blew a scattering of gold and red leaves around them. "Yes, it's time you all cleared out of here. Winter will be coming soon."

He shrugged. "Don't reckon it will matter to us."

She winced at the thought and put her hand on his shoulder. "Will, do you trust me, I mean, *really* trust me?"

He seemed to think a moment. "Yes, I do. I don't think you would do me wrong."

"And I trust you. Today I can legally draw out the money in my own account and I will."

"Will you?" His face mirrored disbelief.

She nodded. "So let's ride into Prairie View and you wait for me to draw it out. Then we'll go to Texas together."

"Won't your stepfather howl about that?"

She smiled. "Yes, but he can't do anything about it. To hell with the bank and the big house, I don't care."

Waco seemed to think it over. "But how can you trust me, Rosie? Suppose I say yes and then when we get away from the bank, I dump you and take your money?"

She shook her head. "I trust you, Will, because I love you. I can't believe you'd do that."

He grinned. "In Texas, this is what we call a Mexican standoff. We both got to trust each other."

She reached to brush the hair off his dear forehead. "Love means trust, Will. Do you love me?"

He pulled her to him and kissed her. "You know I do."

"It's settled, then."

"I'm not gonna risk my men, though. I couldn't ask them to ride into Prairie View on your word."

"Let them make that decision," she said and stood up, brushing the grass from the blue gingham dress.

Prince stirred and woke up, wagging his tail.

The trio walked slowly back to the cabin, where the men were already up. Zeb had the coffeepot going and the frying pan sizzled with bacon. The three turned and looked as the two entered, and Rosemary felt her face redden.

"Well," Waco said, "it's Halloween and Rosie's birthday."

"Congratulations!" all the men said and smiled.

Zeb grinned. "If we was in Texas, missy, I'd bake you a birthday cake."

"You know we're ridin' back to Texas today," Waco reminded them.

"And about time," Zeke said. "It's gettin' colder than a mother-in-law's heart here in Kansas."

"Amen!" The other two nodded.

Waco took a deep breath, knowing he was about to do something he wouldn't have dreamed of only days ago. "Now you men can make up your own minds about what I'm about to tell you, but here's what Rosie and I are gonna do."

The three seemed to sense that something serious was about to be said and gave him their full attention.

"Rosie says she has a lot of money in her own account, and since she's twenty-one today, she can draw it out."

The three looked at him in dumb surprise.

"Will the bank let her do that?" Tom asked.

"Yes." She nodded. "In fact, nobody can stop me."

"And?" Zeke asked as if waiting for the other shoe to drop.

"And I'm going to give it to Will." Rosemary smiled. "Then we'll all ride back to Texas together."

There was a long silence while the three looked at each other, then back to her and Waco.

"Well?" Waco asked.

No one said anything.

After a minute, Rosemary said, "Zeb, your bacon is burning."

"I plumb forgot." He rushed to the stove and moved the skillet.

Waco saw the distrust in the other men's faces. "Look, I'm not askin' any of you to go into Prairie View. You can all ride on or wait outside town while

Rosie and I go to the bank. That way, if anything goes wrong, you can light a shuck for the border without the money. You won't be any worse off than you were."

Zeke frowned. "And let you maybe ride into a trap alone? No, sir. We all come through the war this far together. We wouldn't let you ride into that nest of Yankee soldiers by yourself."

Rosemary shook her head. "I don't think there'll be any trouble. In fact, Will and I will pretend not to know each other. Then we'll mount up and ride out of town separately."

"What about the rest of your wealth, the big house and everything?" Zeb asked as he forked the bacon onto the tin plates.

"I don't care about any of that," Rosemary said.

Zeke frowned as he walked over and poured himself a cup of coffee. "You know, Waco, this could be a trap. And I wouldn't blame the lady none after what we've put her through the past several weeks."

Waco took a deep breath, knowing that he loved her enough to take the chance. "I've decided to trust her. After all, once we get the money, she's got to trust us that we aren't gonna take it and run off and desert her."

Zeb didn't look too happy. "Well, I reckon if you trust her, Waco, the rest of us has got to. I just hope it don't get us all ambushed."

Waco looked into Rosemary's eyes and smiled. "I'm puttin' my life in the lady's hands," he whispered. "And I'm takin' her back to Texas with me. This war can't last forever, and then we'll all be back on the ranch raisin' cattle."

"That settles it, then," Tom said and strode over to get a plate and a tin cup. "Now let's all eat."

After breakfast, they rolled up their bedrolls and gathered up the few things they owned, then saddled the horses. Finally all four of the men loaded and double-checked their weapons. Then all five mounted up. Waco's trio of men looked as stern and sad as if they were going to a funeral. It was clear they thought they were riding into a trap and didn't quite trust the banker's daughter.

In silence, they rode into the outskirts of Prairie View, the mongrel dog trailing along behind them. Waco sensed trouble right away when he saw all the buggies and activity happening on Main Street. "Oh, no, I forgot about the big Halloween celebration," he muttered. "There'll be farmers and soldiers in town for the dance."

"We still got time to back out of this," Tom said.

Waco looked over at Rosemary and she mouthed the words *I love you.* "No, you all scatter around the outskirts of town. If there's any shootin', that gives you a chance to get away."

"We ain't gonna let you walk into the bank alone," Zeke protested.

"Then scatter up and down Main Street," Waco ordered. "I don't wanta hit any women or kids if shootin' starts. Go on ahead, Rosie."

She took a deep breath and nodded, then nudged Lady Be Good into a trot and started down Main Street. Waco was right, she thought with alarm. There were lots of people in town for the celebration. Pumpkins and jack-o'-lanterns displayed all along the wooden sidewalks and in store windows. The streets were full of buggies and wagons. People thronged the streets with lots of blue uniforms visible everywhere, soldiers coming into town for the dance.

What have I done? Suppose something went wrong and the soldiers got suspicious? If they captured her cowboys, they could hang them all as spies since they weren't in uniform. And if anything went awry at the bank, if anyone suspected anything, the bank could be turned into a shooting gallery. Zeb, Zeke, and Tom might escape, but if Waco came into the bank, he wouldn't have a prayer of getting out alive.

She realized people were staring at her. Old Mr. Jones in the general store across the street from the bank was gawking out his plate glass window at her. Her heart in her mouth, she dismounted and tied Lady at the hitching rail before the bank. Out of the corner of her eye, she saw Waco riding down the street, dismounting, and tying up in front of the saloon a few hundred feet away. Then he ambled toward her, stopping to look in store windows as if he hadn't a care in the world.

It's now or never. Taking a deep breath for courage, she crossed the sidewalk and entered the bank. The place was crowded with local farmers and a dozen soldiers. Oh, no, even two deputies stood near the teller's cage, doing their banking business. She pushed through the crowd to old Bill Wilkerson's cage. "Hello, Bill."

"Miss Rosemary?" His white eyebrows went up in

surprise. "Haven't seen you in here in a while. Thought you was over visiting in Thackerville?"

So that was how Godfrey had covered her absence.

"Well, I'm back now." She forced herself to smile although her lips felt too frozen to move. When she glanced around, she saw Waco enter the bank and stand over at a table as if filling out a bank deposit. "Bill, it's my birthday today. I'm twenty-one."

"Well, land's sake, we all forgot." He reached through to shake her hand. "Wished you'd let us know, miss, we would have had a cake and everything."

"Oh, that's okay. I just need to make a withdrawal. How much is in my account, anyway?"

"Oh, you don't need to worry about getting overdrawn," the white-haired old man assured her. "You need a little spending money?"

"I'd just like to know how much is in the account anyway." *Does he suspect anything?*

The teller gave her a strange look. "All right, I'll check for you. Quite a bit, I reason."

The seconds seemed to drag as the old man went over to check his books. Waco stood by the door and she could see sweat on his forehead although it was a cool, crisp day. About that time, young Major Mathis entered into the bank. "Why, Miss Rosemary, so good to see you. You've been gone?"

"Uh, yes." She didn't want to get into a conversation with him.

"I hope you'll be coming to the dance tonight," he said and twirled a blond curl.

"If I do, I'll certainly save you a dance." She smiled. By tonight, she hoped to be heading south to Texas. "If you don't mind, I'm in too big a hurry to visit."

"Oh, of course." The prissy officer looked disappointed.

Old Mr. Wilkerson came back to his teller's cage. "Miss Rosemary," he lowered his voice, "I checked and you got a little over fifty thousand dollars, so you needn't worry about overdrawing your account if'n you want to buy a dress or something."

"How much over?"

He looked at his figures again. "About five thousand."

"Good," she said briskly. "I'd like to withdraw it all."

"What?" He blinked as if he hadn't heard her correctly.

"You heard me, I want to withdraw it all."

He looked as if he didn't know what to do. "Mr. St. John is here. Do you need to speak with him?"

"No." She shook her head. "Now that I'm of legal age to control the bank, I'd like to withdraw what's in my account. That's all. Oh, and Bill, as of today, you are in charge of the bank. I have that authority."

The old man blanched as if she'd lost her mind. "I—I think I'd better call Mr. St. John."

"No, let me talk to my stepfather. I've got a lot to say to him." She felt a sudden resolve. She was as brave as one of her story heroines as she marched across the bank lobby into Godfrey's office and slammed the door shut.

"Hello, Godfrey." She didn't smile.

He put down the pocket knife with which he'd

been cleaning his nails and blanched. "Why, Rosemary, dear, what a surprise."

"I'll just bet it is." She wasn't intimidated by him anymore. Her love for Waco had given her courage. "You thought I was dead and happy about it."

He made a soothing gesture. "Rosemary, please lower your voice. Half the town is out in the lobby."

"I don't give a damn. I've come to make a big withdrawal and to fire you."

"Fire me?" he squeaked. "What do you mean, coming into my bank, creating a ruckus and—"

"In case you haven't read the will, Godfrey, I inherit the bank on my twenty-first birthday, which is today, so I'm firing you and putting Mr. Wilkerson in charge. Also, I'm turning over the house to Reverend Post for his orphans' home."

"You can't do that!" Godfrey was on his feet and raging now.

"Oh, but I can. Talk to my lawyer about the terms of the will." She knew people outside in the lobby were straining to hear every word. She could see Waco's tense face through the glass door. Evidently he was about to come into the office to protect her. She shook her head, aware that she was a changed person—she was proud and independent, and she could handle this weasel alone.

Godfrey sputtered with anger, his handsome face blotchy and red. "You're an ungrateful girl," he snarled, "didn't even appreciate the lovely coming-home party and that fine silk scarf I gave you."

"Godfrey, you may be fooling some of the people in this town, but not me. I know you only married my mother to get control of this bank, and you aren't the saint you pretend to be."

She thought she heard a gasp from the people outside.

Now Godfrey seemed to be aware of the crowd in the lobby and that they were listening to every word. "Now, dear, we need to have a little talk—"

"I've had all the talk I want. I'm withdrawing some money, then I'm going out to the house. I expect you to be out of that house and out of town by sundown. I'll ask the sheriff to make sure you do."

"How dare you!" He grabbed her arm, but she slapped him and pulled out of his grasp.

He looked toward the crowd outside the glass door, his face mottled with angry color from her hand. "We'll talk at the house later, my dear."

She didn't intend to ever see him again. Without another word, she turned on her heel and marched out of his office, pushed through the curious crowd to the teller's cage. Mr. Wilkerson's wrinkled face was pale as she held out her hand for the money. He counted it out for her. "Put it in a bank bag, please," she said.

He did, wordlessly.

"Bill, you will be running the bank from now on. My father trusted you and I do, too. Tell Reverend Post to talk to my lawyer. I intend to give him the mansion for his orphanage. I never liked that house anyway."

"But Miss Rosemary—" he protested.

"Good-bye, Bill, I'm headed for the house."

The whole crowd stared in fascination as she strode out of the bank. Waco still stood leaning against a desk; now he ambled out of the bank and onto the sidewalk. Behind her, she heard the excited buzz of people exchanging comments about the scene so many had just witnessed. She didn't care. It was time everyone knew about Godfrey.

Oh, there was one more thing she needed to take care of. She crossed the dusty street toward the general store. Uh-oh. The sheriff strode toward her on the sidewalk. Out of the corner of her eye, she saw Waco freeze, his hand on his pistol. He thought she was about to turn him in. Instead, she smiled and caught the officer by the arm. "Sheriff, I've had a little set-to with my stepfather, and he's pretty mad. You'll make sure the terms of my father's will are carried out, won't you?"

The man took off his hat, looking puzzled. "Sure, Miss Rosemary."

Mystified, Waco watched her cross the street and stop to talk to the sheriff. *What is she doing? This wasn't part of the plan.* Rosie was supposed to get on her horse and ride out. He looked up and down the street for his men. All three looked like they were ready to mount up and run for it. Prince lay near Zeke's feet, sleeping through the whole drama. Had she been telling the sheriff the plot? Waco wasn't sure what to do as she disappeared into the general store. *We don't need any supplies, what is she up to?* Everything in him warned him to mount up and ride out, that a woman couldn't be trusted.

Love means trust, and he loved Rosie with all his heart. He had to trust that she wouldn't do him wrong. Seconds seemed to tick past while he held his breath. *What is she doing?* Was she betraying him to that old man in the general store? Any moment,

would the old man run outside, shouting for the
sheriff to grab Waco and his men?

Then she came out of the general store, still carrying her bank bag. Hundreds of people seemed
to be watching as she strode over to her horse,
hung the bag on her saddlehorn, mounted up,
and rode down Main Street.

She glanced back and saw Waco leaning against
the hitching rail as if he had nothing else to do.
Good, everything was going according to plan so
far. She headed for the mansion. There were a few
personal things there she wanted to pick up.

Waco waited until she was out of sight before he
mounted up and rode out of town. As he passed
Tom, Zeb, and Zeke, he nodded to them. When he
was far ahead of them, he knew they would mount
up and follow, the lazy dog trailing along.

Rosemary glanced back only once as she rode
out to the big mansion. She could just barely see
Waco in the distance. So far, the plan was going
as hoped. When she reached the house, she
dismounted, tied up her horse, and went inside.
Puzzled, she looked about for servants, then remembered that today was their day off. She was all
alone in the big house. That was just as well. She
didn't want to answer any curious questions about
where she'd been or what was happening.

First she marched into the conservatory, yanked
some of Godfrey's precious orchids up by the
roots, and knocked over the pots, making a big,
dirty mess. An orphanage would want to use the
conservatory for children to have a sunny play
place, not a haven for exotic plants. Then she
yanked Godfrey's favorite. What had Waco called

it? A castor bean, up by the roots, cockleburrs and all, and carried it toward the library, leaving a trail of dirt through the house. She carried it into the library and threw it on top of Godfrey's pristine desk, scattering dirt and leaves across his papers. She pictured him finding it there and how angry he would be and smiled without mirth. Him and his damned French silk scarf. She couldn't even remember what she had done with that.

What to take with me? There was so little she cared about in this ostentatious, grand mansion. Rosemary ran up the stairs to her room, grabbed a small valise from the closet, and threw a few clothes and personal items in it. Should she take all her books? No. She shook her head. She intended to participate in life from now on, not just daydream about it. She paused, looking around the room. There was nothing she cared about here in Kansas—a whole new life awaited her in Texas.

A noise. She froze in her tracks. She had definitely heard a noise downstairs. Good gracious, what could that be? It wasn't time for the servants to be back. Godfrey. Oh no. She intended to slip out of this house without ever dealing with her stepfather again. She braced herself against her bureau and watched her almost closed door. Taking a deep breath, she grabbed the only heavy item within reach, a silver hand mirror. Then the door moved and her heart almost stopped.

Prince stuck his head around the door, and when the yellow dog saw her, he ran toward her, tail wagging. She knelt and put her arms around him. "You precious mutt, you nearly scared me to death. Let's get out of here and join the boys."

She grabbed the small valise and finished packing the few things she needed, the happy dog lying on the carpet beside her. She knew she was taking a big gamble that the four cowboys might take her money and head for the border without her, but she loved Waco and because she loved him, she had to trust him.

Meanwhile, back at the bank, Godfrey took a long moment to compose himself and then he pasted a smile on his face and walked out into the lobby to face the curious crowd. "It was just a little family spat," he assured one and all, "nothing to it. Why, I'm sure when my hysterical stepdaughter and I can talk it over, we'll work everything out."

He turned to the teller. "Bill, where did she say she was going?"

The old man didn't look too convinced. "Why, she said she was going to the house, but—"

"Have someone bring my buggy around," Godfrey snapped. "I'll go home and get this all straightened out. Don't worry, everyone, things will be back to normal right away."

He was seething as he jumped into the buggy and whipped up the startled old horse. That damned girl had put him on the spot and humiliated him in front of all his customers.

Where has the little bitch been the past several weeks? Thank God it was the servants' day off so there'd be no one at the house to overhear the fierce argument that Godfrey knew was coming when he confronted her. He wasn't sure what he was going to do about Rosemary yet, but he'd think of something on the way home. He had to murder her and hide the body. He'd tell everyone they'd had an argument and she'd left town.

Yes, he was going to have to kill her to keep control of the money and the mansion and especially to get back all that cash she'd just taken. He could hide that and no one would ever know she hadn't taken it with her when she left town. Why was she now so willing to confront him? Had she guessed that he had murdered her mother?

However, when he arrived at the fine mansion, the front door was standing wide open. Now what? He got down, tied up the buggy, and strode inside. "Rosemary? Rosemary? Damn it, where are you? We've got to talk!"

No answer. He grew more furious as he strode through the house, looking for her. In his conservatory, he discovered she had yanked up all his precious plants and tossed them about. His anger knew no bounds. He was livid and almost frothing as he followed the trail of dirt across the fine Oriental carpet and into the library, where he found the castor bush thrown on his desk. *So she guessed. Well, what difference does that make?* "Rosemary, where are you?"

Up in her room, Rosemary froze and held her breath while the dog growled softly. She heard Godfrey stomping through the rooms down below. He was certainly angry enough to be dangerous, and Waco and his men were probably too far away to help her. She'd have to handle this all by herself. What would one of her willowy beautiful heroines do?

No, she thought, *damnit, no. I don't care what some*

thin, vapid storybook heroine would do. I am Rosemary Burke and I am a strong, capable woman. I can handle this myself, and if I have to, I'll defend myself. However, time was of the essence and she needed to get away as fast as possible.

Picking up her small valise, she whistled softly to the dog and tiptoed through her bedroom to the next one, then closed the door. If Godfrey came into her room, maybe she could slip out into the hall and down the stairs before he found her.

Godfrey's rage knew no bounds as he hurried through the house looking for her with no results. She was probably up in her room. He ran up the stairs, gritting his teeth. The servants would be home soon, and he wanted to have this out with his stepdaughter before the servants returned to overhear the heated argument. He ran into her room, slamming the door so hard, it rattled.

Damn her, where can she be? He was so enraged, he picked up a small stool and threw it against the big mirror over the dresser. The glass shattered into a million pieces. He kicked the rocking chair and it went over on its side, then he opened her drawers and threw clothes and personal items all over the floor. When he found her, he was going to kill her and maybe bury the body or throw it in the river where it would never be found. He'd tell everyone she was hysterical and maybe even insane when she had come into the bank. He would say she was gone when he got to the house. Yes, he smiled to himself. He knew his oily charm would convince everyone. Besides, then he would be over fifty thousand dollars richer.

Rosemary could hear him in her room, wrecking it. He was making so much noise, maybe he wouldn't hear her as she took her valise, motioned to the dog, and tiptoed out into the hall and down the stairs. The dog wagged its tail, barked softly, and loped into the library. Gracious! Had Godfrey heard that? She wasn't about to leave her dog behind and she couldn't whistle for him. She put down her valise and ran into the library to get her dog.

Godfrey paused in wrecking her room. What was that noise? It sounded like a dog, but they didn't own a dog. Godfrey hated them. He tiptoed down the stairs and stormed into the library, confronting Rosemary with a small yellow dog in her arms. "So here you are!"

She put the dog down on the floor. "Get out of my way, Godfrey, I'm leaving!"

"Not with that fifty thousand dollars, you're not!"

The dog growled and bared its teeth at him.

"Get out of the way, mutt!" He kicked at the dog as he strode toward his stepdaughter. "You fat wench, how dare you try to take everything I've worked so hard to get? How dare you destroy my fancy castor bush! You must know about your mother!"

"What?" She had no idea what he was talking about. "Step aside, you weasel, I'm leaving."

He took his pocket knife out, lunging toward her as the dog growled again and leaped for his wrist. Godfrey screamed and slapped at the dog. "You damned cur! Rosemary, call him off or I'll—"

However, the dog hung on to his wrist, sharp teeth going through to the bone. Godfrey couldn't seem to shake him loose, and in the meantime, Rosemary picked up the big exotic plant by the roots and swung it at him. The cockleburrs caught him across his handsome face and he shouted a curse as he stumbled backward. Now he came at her again with the knife, and at that point she screamed.

Waco ran into the room, jerked Godfrey up by the lapels of his fine suit, and hit him in the mouth. "You low-down skunk, you're as rotten as she said you was."

Godfrey stumbled to his feet, his face and wrist bleeding all over the fine carpet. He lunged toward Waco again as Rosemary picked up a heavy book and threw it at him. Prince now had Godfrey by the ankle, biting and growling. Rosemary could only watch now as the two men fought, the fine room in shambles.

Waco knocked Godfrey into a bookcase full of expensive glass knickknacks that fell on him, burying him in a crash of tinkling crystal. Waco wiped the blood from his mouth. "Let's get out of here, Rosie."

"Come on, Prince!" she called, and the dog turned loose of Godfrey's ankle. She grabbed her small valise and the three of them ran for the door, leaving Godfrey bleeding and writhing on the floor.

They mounted up, the dog gamboling next to the horses.

"What made you come?" she gasped.

"I know I was supposed to wait for you up on the hill, but when I saw that buggy pullin' up, I knew you were gonna need help. I reckon Prince knew it before I did because he took off toward the house and we couldn't stop him," Waco said.

"Let's go!" She slapped Lady with the reins and

Waco nodded. The two riders and the dog raced for the top of the hill where the other three men waited.

"What in tarnation happened down there?" Tom asked.

Waco grinned. "We'll tell you about it later. Prince about chewed that banker up."

Zeke smiled. "I always said that was a smart dog. Prince, you'll make a good dog for the ranch."

Rosemary paused and looked back at the big mansion, then she nodded to the men and they turned south.

"You aren't regrettin' what you're leavin' behind?" Waco asked her.

She shook her head. "No, I have no fond memories here. I hated that house. It was only a monument to my mother's pride and vanity." She handed him the bank bag. "You've got the money you need and a few thousand extra besides to fix up the ranch after the war."

"You trust me?" he asked earnestly as he took the bag.

"You just trusted me with your life, I guess I can trust you with mere money," she said, her eyes misty. "Now let's put some distance between us and Prairie View."

Waco said, "What did you say to the sheriff and why did you go into the store?"

She smiled at him. "I see you didn't cut and run when that happened."

"I love you," he said, "so I had to trust you."

"Well, I told the sheriff to enforce the terms of the will, and there was something I wanted in the general store."

"We had enough supplies," he protested.

"I know we did." Rosemary smiled as the five broke into a gallop, the dog running along beside. She wouldn't tell Waco until later that she had bought back his silver spurs and his grandfather's gold watch. "I love you, Will," she said as they rode toward the sunset.

"And I love you, Rosie, more than you know!" Waco nodded to her and they headed south to Texas.

Chapter Nineteen

Back at the mansion, Godfrey finally swayed to his feet, shook off the shattered glass, and got a bottle of whiskey from his desk. He took a long drink, attempting to think clearly. *That damned girl.* He took another drink, trying to decide what to do. His brain seemed dazed, but he knew he must chase her down and kill her, get that money back.

Taking the whiskey with him, he stumbled outside and climbed into his buggy. *Where has she gone?* It could be anywhere, and now it was turning dusk. He took another drink, trying to make a decision. Maybe she had gone back to town to turn him in to the sheriff. He must not let that happen. His mind seemed fuzzy from the fight and the whiskey, but he figured he could still stop her.

Vaguely, he tried to keep his mind on his task, but he felt the reins slip from his hands and the horse wandering off the road. Maybe if he'd take a little nap, he'd still be able to catch up to Rosemary.

* * *

An hour after dark, the servants coming home found him unconscious, dirty, and bloody in his buggy. They hurried to the house. They found the door open and the house in disarray, blood, dirt, and plants scattered everywhere.

Mollie, still in shock, ran up the stairs to check on Miss Rosemary. She gasped when she lit the lamp and found the room destroyed and furniture overturned. Evidently there had been a big fight here. She began righting the furniture, picking up the jewelry off the floor. One piece lay half under the bed. "What in the devil and all the saints—?"

She knelt and reached for the ornate pin. That's when she saw the crumpled white silk scarf under the bed. She pulled it out and shook it. When she saw the dried blood, she bolted for the door, shrieking all the way down the stairs. "Go for the sheriff quick, he's murdered her!"

Three days later, the five riders reined in at a town on the south Kansas border to rest and buy supplies.

Rosemary had never been so happy. Never again would she dream of being a storybook heroine. She was Rosemary Burke, and she was a competent, strong woman. She might not be a great beauty, but the man she loved, loved her just the way she was, and that was all that mattered. No longer would food be the main priority in her life.

The five rested under the shade of a tree while they ate bread and cheese, the dog, Prince, happily sharing with them.

"Yes, sir," Zeke said as he fed the mutt a bite, "didn't I always say that this was one smart dog?"

Waco winked at Rosie and she winked back.

"By the way," she said, putting her hand on her love's knee, "Godfrey said something I didn't understand. Something about me finding out about my mother's death."

"When was that?" Waco asked.

She shrugged. "Just before you came bursting into the library to save me. I had thrown his precious exotic plant on his desk."

"The castor bean plant?" Waco said.

She nodded.

"We all wondered what you were doin' with castor beans in your pocket," he said. "Rosie, they are deadly poison. We use them down in Texas to kill gophers."

"Gracious," she gasped, "he must have mixed them into the pinto beans Mother ate at the dinner that night, and old Doc was too incompetent to know it wasn't appendicitis."

"That's about the size of it," Waco said.

"I hate it that he'll get away with murder." She gritted her teeth.

Waco shook his head. "Well, we can't do nuthin' about that. What goes around comes around, they say, and sooner or later, he'll get what's comin' to him." He turned toward the other three. "You boys about ready to mount up?"

The other three nodded.

"I can hardly wait to get that money to the colonel." Zeke pulled out his mouth organ. "You suppose this war's gonna be over soon, Waco?"

"It can't last much longer, even with the little bit

we're addin' to their treasury," Waco said. "We Scotch-Irish have done more than our share in this war, but I reckon we was outgunned from the first."

Tom frowned. "It wasn't from a lack of bravery."

"Amen to that," Zeb muttered. "Texans, especially the Scotch-Irish, would charge hell with a dipper of water."

Waco nodded. "Soon we'll all be back on the ranch, raisin' some fine colts from Amigo and Lady."

Rosemary smiled at him and leaned over for a quick kiss. "And some fine children between Waco and Rosie."

Tom pushed back his hat. "What time is it?"

Waco shrugged. "Gawd Almighty, now how would I know?"

Rosemary smiled at him. "Oh, by the way, I've got some gifts for you." She walked over and dug in her saddlebags.

Waco pushed backed his Stetson. "For me? Now, what the—?"

"I got them at the general store after we left the bank." She came back to him with a small package wrapped in brown paper.

He took it, puzzled. "I wondered why you went in there."

"But you trusted me enough not to make a run for it."

"I was tempted," he admitted as he opened the package. "Well, lookee here, boys."

The sunlight glittered on his silver spurs and the gold watch.

His three men made sounds of wonder.

Waco's eyes teared up and his jaw worked. For

a long moment, he seemed to have trouble speaking. "I—I don't know what to say, Rosie."

"Say you love me and *gracias*," she whispered.

"I'll do better than that." He laid the treasured gifts on a stump and pulled her to him, then kissed her thoroughly.

Tom grinned. "Now what time is it?"

Waco grinned even wider as he put the spurs in his saddlebags and held the gold watch a long moment, looking. "Noon. We can be deep into Indian Territory by sundown." He stood up, tall and lean, and every inch a Texan.

She brushed crumbs from the blue-flowered gingham dress she wore. "I wish I knew what was happening back in Prairie View. I hate to think Godfrey isn't paying for all his crimes."

A stagecoach pulled in just then at the rest stop, and the passengers got out and went inside for lunch. One of the traveling drummers threw aside a newspaper and Rosemary hurried to pick it up.

"Look," she said, "it's a *Prairie View Gazette*." She paused and looked at the headlines, then gasped. "Well, I'll be." She handed it to Waco as the others gathered around to look.

Waco read aloud the big headline: BANKER INDICTED IN STEPDAUGHTER'S MURDER.

"'Banker Godfrey St. John has been indicted for the murder of his missing stepdaughter, Rosemary Burke. Servants say a wrecked house spoke of a violent struggle, and a maid found a bloody monogrammed scarf. Others spoke of disagreements between the banker and his stepdaughter, leading the sheriff to believe that St. John killed her and disposed of her body, possibly by throwing it in the river.

"'Further investigation finds that St. John's name is actually Elmo Croppett and that he is wanted in three other states. The man is expected to hang for his stepdaughter's murder.'"

The five looked at each other open-mouthed.

"Gawd Almighty!" Waco shook his head. "He killed your mother, but they're gonna hang him for killin' you."

"I reckon that's justice, Waco," Rosie said. "What goes around, comes around." She swung up on her horse. "You boys ready to ride?"

"I love you, Rosie." Waco grinned as he and his men mounted up. "You are gonna marry me, aren't you?"

Her heart melted when she looked at him. "I sure am, Will. I can hardly wait to be Mrs. Will McClain."

Prince ran ahead of them on the road, barking. The five of them laughed and spurred their horses toward the south, crossing into Indian Territory and the bright future that awaited them in Texas.

To My Readers

Where did I find the basis for this story? I found it in a few paragraphs by J.B. Nation from the Kentucky Historical Society and a *New York Times* reprint of the *Louisville Journal* newspaper, dated August 30, 1864, titled REBEL ATROCITIES: A BATTALION OF NEGRO TROOPS SLAUGHTERED IN COLD BLOOD—MURDER AND OUTRAGES IN KENTUCKY.

Kentucky was one of four slave states that decided to stay with the union when the Civil War tore the country apart. These were the so-called "border" states. The Kentucky bank robbery under Captain Jake Bennett, including the massacre of the Union black troops guarding the barge, is a small true snippet of history. Of course, my main characters are fiction.

And yes, the Confederacy got so desperate for money, they gathered up jewelry and attempted to invade Nevada and California to capture gold and silver mines. The Rebels were turned back in defeat at the battle of Glorieta Pass, in present-day New Mexico. I have been there and walked the battleground.

As far as poisonous plants, the castor bean plant originated in Africa and was brought to this country. It is an interesting, exotic plant that grows commonly in many states. Processed one way, the beans become an old-fashioned medicine, castor oil. Processed another way or raw, they are very, very poisonous. Castor beans are the basis for the terrorists' deadly ricin, which is six thousand times more deadly than cyanide. In 1978, ricin was used to assassinate Bulgarian dissident Georgi Markov with a tiny pellet in the tip of an umbrella that was poked in his leg as he passed the killer on a London street.

I want to say a little about the Scots-Irish or the Scotch-Irish, or Ulster Scots as they are sometimes known. I have covered many nationalities in my stories, but I find the Scots-Irish particularly interesting, maybe because my maternal grandmother was a Scots-Irish Texan and her mother was originally from the hills of Kentucky. This ethnic group has given us some of our best soldiers, a dozen presidents, good whiskey, country music, and NASCAR. I recommend an excellent book by James Webb, *Born Fighting, How the Scots-Irish Shaped America*, published by Broadway Books, New York, 2004.

Coming to America, the Scots-Irish found the best lands already occupied by the snooty English. While the Catholic Irish generally migrated to the big cities such as Boston, the Scots-Irish scattered into the mountains, particularly the Appalachians and the Alleghenies. Protestant, proud, and usually poor, the Scots-Irish worked the coal mines, hunted, fished, and trapped for a living. The words "redneck" and "cracker" were used by the British to describe this group several hundred years before disdainful Northerners began to use them. I have read that they might have been called "hillbillies" because, coming out of Scotland and northern Ireland, they were followers of William of Orange.

Their only cash crop was excellent whiskey. The legend of NASCAR racing says the sport began when the mountain folk souped up cars to carry the illegal moonshine and outrun the federal agents. A good movie on this subject is *Thunder Road*, starring Robert Mitchum.

Forty percent of the Revolutionary army and much of the Civil War armies, particularly in the South, were Scots-Irish, even though the majority owned no slaves. Stonewall Jackson, George S. Patton, Davey Crockett, Sam Houston, Lewis and Clark, Mark Twain, Daniel Boone, and John Wayne are but a few of the American Scots-Irish. It is probably not a coincidence that the biggest hero of World War I, Sergeant Alvin York, from the Tennessee hills and the biggest hero of World War II, Audie Murphy, from Texas (whose kin came from North Carolina), were both Scots-Irish.

To this day, the group is independent, stubborn, and clannish; the Bible Belt blue-collar working class that believe strongly in the Second Amendment (the right to bear arms) and provides an army when the nation needs it. They are still found mostly in the South, although there is a large group of them around Bakersfield, California. If you want an unprejudiced look at these people, I suggest a movie, *Coal Miner's Daughter*, about country singing legend Loretta Lynn.

As far as the bushwhackers of the Civil War, Bloody Bill Anderson and Quantrill were two of the leaders of these guerilla groups that robbed and killed without mercy, particularly in Kansas and Missouri. In those early years, Frank and Jesse James and Cole Younger rode with Anderson, and that's where they got their training to become outlaws. Quantrill and Anderson sacked and burned the town of Lawrence, Kansas, murdering most of the men and boys, in the summer of 1863. Bloody Bill was finally killed by federal troops October 27, 1864, near Albany, Missouri. Quantrill was killed in the spring of 1865, about the time the Civil War ended.

If you've read my previous books, you know they all connect. Waco McClain is a cousin on his mother's side to Blackie O'Neal (*To Tempt a Texan*), Brad O'Neal (*To Love a Texan*), and Bonnie O'Neal Purdy (*To Wed a Texan*).

If you've never been to Waco, Texas, it's an interesting city to visit. There you'll find the Texas Ranger Museum, the Dr Pepper Museum, and Baylor University.

If you have been reading my books for a while, you know I have connected all my stories in one long, long saga of the West that begins in the 1850s and stretches into the 1890s. So far, there are twenty-eight books and two novelettes in the Panorama of the Old West. The earliest novel begins in 1857, *Warrior's Honor,* the latest one begins in 1895, titled *To Wed a Texan.* Some of these can still be ordered at your local bookstore or online or phone from kensingtonbooks.com.

Wishing You Your Own Handsome Cowboy,
Georgina Gentry

Put a Little Romance in Your Life With
Georgina Gentry

Cheyenne Song
0-8217-5844-6   **$5.99**US/**$7.99**CAN

Apache Tears
0-8217-6435-7   **$5.99**US/**$7.99**CAN

Warrior's Heart
0-8217-7076-4   **$5.99**US/**$7.99**CAN

To Tame a Savage
0-8217-7077-2   **$5.99**US/**$7.99**CAN

To Tame a Texan
0-8217-7402-6   **$5.99**US/**$7.99**CAN

To Tame a Rebel
0-8217-7403-4   **$5.99**US/**$7.99**CAN

To Tempt a Texan
0-8217-7705-X   **$5.99**US/**$7.99**CAN

Available Wherever Books Are Sold!

Visit our website at **www.kensingtonbooks.com**.

More Historical Romance From
Jo Ann Ferguson

Available Wherever Books Are Sold!

Visit our website at **www.kensingtonbooks.com**.

More by Bestselling Author
Hannah Howell